IN SEARCH
of a
GOOD FEELING

IN SEARCH *of a* GOOD FEELING

ANTHONY WEBB

IN SEARCH OF A GOOD FEELING

Copyright © 2018 Anthony Webb.

All rights reserved. No part of this book may be used or reproduced by any means, graphic, electronic, or mechanical, including photocopying, recording, taping or by any information storage retrieval system without the written permission of the author except in the case of brief quotations embodied in critical articles and reviews.

iUniverse books may be ordered through booksellers or by contacting:

iUniverse
1663 Liberty Drive
Bloomington, IN 47403
www.iuniverse.com
1-800-Authors (1-800-288-4677)

Because of the dynamic nature of the Internet, any web addresses or links contained in this book may have changed since publication and may no longer be valid. The views expressed in this work are solely those of the author and do not necessarily reflect the views of the publisher, and the publisher hereby disclaims any responsibility for them.

This is a work of fiction. All of the characters, names, incidents, organizations, and dialogue in this novel are either the products of the author's imagination or are used fictitiously.

Any people depicted in stock imagery provided by Getty Images are models, and such images are being used for illustrative purposes only. Certain stock imagery © Getty Images.

Scripture quotations marked NIV are taken from the Holy Bible, New International Version®. NIV®. Copyright © 1973, 1978, 1984 by International Bible Society. Used by permission of Zondervan. All rights reserved.

ISBN: 978-1-5320-4658-2 (sc)
ISBN: 978-1-5320-4657-5 (e)

Library of Congress Control Number: 2018904186

Print information available on the last page.

iUniverse rev. date: 05/19/2018

May your

Search for

a Good Feeling

be wonderful

ACKNOWLEDGEMENTS

I would like to thank my friends and family for their support throughout this process, especially Chinky, Jo-Ann and Deb without their assistance this project would not have been completed.

PROLOGUE

In Search of a Good Feeling
"What am I to you?"
"You are my good feeling."
"A good feeling? Is that all?"
"That's everything sweetie. Love is a good feeling that causes a person to do things that they would not do if they did not have that good feeling."

In search of a good feeling is man's endless quest for a homeostatic state of pleasure. Pleasure derives from the interaction of positive expectations and channeled joy. It's almost animalistic in a way. Animals get up every day in search for a meal. Their whole existence is depended on obtaining a meal…so they go searching. Not unlike humans….we search daily for that good feeling. Without it our life has little meaning.

Obtaining a good feeling confirms us and gives meaning to self. That explosion of dopamine in our brain identifies the sought out sensations for the individual. When obtained, the neurological process has the power to change the emotional state of the person. Many successful exposures of a good feeling can trigger an addictive state to manifest within the person causing the individual to begin that endless journey in search of a good feeling. Consequently, being able to create a good feeling inside of someone is a very good thing.

CHAPTER 1

"Mmmm," quietly moans Boswell. *Shoot those cinnamon rolls smothered with the maple icing and pecans sure look good.* The sight and smell of the tasty treats instantly ignites Boswell's sensory memory taking him back to a time where having a maple cinnamon roll was the reward he would receive from his mother on Saturday morning after helping her put the groceries away. She would have stopped at Hough bakery on the way home from grocery shopping and picked up some sweet goods for the family. After bringing the many bags of groceries in the house and carefully putting them away, his mother would open up a box of cinnamon rolls and let the good times begin. The tasty combination of bread, cinnamon, sugar, and nuts formed an incredible sensation in the mouth. Simply delicious! The thought created that "good" feeling in Boswell.

Quickly returning to reality, Boswell inspects the menu on the wall of the eatery to see what he could purchase. This situation always possesses a dilemma for Boswell due to the fact he recently gave up sugar, corn syrup, and artificial sweeteners which can be a problem when you're looking for something to eat. Generally, there was nothing that he could purchase for the exception of water or a hot drink without sugar. The decision for giving up sugar was reached in a very Boswell like way. One Sunday night after watching a segment of 60 minutes on the evils of sugar, he decided to go cold turkey and give it up immediately.

With the presence of diabetes in his family history and a need to lose weight the decision made a lot of sense to Boswell. Eliminating sugar from his diet was not as difficult as he thought it would be except for the time Boswell would eat out for breakfast. Either the menu was full of dishes with a ton of salt, like bacon, sausage or ham, or drowned in sugar like pancakes, French toast, cinnamon rolls and donuts. Boswell even found out that the innocent bagel was not so innocent. It was packed with calories and sugar. On most mornings, Boswell would fix a breakfast of oatmeal with raisins and cinnamon, somewhat bland but filling while having no added sugar. Today he had run out of oatmeal for breakfast so had decided to stop at a familiar haunt where in the past he purchased with gladness his daily hit of sugar-drenched breakfast delights.

This morning he was obtaining unsolicited advice from the yin and yang influences in his life. Others may see these influences as voices inside your head which Boswell might agree to…but he also sees those "voices" as a part of him which state their opinion whenever Boswell faces a dilemma. The little devil on his right shoulder was supplying him with juicy reasons to purchase the maple cinnamon rolls with nuts. Reasons such as, "You know you want it…its only one…you deserve it." And the mother of them all, "You know it's makes you feel so good."

In Search of a Good Feeling

On the left shoulder the angel was not going to be out done. He was going nonstop saying, "Sugar is no good for you….it sucks…you are better than this…just say no." He even used conspiracy theory assertions, "It's a government plot to destroy you…." But before Boswell could develop an argument for either side, the voice of Sister Juanita pierces through his confused state to get his attention.

"Well lookie here, it's the good doctor …have not seen you for a while. I thought you put ole Sister Juanita down, but I see you back like everybody else. Nobody can get enough of Sister Juanita's good stuff…always coming back for more. So what are you going to do Doc…this isn't the zoo? My food is for purchasing …not to be looking at… C'mon baby, money talks…BS walks…so what will it be this morning? So where have you been? You too good now to stop by and give a poor woman a little attention since I heard you gotten your doctorate or something like that?" Can you fix what ails me since you now a doctor? Can you be your doctor Feel Good?" laughs Sister Juanita.

The early morning regulars were getting their laugh on for the day. When Boswell walked into the restaurant they saw Sister Juanita sizing him up, like a lioness looking to devour an antelope. So they waited in silence at their tables slowly drinking their coffee, peering over their cups always with their eyes in the direction of Sister Juanita. Closely watching her daily ritual of nibbling, teasing then pouncing on her victim. After waiting all morning for their appetite of victimization to be fed, they roared in laughter half listening for Boswell's reply.

The more things change the more they stay the same and Sister Juanita is a prime example of that saying. Boswell has known Sister Juanita for over twenty years. She used to have a coffee cart not far from the school where Boswell works. Now, she owns a little greasy spoon around the corner from his apartment. New location but the same old Sister Juanita. Half flirt, half business woman. She remains one of the most talkative, opinionated, politically incorrect individuals that he has ever met. She has the ability to embarrass you while at the same time producing the biggest smile on your face.

Boswell wonders how Sister Juanita found out that he had finished his Doctorate and why did that become a news item around here? Boswell realizes he could figure out the connection later but for the moment he had to concentrate on Sister Juanita, which on a good day is quite a difficult task. He thought he would attempt to deflect her many questions and flirts by getting a cup of coffee and quickly leaving but he had underestimated his foe.

"Just a black coffee Sister Juanita."

"Any sugar or cream?"

"No, I said black. That means no sugar and no cream… black like me."

"Black like you? You ain't black sweetie. You are mahogany brown to me. Look like you got a little cream in you doc. Is there something the matter with you? No sugar hmmm? Everyone needs a little sugar. Would you like me to stick my finger in your coffee so that you can get some of this natural sweetness? Hmmm?"

The restaurant patrons explode with laughter. Sister Juanita is on a roll and they were enjoying the show. Boswell stood there frozen, unable to say or do anything as a warm feeling was quickly moving across his face. The lioness had pounced and was showing no mercy causing the laughing hyenas to howl with glee. So, Boswell did what any animal found within the clutches of a hungry lioness would do. Run as fast as you can and lick your wounds later hoping to get away with some pride left.

"No Sister. Forget about the coffee. I got to go. Nice seeing you again."

The hyenas had become bold as they began nipping at his heels.

"Boy, Doc I never seen someone as dark as you get that red before!"

"Hey youngin, you better go before she has you back behind that counter asking you to play doctor on her!"

To finish off her morning meal…Sister Juanita replies, "Doc what's the matter I got you nervous? I know that you want me. I'm all the sweetness you will ever need. Don't be a stranger. Come back and see your Sister Juanita soon and next time buy something with your cheap self. I told you this ain't no zoo."

Boswell quickly retreats out of the restaurant, waving goodbye with head down. He suddenly stops at the door, turns around and blows a kiss in Sister Juanita's direction causing the hyenas to go wild. Boswell has always admired Sister Juanita for her assertive flirty nature. Once again he had gotten in over his head and found his way out even though his way of escape was a little puny by his own standards. Today he entered into her den unprepared and that was his mistake. But, he who laughs last laugh best, so despite the fact he has not eaten anything for breakfast Boswell is feeling good. That was until he received a text from his present romantic interest Michelle.

It's not that Boswell does not look forward to hearing from Michelle, he does. Boswell is not an avid supporter of using texting as a communication medium. He views texting as a regressive method of expressing oneself and ideas comparable to using Morse code. He cannot understand why someone would rather type than talk. But his biggest problem with texting is the assumed expected reciprocal behavior that people expect him to text them back and get offended if he does not. In his attempt to disconnect himself from pop culture Boswell has explain to family and friends that he rarely texts, so do not expect one in return.

The conversation sometimes goes like this... sometimes they call and say, "Boswell did you get my text?"

"Yes I did."

"So why didn't you answer it?"

"I told you I do not text."

"But I TEXTED you!"

"Yes I know...so what do you want?"

"Nothing, just nothing."

"Just what I thought."

It's like if someone texts you it's your moral obligation to text them back to acknowledge the reception of the text. In Boswell's mind it's a choice to return a text not an obligation and not a choice he wishes to do. Instead of thinking, *it's a text from Michelle, I can't wait to read it,* Boswell's mind goes immediately to why she didn't call me. What Boswell really would like to express to his family and friends is that he enjoys engaging in conversation. It allows him to become more connected to the person by hearing their voice and sensing their mood by listening to the rhythm of their words. Texting is a decent way to send words but not meaning

In Search of a Good Feeling

and feelings which are the essential parts of conversation. Boswell's self-imposed ban on texting forces people to see him as someone who cannot conform to today's standards, instead of being a lover of expressive language.

The text reads: "Hi baby can't wait to see you tonight☺."

It can be said that Boswell is not a fan of the emoticon either. How Boswell and Michelle met was a combination of luck and charm. Boswell was in luck that day and was overwhelmed by Michelle's charm. They shared a table in a coffee shop in the Olde City part of Philadelphia. Olde City is located in the historical part of Philadelphia right off the Delaware River. It is populated with antique shops, music stores, live theatre and a couple of coffee shops. This is an area where Boswell enjoys going due to the informal atmosphere. His version of their initial interaction goes something like this.

Michelle spoke first. "Hi is there any one sitting here?"

"Nope."

"May I?"

"Sure, let me move my laptop out of your way."

(About 3 minutes later)

"Excuse me, the cologne you are wearing smells good. What's the name of it?"

"I can't tell you."

"Ok, why not?"

"Because if I tell a woman whom I do not know the name of the cologne that I am wearing, she will go purchase it for her man, and he will smell as good as me. I then lose my advantage."

"Hmm, you are pretty smart. What a man. You smell good and are smart, too. But, for your information I do not have a man, so the advantage is still yours. And if you are smart as you think you are now is the time to use it. By the way my name is Michelle, what's yours?"

"Glad to meet you Michelle, my name is Boswell and the answer is still no, but thank you for informing me about my present advantage, that's so cute. Are you attempting to pick me up?"

Michelle's version is quite different. She remembers that it was raining and she had run in from the rain into the crowded coffee shop. Looking like a wet cat with foggy glasses Michelle looked for somewhere to sit and regroup. That's when she spotted the empty chair at Boswell's table. She was torn about what to do. Michelle wanted to sit down but she did not want this guy to come on to her. Quickly, she weighed the pros and cons of her situation and decided to sit down anyway, but if he initiated anything... to be very distant with any responses to him.

Michelle walked over to Boswell's table and asked him if the empty seat was taken. He looked up from what he was doing and a great big goofy smile came over his face when he said, "No I would be honored for you to sit here."

From that moment on, Boswell attacked, attacked and attacked. He offered to buy her a hot drink, he asked her name, he told her about the book he was reading, he asked if she was single, asked, asked, and asqked some more. Michelle strangely found him charming, but really she is a sucker for a smile, and Boswell had a great one. So in the end, Michelle gave in and they have been a couple for the last year.

Dating has not always been Boswell's strong suit. He is a victim of the relationship wars, and wears some scars

In Search of a Good Feeling

to prove it. Never married, he has been in a couple of long term relationships that, depending on who is telling the story were either great or terrible. Boswell likes to believe that his relationships are like chapters written in his book of life. Some of the chapters are long and loving and others are short with problematic endings.

The oldest of three children, he has twin sisters, Wendy and Wanda who are three years younger than him. His father drank himself into an early grave. Soon after his father's death, his mother quickly remarried, to Boswell dismay. The suddenness of the marriage caused a major rift between Boswell and his mother which continues today. He refuses to acknowledge his stepfather's existence and his mother's marriage status. He generally sends messages to his mother through one of his twin sisters and those messages are infrequent.

While studying communications at Ohio University, Boswell joined the Air Force ROTC resulting in an eight year stint as an officer in the Air Force after graduation. He served in the Iran war, and is presently in the Air force reserve as a captain. He settled in Philadelphia after being stationed in Dover Delaware. His time in Philadelphia has been interesting. While in the Air Force, Boswell finished his Master's degree in communication and once out of active duty he used his GI bill to complete his Ph.D. Presently he is teaching at Temple University in the communication's department.

CHAPTER 2

At 8:30 am, Michelle finds herself in jury room 101 of the City of Philadelphia listening for her jury number to be called. Michelle Waterman can best be described as just a beautiful person in looks, actions, and mannerisms. Her world view of life is simple and innocent, while being uncluttered with any pop culture idealism. She sees her role in the world to be an observer and not a judge. Being one to interpret a person's behavior within the context that it occurs. Believing that an active mind requires the same type of body, she participates in yoga, refuses to eat red meat, rides a bike to work on most days and swims at least three times a week at the downtown Y. She volunteers as a tutor to older adults who are attempting to obtain their GED while being involved in the city wide Red Cross disaster team.

Michelle is the only child of a multi-ethnic family. Being from a mixed family has its plusses and minuses, especially for Michelle. She refuses to be blamed for the negative things that one side of her family committed. Her father, John Waterman, was born in South Carolina and studied engineering at the University of South Carolina. After graduating, he obtained an engineering position at Sharpe Industries, a leading firm in the production of plastics at their home office in Charleston SC. He met Michelle's mother, Cordelia Specht, a German woman while in Germany on company business. During his three year assignment in Germany they fell in love, got married and began their family. At the age of two, Michelle and her parents moved to the states. Soon after Michelle turned ten, her mother was killed in a car crash. Michelle was sent to be raised by her paternal grandparents in South Carolina while her father moved to Texas to tend to his business pursuits.

Michelle remained with her grandparents until her graduation from her father's alma mater. When she looks back at her time at the University of South Carolina Michelle smiles. Experimentation with whatever and whoever was her motto. The shyness that she brought to college was soon abandoned and traded in for the spirit of the butterfly. She bounced from one major to another until surprised at the end of four years she had amassed enough credits to receive a Bachelor's degree in General Studies, which pleased her grandparents and father especially.

Determined to be her own person, Michelle set off on a path of self-discovery that was littered with potholes and boulders. Within the next fifteen years, she had been married and divorced twice, lost her father, completed a stint in the Peace Corp, obtained an advanced degree in anthropology, found Christ, lost Him, and is presently looking for Him again.

Her failed marriages reflected besides what she believes were two bad decisions, a belief in the power of love. Her anthem song for her marriages could have been that old Beatles' classic "All You Need is Love." She holds strongly to the belief that despite differences between two people love has the power to overcome the gaps and unite. Michelle fondly refers to her first marriage as her get out of jail card. She wanted to get out the watchful eye of her grandparents so Michelle married her college boyfriend. The marriage was brief with a sad ending. Due to the fact it was her first love, Michelle had overestimated her ability to love someone who did not love her back. Defeated, but not out, at the age of 24, Michelle sought out the outcome of loving someone without much success.

Michelle's father died in a car accident soon after her 25th birthday, leaving her emotionally numb but financially secure for life. One relationship soon slid into another, until a she finally bottomed out at age 28, and went seeking new inspiration. Michelle's journey brought her to the doorsteps of Temple University's anthropology department. Her interest in the subject matter was an extension of Michelle's search for self. Born in one continent and raised in another one has caused her to develop a diffused sense of self.

The only child of American-German couple with dual citizenship left her feeling like a woman without a country. With no desire to give her allegiance to either country she appeared indecisive and lost to her friends. So she enrolled at Temple University to study different cultures in hopes of finding herself. Why Temple University in Philadelphia? Hmmm, because it was on the other side of the country and hopefully her past would not follow her.

While at school, Michelle met her second husband George, a student not unlike her in search of self. After a brief moments sprinkled with romance, raw sex and deep discussions about the power of love they became a married

In Search of a Good Feeling

couple. They thought that if marriage would allow them to become one or we, and with the combined forces of us, they could find their own you and me. It was a tactical mistake unforeseen by the naive couple. Their search for their individual self, took the couple in opposite directions and never back to the comfort that the we provided. The bones of love are everywhere said one song writer.

Internalizing her marriage failures caused Michelle to feel like a piece of driftwood on a lake, just being pushed and pulled by waves of emotions with no destination in sight. Soon after the ink on her divorce had dried, Michelle interviewed with the Peace Corp, and three weeks after graduation she found herself in a middle of the rain forest giving locals instruction on how to disinfect water.

Frustrated with her love outcomes, Michelle attempted to revive her soul by focusing on others. Her Peace Corp travels took her first to Costa Rica and then to Chile. Among the bugs, heat and constant rain, Michelle began to develop a sense of self due to the fact no one cared about her past life, everyone was focused on the present and future. This new perspective forced her to stop her pity party and start caring for someone else, at the moment it's Boswell.

She returned to Philadelphia and took a job at Community College of Philadelphia teaching sociology and anthropology full time. Dr. Waterman as she hates to be called recently took a yearlong unpaid leave of absence for the purpose of what she calls, "to sit on the park bench and just check out life." From this year of checking out life, Michelle intends to write a book about her observations.

She has just finished texting her boyfriend, Boswell, a term anyone else would use to describe Boswell's role in her life. Neither are comfortable with the terms boyfriend or girlfriend nor the role that it designates. The terms seems too juvenile to them since both of them are past thirty but by saying that they are just friends does not do it for them either. Michelle was adamant in stating that she did not want a boy-friend…she wants someone who "takes delight in her" not someone with a title. When asked by Boswell what does delight looks like, she describes it as the feeling you get when you eat your favorite food. So after a little discussion they settle on the novel concept that they were just dating, and their interactions together were just a date. Therefore, nothing is taken for granted and the goal is to string as many good times together as possible. Until last week all of the interactions could be described as good times, but the good times may be coming to an end.

Sleepy from another restless night of tossing and turning, Michele yawns in unison with the other less than stimulated perspective jurors. Her mind drifts back to her present situation as people mill past her attempting to find a seat that meets their personal space requirements. They wander around looking but their selection is limited and stress begins to appear on their faces. The awkwardness of placing a large number of people together who do not know each other results in eerie silence. No one talking, all nervously awaiting their fate, with no desire to self-disclose to anyone.

At 8:45 am, the jury selection officer welcomes 300 jurors and expresses to them the importance of the civil duty they are about to perform. The officer describes possible scenarios that may occur today and reminds the group that their requirement is either be placed on one jury or serve

In Search of a Good Feeling

as a participant in the jury selection pool for one day. The instructions for the day are finished and the calling of names begins.

"Michele Waterman," a voice calls, "Juror 37". Michelle says, "Here," and lines up with 40 other potential jurors of a mixed bag of races, gender and ages.

This group weaves their way through the corridors of justice to the fifth floor courtroom of Judge Robin Bush. As the jurors awaits permission to enter the courtroom, Michelle notices that some jurors are pulling out cellphones despite instructions given to turn them off. She slowly shakes her head…*freaking sociopaths.* While they wait several members of the Philadelphia Police force in different stages of physical conditioning walk by. Michelle wonders silently if "*misphysical*" is a word. Attorney looking people with expensive suits and flashy ties continue to exit the fifth floor elevators then scatter like chickens into various courtrooms.

The jurors are finally asked to enter into Judge Bush's courtroom and sit in numeric order. In their chair each juror finds a card with their jury number on it. Stress is visibly high in the courtroom. Most of the jurors sit and wait hoping not to be chosen, so for good luck Michelle rubs her belly. The prosecutor and the defense lawyer proceed to question the jury pool. The jury pool responds in the negative by raising up their jury number. Michelle's strategy is to raise her number as much as possible even if it means lying. It's not that Michelle does not want to do her civic duty, she truly does, just not this part of it. Just to participate in the jury pool selection is civic duty enough for her, to be selected on a jury is beyond the call of duty. Although there are those civic conscious individuals who see jury duty as one of the privileges that the constitution bestows upon every American, Michelle just is not one of them.

The questioning ends and the lawyers leave the courtroom to determine the fate of the jury pool. As soon as the lawyers leave, something remarkable occurs. People start to talk to each other. It must be the built up anxiety caused by the wait. Waiting to be called to a prospective jury. Waiting in the hallways to be called in the courtroom and finally waiting in the court room that turns the same group of cell phone gawking individuals into social creatures.

Juror 38, a redheaded older woman from South Philly whose name is Betsy, shares with Michelle her anxiety about the process along with asking Michelle where she bought her sandals. Michelle listens intently to Betsy as the conversation goes in a million directions over the next fifteen minutes. Betsy talks about her two grandchildren, her the job at Macy's and sorry husband, but concludes that life is good. Not one to disturb someone's stream of consciousness, Michelle smiles, nods, while interjecting some umps and wows.

Suddenly, a door opens, and the room becomes quiet again. The judge and the rest of the court officials return as anxiety in the room climbs. After clearing her voice, a court staffer states, "If your number is called you can leave the court room. Your duty is over and you can pick up your stipend on the way out. If your number is not called please remain in your seat." She began to read off the numbers, "1, 5, 7, 11, 18, 19, 20, 27, 36, 37……..*"*

That's is all Michelle needs to hear as she rises quickly but is torn about what is the correct etiquette in this situation. Should she turn to say bye to Betsy, or should she quickly leave the room with her good fortune? Michelle turns to Betsy and says, "Nice talking to you and good luck."

Betsy smiles back and waves goodbye. Free at last, free at last thought Michelle as she ran out of the courthouse doors with the nine dollar stipend in her hands. *But what to do now? I got money, I got time.* Since she has the rest of the day to herself, Michelle decides to walk down to river, pick up something to drink on the way and lose herself in a book.

Along her way down Market Street Michelle is greeted by catcalls from a group of high school males. She smiles in embarrassment, picking up her pace to distance herself from the young admirers. *I am old enough to be their mother, what the heck do they want with me? Men young or old seem to not understand the difference between good attention and bad attention.*

Crossing at 2nd Street Michelle makes her way to Penn's Landing, a city park on the Delaware River; the river that separates New Jersey from Pennsylvania. She buys a water from a vendor for a dollar and goes in search of the perfect park bench to read her book. An avid reader of fiction, Michelle has decided to go in another direction in her literary quest for knowledge and read a nonfiction book titled, "The Meaning of True Love". The book was suggested by Deb, her yoga buddy who is always reading something about the true meaning of something. Deb convinced Michelle to read the book by saying it would change your life by allowing you to experience true love at a higher and more meaningful level. Michelle doubted her claim but with no book in mind to read she reluctantly accepted the book with the promise to report back to Deb when she finished it. It has been two weeks since she received the book, so Michelle thought this is as good of a time as ever to read it, since she was really tired of ducking Deb at yoga.

She thinks, *This book is a good distraction for the moment... the true meaning of love, that's what a girl needs right now. I have been anxious for a couple of days about discussing something with Boswell. I have delayed the discussion a couple of times due to the fact that Boswell can be quite difficult about some things. But tonight is the night, so in the meantime let me find out what love truly is*". Michelle sighs, as she open the book to page one and reads the following:

Chapter One: What True Love Is

John 3:16 New International Version (NIV)

[16] For God so loved the world that he gave his one and only Son, that whoever believes in him shall not perish but have eternal life.

The Verse teaches us that True love begins and ends with you giving your most precious possession (self) for the survival of someone.

Whatever came after the first sentence is lost to Michelle. She closes the book and just fixates on the first sentence repeating it over and over in her head. The words dance in Michelle's mind as she attempts to makes sense of what she just read. *Hmm, to love is to be willing to give up self for someone else. That's deep. I think that I am there with Boswell but I am afraid to admit it to him. I'm afraid of his reaction and that sucks.*

In Search of a Good Feeling

Michelle places the book back in her bag and drinks her water. She remembers one day talking with Boswell about his first love and a smile came on his face. She asked, Why the smile?"

"My first love was my 6th grade Spanish teacher named Ms. Negron," he said. "I was crazy about her. I can remember she called my eyes so "tan vivo", which in Spanish means so alive."

"So what happened to your first love?" I asked.

"Well unfortunately she got married and moved back to Puerto Rico, never to hear from again. I was crushed... and broken-hearted when she announced her marriage to the class. I vowed never to fall in love again."

"That's cute."

"Cute! Are you making fun of me?"

"No just commenting on a past experience…it was cute, your first love."

She smiles about the memory, and sits for another hour before returning to her apartment to change for her date with Boswell tonight.

CHAPTER 3

Boswell with drink in hand looks around the coffee shop for a seat. Early as usual, he spies out his favorite spot. He sits at the table, pulls the adjacent seat close to him, and smiles. *Perfect,* he thought. Boswell likes to come early to check out the crowd, and anytime you deal with Michelle you are going to be early.

The coffee shop slowly transforms from a quiet sleepy place to a crowded and noisy one. It's getting close to show time and the place is becoming more alive in a sense. After the mike check ends the next voice that is heard is that of Joe Brown, the MC of tonight's show. Boswell slowly scans the crowd of multiracial, multiethnic everything. He nods in the direction of a couple of regulars and gets up to shake the hand of his longtime friend Bill, a relic of the Black power movement. He is a musician in his own right, but like a lot of people, Bill is truly in love with himself.

"Yo brother, how you be?" smiles Bill.

"I'm good, you know I'm just here to chill out after a crazy day at work", remarks Boswell.

In Search of a Good Feeling

"Well I think I understand, but tonight I am on the prowl for some bed time fun if you know what I mean. There are some nice looking honeys up in here tonight."

Both men laugh.

"So, where is your lady?" asks Bill.

"You know she is a lady and she appears when she appears," replies Boswell.

"That's that crazy talk. If she was my lady she would be here waiting on me. You got it all wrong. Talk to you soon, time is a wasting. I'm going to slide over to that sweet honey over there and see what's up for tonight," remarks Bill.

But before Boswell can reply Bill walks quickly towards his next victim with a silly smile on his face.

Women beware, fathers hide your daughters because Wild Bill, the dog of all dogs is on the loose.

It's not that Bill is a bad person, it is just that his view about women is somewhat screwed up and detrimental to the human race. But that's Bill.

Boswell checks his watch again. *She is late.* He takes a deep breath in an attempt to become mentally centered. Known by all who know him, Boswell has little patience for being late. Surprisingly, he does understand that things happen, but he has come to recognize in his own behavior that if he is late is it is because he has not managed his time wisely. So he generalizes this type of reasoning to other people's behavior. He has developed a belief that people are more alike than different, that everyone has the same basic needs of attention, desiring a connection, and being confirmed. He sees these as basic needs for every human being. What he identifies as the difference is how individuals express those needs through their outward behavior. So, Boswell uses his basic understanding of self and generalizes his behavior to others to understand why they do what they do. It does not manner to him that his judgment might be wrong. In Boswell's world, he would rather be wrong than right. In being right, it only confirms what he already knows, but being wrong allows learning to take place and allows his knowledge base of human behavior to expand. Thus, Boswell sees a person's lateness, especially Michelle's, as a function of poor time management rather than a character flaw.

Although Boswell is somewhat disturbed by Michelle's lateness, all is not lost because there is music in the air. Wednesday night is open mike at the Wired Bean, the coffee shop where Boswell and Michelle first met. After their initial meeting, it has become their regular water hole for hanging out and Wednesday night at the Bean is one of the couple's week day standing dates. Boswell enjoys live performances of any type of music. There is something about getting in front a group of people and doing your thang that impresses him.

Tonight's opening act is a newcomer named John, an older gentleman who is wearing a Philadelphia Eagle's jersey. It always amazes Boswell about the musical talent of some of the performers. John, like most of the performers at open mike night does not have the greatest voice. His is raspy and sounds like he is talking instead of singing. Despite his apparent vocal music limitation, John is strutting like crazy on that acoustic guitar. He is what Boswell calls an entertainer, a person with average music skills but who has the ability to get the crowd moving. There are individuals with great musical talent who will never move to the level

In Search of a Good Feeling

of entertainer, but John is not one of them. He may never be a great musician, but entertain he can.

John finishes his four song set with an original song titled, "Curb your Dog" and everyone is loving it. After a brief pause, Boswell's favorite performer, TJ is announced just as Michelle appears walking towards him. She is simply dressed wearing an orange T-shirt with a long flowing colorful skirt with sandals. A warm sensation slowly comes over him as his heart seems to speed up, his pupils become larger and a smile appears on his face.

"Now," says Michelle, "Is that smile for me?"

"Of course dear even though you are a little late. Hmm, 15 minutes to be exact, but the smile is for you. Just seeing you makes me feel good."

"Oh that's sweet or is the smile because TJ is about to perform?"

"TJ who?" smiles Boswell as he looks quickly towards the stage "It's all for you dear, all for you!"

Boswell leans towards Michelle and gives her a kiss on the lips. As Boswell listens to rhythmic tone of TJ's voice he realizes that he loves Michelle, but not the type of love that one expresses in verbal conversation like saying, "I love you" at the end of a phone call. It's more like the love that creates a feeling inside that you cannot shake. It warms, delights you and scares you at the same time. It was the scared part that concerns Boswell. As he sits in the middle of the coffee shop with his woman on his side, and TJ on the mike, Boswell smiles thinking, *This is good.*

Michelle glances over at Boswell to study his face. She thinks, *Smiling does allow a softness to come to his face. Why do men attempt to hide that part of them? I wonder if being a man is as difficult as being a woman? I doubt it.* Michelle chuckles quietly. Boswell touches Michelle's arm and asks,

"What's funny?"

Before Michelle could answer applause fills the air. TJ had just finished her first spoken word poem. After the applause ceases Boswell did not re-ask the question nor did Michelle offer an explanation. His mind was somewhere else slowly connecting the dots of all of the good feelings surrounding him. TJ's voice stimulates his mind while Michelle's touch and presence sends him to that good feeling place, where time stands still and there is no restriction on the wrong and right. After TJ's set was over Michelle leans over and whispers in Boswell's ear

'I'm pregnant."

Immediately Boswell's mind goes into panic alert. With the words "I'm pregnant" echoing rapidly over and over in his mind his amygdala that controls road rage and high emotional states in the brain wakes up. The brain automatically transfers blood from Boswell's non-essential areas like digestion and sexual urges to his outer extremities to execute the flight or fight response. While blood is being moving from one organ to another the brain multi-tasks to search his memory banks to find when Boswell has been faced with a similar situation in the past and its outcome. The brain finds none. Instantly Boswell knows that he is stuck, his body is saying run or fight, his brain is indicating that he is in a high emotional state, and his history of past responses is empty. This all occurs in a micro-second. Boswell assesses the situation and realizes that he is scared but without missing a beat he takes Michelle's hand into his, looks in her eyes, and replies,

In Search of a Good Feeling

"Cool, it's going to be fine baby."

Boswell's thought processes continue into hyper drive asking the questions to himself, *What just happened? She said that she is pregnant….what…by whom...Me??? Oh shoot!,* as he awaits Michelle's response. She kisses him on the cheek and places her head on his shoulder.

As Boswell's anxiety grows, Michelle's anxiety quickly disappears, her heart slows down, and now she is able to breathe again. Unfortunately for the past two weeks Michelle did not radiate with such a glow. Feelings of doom, depression and rejection were her constant companions. Questions seemed to attack her constantly,

Why? How? What will Boswell say? What the heck am I doing pregnant? This was not in the plan….Oh God this is not funny. Due to the scientist nature in her, Michelle had tried four different pregnancy tests and all came back positive. Now what? She wanted to tell Boswell immediately, but she was afraid. Knowing Boswell's past responses to personal events in their relationship Michelle thought his reaction to her announcement would be typically low key without any indication of emotional stress. *I was right,* thought Michelle. *Boswell did respond like I thought he would buts it's alright. I told him and I feel good about it. Let him freak out for a moment to ponder about being the father of an unborn* child.

Boswell's thoughts continue in their circular path. Without any previous experience with getting anyone pregnant he is lost about the next step. He wants to excuse himself and run. In later discussions about the moment, Boswell admitted that he did not know what to feel, he was scared in to numbness. The news was unexpected, overwhelming and powerful. It reminded him of the time that he received the news of his father's death. He did not know how to feel so he waited for his feelings to attach themselves to his thoughts and it took a while.

Her announcement made them quiet. Before TJ started her next set they left the coffee shop, walking around Olde City hand in hand but silent in their own thoughts. Initially the silence comforted Michelle but after a while it troubled her. *I just stated that I am pregnant, and this fool is quiet. Why the heck doesn't he have anything to say?"* They occasionally break to kiss, look into one another's eyes, then continue to walk. Under the streetlight at 2nd and Market, they stop. Still holding hands Boswell turns to Michelle.

"How are you feeling?"

"I'm ok."

"Just Ok?"

"Well yes, just ok. This is scary. I did not know how you would respond. I know my initial response was one of, "What the Fuck!" For two weeks I have been an emotional train wreck. I was just scared. Scared of your reaction and more scared of my own. Aww, what now! What are we going to do?"

Boswell hesitates. He wants to pull her close, but believing she will stop talking if he does, he just waits.

"I need to know how you feel. I do not want the cool calm laid back crap that you serve me in the coffee shop, and I need to know how you really feel about our situation. Talk to me because I'm scared. Say something to me other than its cool, It's going to be alright."

Boswell now pulls her closer. "I do not know how I feel. My emotions have not connected with my brain yet. When you told me the news I was in shock. You pregnant…that was not in the plans. My mind kept on turning faster and

In Search of a Good Feeling

faster while the questions keep coming. I needed to think so I got quiet, had to let my mind slow down. Not surprisingly I feel so close to you. At this moment I'm good with the idea. I'm good with you, and happy for us but I'm also scared as hell, which is an ok place to be because it forces me to think clearly."

Tears form in Michelle's eyes as she slowly shakes her head and begins to cry. Boswell is caught off guard with her tears. He reaches for Michelle but she backs away from him not wanting to be comforted.

"Boswell, I do not need you to hold me. I need you to be a man. Stop giving me more of your crap. Give me a freaking answer and start thinking. Let's look at reality Boswell. First of all, the fact that this happened, pretty much alters the nature of the relationship no matter what we decide to do. The thing about "I'm pregnant" is that, no matter what, "what we did" is over. It might still be good or maybe even better, but our time spent like that is over. There is a bit of a sadness. That "little special thing" we do, sharing music, spending time exploring together now has a little nail of reality hammered into it even if we don't keep the baby, it happened. If we decide to make a clinic trip, life pretty much tossed us a ton of sadness that we can't go back on. We will act together like things are right again but it won't be quite the same, ever. I know you don't want to get married and neither do I. So, what if we did that? You will be a dad and I will be a mom and we will be parents together with "date night." Really?"

Boswell remains silent. He feels powerless. He ponders for a moment for a response. "Yes, we are going to have the baby. The only reason that we wouldn't would because you do not want to have it. Michelle, the baby resides in your body, and I cannot tell you what to do with your body. Whatever you desire to do you have my full support. Yes, there are other future considerations that as of yet have not been figured out but like you said the relationship has been changed and there is no going back. Let's get some sleep tonight and deal with some of these issues tomorrow with a clear head."

They walk until ending up at Michelle's apartment on 5th and South Street. Michelle looks at Boswell saying, "I want to stay at your place. I'm tired of dealing with all of this mental crap at night in my apartment. I need to be in your bed, in your arms to be energized, to be loved, and to eat because I'm crazy about your cooking. I'm eating for two now you know."

"Good, that was going to be my suggestion also but for other reasons."

"What other reasons?"

"Well my bed is bigger, so is my bath tub and I have real food."

But what Boswell really wanted to say was, *I want you to stay with me tonight because you make me feel good. Your presence in life makes me feel more alive. I want you to stay with me tonight so that we can comfort each other. I want you to stay with me tonight because I am very scared.*

The couple walk up three flights of stairs and enter Michelle's apartment. She runs into her bedroom as Boswell checks out the frig. He slowly shakes his head at what he saw, containers of organic yogurt, cottage cheese, bottled mineral water and packages of salad mix huddle together in the middle of the frig seeming to keep each other warm.

In Search of a Good Feeling

Boswell thinks, *Oh my God, just as I thought... when did cottage cheese became a food? No wonder she wants to stay with me tonight. There is not anything in here to eat unless you desire a lettuce wrap filled with unsweetened plain yogurt.* Out of the corner of his eye Boswell spies a jar of unsalted almonds on the kitchen table. *Saved!* Michelle reappears from her bedroom with an overnight bag. Boswell stares at the bag.

Michelle notices Boswell's puzzled look and says, "What's the manner Boswell?"

"What you have in that bag? You have some clothes at my place remember?"

"Just some reinforcements. You like me looking good."

"Yes I do but I like your inner beauty also. Aww, forget it lets go."

They hail a cab on the corner which is generally not an easy feat at this time of night for Boswell, but with Michelle as his partner in crime there was no problem. After a twenty minutes ride they arrive at Boswell's apartment where Michelle remains for the next four months.

CHAPTER 4

The first night at Boswell's apartment, Michelle wakes up in the middle of the night in a semi-panic mode. Trying not to disturb Boswell, she slips out of the bed into his living room. She finds a quilt on top of the book shelf and situates herself on the old green couch where she remains the rest of the night. Despite the warm quilt, Michelle's body trembles as thoughts of the possibility of rejection by Boswell races through her head. *He is always so non-committal in his answers. Mr. Be Cool So Cool. What did he mean when he said that we are going to figure this out? He makes me so freaking mad at times not wanting to share what he is thinking. UUUGH.* Michelle fingers his t-shirt that she is wearing. It's an orange one with the words Cleveland on the front. She can remember when he bought the t-shirt on a trip to his beloved home town. She realizes that something about wearing it makes her feel good. Michelle sniffs it and her body tremor subsides while a feeling of warmth replaces it. *I really do like his smell that must be it.* She pulls the quilt closer to her and falls asleep on the couch.

The next morning conversation starts out fine but turns poorly quickly. Boswell awakens alone in the bed with his

In Search of a Good Feeling

thoughts. He quickly panics when he realize that Michelle is not in the bed with him. Calling her name Michelle appears in his doorway wearing the quilt. With a sleepy smile on her face she says,

"You rang master?"

"Good Morning. When did you get up?"

"Hmm, soon after you went to sleep. I was restless so I got up and went to the sofa as so not to disturb you. What's the matter, you look like crap?"

"Thanks I needed that compliment. I did not sleep well because of this freaky dream I had."

"Ok, I'm listening,"

"Well you will not believe this but I dreamed that I was pregnant!"

"PREGNANT? Wow, that's makes two of you. Who is the lucky mother?"

She laughs and gives Boswell a hug. Boswell playfully pushes her away.

"It's not funny, it was terrible, and I just got bigger and bigger and bigger. I could not move. I was scared. Then I woke up looking for you."

Michelle sits down on the bed next to Boswell and begins to rub his back.

"Sorry you had a bad dream baby. Once I laid down on the sofa I fell straight to sleep."

Boswell slowly shakes his head. "No doubt, but back to my dream. The other weird thing that I remember was there was a crow in my room."

Michelle stops rubbing Boswell's back and looks at him strangely. "A crow?"

"Yep it was the damnest thing".

Michelle takes Boswell by the hand and leads him in the direction of the kitchen. "Sounds freaky to me. A crow and you pregnant. I think you need some coffee."

Boswell looks into Michelle's eyes and speaks with a very sincere tone. "But Michelle do you think it means anything? You are the expert in ancient tribal rituals."

Michelle holds in her laughter due to the fact she realizes that Boswell is serious. She kisses him on the head saying, "Now, it is nothing. Just too much mixture of fear, late night eating and imagination. But one of Freud's followers believed that men suffered from uterus envy due to the fact they cannot have a baby. Freud would say that your pregnancy may represent your desire to produce something, and the bird symbolizes the ability to give your idea flight."

"Wow that's deep", exclaims Boswell.

"Ok, now can we have some of the Jamaican Blue mountain coffee that you keep locked up and I will tell you more? By the way do you have any oatmeal cookies hidden up there also?"

"Hmmm…no oatmeal cookies. Maybe next time."

After a breakfast of coffee, blueberry pancakes and maple syrup, the couple remains sitting at the makeshift eating table on the sun porch. The sun rays begin to warm the early morning air. A dog barks in the distance, while squirrels scamper up a nearby tree. Philadelphia was slowly waking up. The warmth from the sun and the recent meal causes Boswell to feel sleepy.

The good times feeling returns for him. With his eyes half open, Boswell smiles at Michelle saying, "You are so beautiful, but can we get back to the dream."

In Search of a Good Feeling

"Well thank you master, you are so gracious. Thanks for breakfast. It was wonderful as usual. Your mama would be proud of you". "The dream, well I have to research what a crow means. I tell you what, let me know if those symbols return in your dreams then we may be on to something."

She leans over a gives him a kiss on his cheek before saying, "So, have you thought about what we going to do? Are we going to have the baby? Are we getting married? Are we going to live together?"

Boswell quickly sits up straight. His eyes are fully open now. He is taken back by the sudden change of subject and increased seriousness in Michelle's voice. The room seem to be get somewhat smaller, and there is a stillness in the air. Leaning forward with his hands up in the air, Boswell says, "Hmmm, did I miss something? Aren't you having the baby? I thought that we talked about that last night?"

Michelle repositions herself in front of Boswell. The reflection of the morning sun on her causes a glowing sensations making her look like she is on fire. With a stern voice which Boswell would later describe to Bill as the voice of a she devil, Michelle says, "Who said that I was having the baby? I did not. I just informed you about the situation. We have yet to discuss what we are going to do about it. You just gave me your opinion about the situation. We have not agreed on anything."

Boswell now fully awaken and fearing bodily harm from Michelle meekly says, "After what I thought was the discussion about what we are going to do last night I just assumed that you agreed to have the baby. I like the idea of us having a child together, I really do."

Michelle folds her hands then unfolds them. She becomes quiet for a moment, her attention focuses on the squirrels playing on the tree. She smiles while saying, "Boswell, having a child is more than liking an idea. It's a freaking commitment. Have you thought about that type of commitment Mr. Noncommittal?"

"That's not fair. I have not had as much time to think about it as you have. What's that Mr. Noncommittal about?"

"We both are 35, we will be 55, 55 years old when this bundle of joy is 20. Can you handle that?"

"Sweetie when it comes down to it, it's not a 'we' decision, it really is yours. I cannot tell you what to do with your body but whatever decision you make I will support".

"YOU WHAT!!! You piece of shit. Are you being a typical guy who does not want to deal with his responsibility? My decision? No sweetheart! It's a WE decision and we make it today, together."

"Wow those are strong words. Me, a piece of shit? I am not going to attempt to defend myself but I told you yesterday I do not have the right to tell you what to do with your body. I am not attempting to get out of my responsibility to you. I just know where my role begins. It may sound like a cop out, but truly it is not. What would happen if I said yes, and you said no? So in the end you have the power not me. We have always worked together to get through our situations. We both bring a different perspective to the decision making which is one of our strengths. So that's my decision. If you desire to have the baby I am there for you. If you do not, I am there for you. I vote in concert with your decision."

There was a long silence which, in Boswell's world is a confusing situation. His interpretation of Michelle's silence is a problem for him. What does silence mean? Boswell believes that it can be a good thing because it gives the person time to make decisions. In class he encourages his students to ponder before answering. Boswell calls it ponder power. But Michelle is not one of his students and her silence is killing him. Yes, he is pissed for being called a piece of shit, but he has been called worse by lesser individuals. He knows that no matter what she says next his world is about to change.

Michelle begins to cry, slowly one tear then two. Her body shivers as she reaches for Boswell. They embrace in silence for a couple of minutes both afraid of letting the other go. At this moment they listen beyond words. Feeling the fear and the uncertainty in each other's body they embrace to find the strength together. Faces wet from tears greet each other with smiles as lips meet lips and tongues begin to dance. The couple instinctively return to the bedroom to continue the moment.

He gently kisses her hand and asks, "So how did it happen?"

"How did what happen?"

"How did you get pregnant?"

"Well your sperm fertilized my egg, so congratulations." Michelle slowly claps. "Yes your boys can swim, and very well I must say."

"But you take birth control, correct?"

"I do, but I periodically stop for a while to cleanse my body of toxins. It must of happened during one of my cleansing periods."

"Well ok, but I assumed….."

"Did not your Mama teach you never to assume? And because you did, you are the father of our child."

CHAPTER 5

The relationship is over? Did I read that right? And she sent it in a text to me, a damn text!!! Let me read it again. Don't I have some say in our relationship if it is over...over? She must be kidding me, over? Boswell's mind suddenly goes silent, and his body limp, tears form in his eyes and stream down his face. The hurt manifests itself physically, his body begins to shake, and he wraps his arms around himself and cries louder.

Boswell awakes the next day on the couch still in his yesterday clothes. He looks around the living room and on the table next to him sits a half-eaten container of vegetarian fried rice and a bowl of melted ice cream. Boswell moves slowly trying to gather himself while attempting to figure out what happened to him last night. He walks into the bathroom and begins to fill the tub with water. Boswell always thinks clearer while relaxing in a tub of bubbly hot water. He eases down in the tub hoping that the hot water will jog his memory. Quickly the water did its job causing Boswell to race out of the tub still covered with suds in search of his cell phone.

In Search of a Good Feeling

Stuck between the cushions of the couch, Boswell recovers his phone and rereads the text from Michele last night. He screams as the suds slide down his body. In an attempt to console self, Boswell returns to his safe place, the tub. He feels like his world is spinning out of control. Questions race through his mind. *Why did she send me that text? What happened? What did I do?* Boswell blasts the hot water and jumps at first due to the temperature of the water then grimaces as he attempts to see how hot he can stand it. He finally turns off the water. The hot water has created a mist in the bathroom causing the walls to appear like they were weeping. He slides deeper down in the tub, as beads of sweat roll down his face uniting themselves with his tears. After 30 minutes of silent mediation, Boswell rises from the tub dripping water all over the floor as he moves slowly to his bed room. He drapes a towel around his waist, walks into the kitchen, gets a glass of water and sits on the couch to ponder.

After I sent the text, I became scared, I did not know how Boswell would respond. But it is his fault, he forced me to do it. We were fine. Yes, the pregnancy issue was an unseen obstacle, but I thought we managed to turn it into a positive. But then he began asking me question. I think he has always asked me questions, but this time it was different. They kept coming and coming. It was too much. Then yesterday he told me that we needed to talk. Needed to talk I thought, talk about what? Oh no everyone knows what that means and he is not going to break up with me first. I heard those same words before and the end result was another relationship ending badly. Oh no, so I decided to end this silly relationship before he can find the words to say it to me. On top of that I texted him that I was ending the relationship knowing how much he dislikes text messages. Serves his ass right. What the heck do we have to talk about? We talk every day, so why did he have to say to me that we have to talk? We are not going to have any freaking talk; talk about what? I am going to do all of the talking now. I decide when we are over, and we are over, but he still has the responsibility to tend to his business. You think that you are going to take and not give back? Have you lost your mind? You really do not know who you are dealing with mama's boy. I should have never sat down at the coffee shop that day. I should have kept on walking pass you. You with that pitiful rap about how beautiful you thought I was. Don't you know how many times I heard that line? Plenty. I just felt sorry for your butt. You make me sick, giving up on me. Oh no. I know that you have been acting kind of funny lately. I thought the idea of being a father was getting to you, but breaking up with me does not stop you from your responsibilities. You are going take care of our child if we are together or not. Hell it took two of us to make this bundle of joy inside of me and the two of us will be responsible for this joy. I do not care if he has three wives, he's still going take to care of this baby. I wonder what his mother would think? It's probably her fault anyway. He is undoubtedly a mama's boy. No wonder he is not married, no one else would put up with his crap. I remember Shirley telling me something like this happened to her. Her husband walked out of her life and left her with two kids. She was married that's a little different. Heck no it's not. Hmm, I am glad the irresponsible butt did not ask me to marry him. I would be a sad state of affairs, pregnant and left at the altar. I'm scared, maybe that's it. I will be getting fat and Boswell will not want to be with me But it's his fault. He could have use a condom but he did not. That cheap fool, and now he does not want me.

Boswell slowly gets dress, he picks up one of his t-shirts that Michelle enjoys wearing. *I feel empty. I thought I would never say or think that way but I do. I do believe that if a person does not want to be in a relationship you should not guilt them into staying with you. So if Michelle desires to leave the best relationship that she has ever been in for whatever screwed up reason that she has come up with, well it's her loss. Wait a minute let me get my wits about the situation. I do know what to do. In the past when something like this occurred in my relationships I generally waited it out allowing my partner to make the first move. It was the best strategy because it allowed me not to risk too much. I have come to believe that a relationship is all about risks, gains and losses. How much of yourself will you risk? The greater the risk the greater the reward or loss. Surprising in my relationship with Michelle I decided early on to risk it all. To be open, vulnerable and to take risks. One thing my dad told me, "A scared man cannot to anything. You have to play to win not to lose. A scared man has already lost, he is just waiting for it to happen. A relationship is a funny thing, you fuss while you are in it and cry when you are without it."*

I can remember how I felt after our first accidental meeting at the coffee shop. I left with a smile on my face and thinking that the dating god has finally found me worthy. My cries had been heard and prayers answered. I thought it was my time to reap the benefits gleaned from the experiences of past relationships that had gone wrong. My time to discover if the myth is true, that a rare sweet nectar flows from the lips of a woman as intelligent and beautiful as Michelle. But in the same breath attempting not too get to ahead of myself, I stopped and pondered. Hmm...people like Michelle tend to be too good to be true. Is the dating god playing a trick on me for screwing up my last relationship? Voices of doubt soon appeared in mind saying, Why you? Is that really her number? Are you on candid camera? Or did one of my sorry ass friends put her up to this? The voices were on their way to staging a massive attack until suddenly I received a text saying:

> Hi Boswell. Just wanted to tell you that I really enjoyed our brief time together today. Sorry for me being a little defensive but you can't just let anyone into your life, however, you seemed to be a good sport about it. Looking forward to seeing you tomorrow and also I was checking out this number to see if it was real, a girl can never be too safe....
> Michelle

Move on voices, it's time for me to break out in my happy dance. Our first interaction had me wanting more and more of her. It was strange, but at the same time wonderful. She gives me a different insight into myself. It was like she gives me something to be proud of about myself. The most amazing thing I realized was that she listened. Michelle really listens to me. It's been a long while since I have received that type of attention. A wise man once told me that all we all desire in life is positive attention and if you were fortunate to receive it from someone, you may end up following them where ever they go. I am a witness that my Uncle Webb was right again. I know my students listen to me, they have to kind of but she would look me in the eye whenever we talked, wait patiently to hear what I have to say and then ponder it. It has never been a contest, it has been a conscious effort on her part to hear me. That type of attention was new to me. I was reinvented in a small way. It started by me educating Michelle about me and ended up with me learning more about myself through someone else eyes.

Michelle and I were open to discuss anything that crossed our mind. We would have long conversations about anything from who is the best singer ever to the best way to roast a duck. She had a love for Bob Dylan's music. Michele called his lyrics musical poetry which I interpreted to mean that sometimes the lyrics are better read than to listen to him sing them. I saw him as a cult figure that the hippies of the 60's flock to because they were stoned and they did not know how bad his music was at the time. Of course once I said that it was on. This discussion led to us to having weekly music listening dates, yep music listening dates where we would listen to each other's music and maybe engage in other activities depending how the music moved us.

Michelle, Michelle, Michelle, hmm, what am I going to do? It's been over 24 hours and nothing, no communication. What could she have been thinking to send me such a text? Maybe it's the pregnancy, maybe the thought of having our baby is too much for her. I never thought about the stress of having a baby. I just know how it makes me feel. Initially it felt very unfamiliar. The last thing was that truly dependent on me for support and its existence was my cat Camille and she died last year. But now a baby, and a baby's mother, that was a lot to deal with all at once. I was just getting my head around being a father when all of this happened. Me, a father? Now that's funny, never thought that would occur. Although I still do not know what it means to be a father, I did have the opportunity to observe a good one. My father and I never entered in a conversation about fatherhood, football yea, but nothing about being a father. Probably it was for the best, it just might have scared the crap out of me.

One night after a meal of beans and rice with plantains at my apartment, Michelle took my hand in her and kissed it. A warm fuzzy feeling came over me and before I could physically respond she looked into my eyes and ask me a very simply stated question: "Boswell how available are you?"

I looked at Michelle and said, "Baby, I'm available for you," as I leaned over to kiss her lips.

Michelle laughed and placed her hands over my lips shaking her head as she spoke again, "No silly really how available are you?"

"What the heck are you asking me, I told you I'm ready right now?" I replied. "Oh, you are just teasing me. You get me all hot and bothered and you ask me a question like that. Shesssssh woman."

Michelle straightened her face. "When I ask how available you silly I mean are you available physically as well as mentally and emotionally? To be in a relationship I need to know your availability. If you are going to limit your availability to me let me know. Just ponder the question Boswell do not say a thing, just think about the ramification of your answer."

I just sat there with this stupid, what just happened look, on my face. As Michelle cleared the table I pondered the question and had a hard time with the final answer. The physical part was easy since there was no one else in my life, so if I wanted to be I was physically available 24/7 for her. Mentally, it was somewhat tricky. I have things going

In Search of a Good Feeling

on in my life and occasionally I do not listen about the things that she talked about because I viewed them as noise. Emotionally, I knew there was limited availability because my last relationship did not end well and I have yet to clean up the mess that was caused by the break up.

Michelle said, "I see that you are sitting there with that weird look on your face, so I will let you in on a little information. At this point in the relationship I do not require all your availability but I may in the future so do what you have to do to get ready for me if you want me."

As I continued to sit there with a stupid look on my face attempting to comprehend what was just said to me Michelle got up took the plates in the kitchen. She placed the remaining food in two plastic containers which she put in her back pack. She quickly got her coat and said, "Again thanks for my lunch for tomorrow, you are truly a blessing in the kitchen. I hate to eat and run but I think you have something to think about, so I will leave you with your thoughts. See you tomorrow my love." Michelle left with a sinful grin on her face.

Michelle looks out her apartment window. The recently brewed green tea just steams away in its cup waiting to be sweetened with honey. A half chewed slice of wheat toast keeps it company on a red small plate while Michelle's mind is consumed with thoughts of her recent actions. *I do know what to do. Yesterday I was mad as hell and scared but today I miss his presence so much. But I do not want to look like I am begging to be with him. There are many men out there that hit on me daily but I refuse them. I had to give into his weak rap and wonderfully clever mind. I do not know what to do. Did I over react? I know the signs. I was right, its him who is* *wrong, setting me up, but what now? I have not heard from him. I know he is quite beside himself at me. I outthink him. I wonder what he is thinking. Revenge probably. Figuring out a way to get back at me. A typical man. Their feelings get hurt and seeking revenge is their next move. He probably was just waiting to get rid of me especially since I'm pregnant. He has little use for me now so bye bye Michelle. Hahaha, I fixed his ass. I struck first. (**A tear appears**) I hope I was not wrong. I miss him. Yes, I know it has not been that long but I could have been wrong. Although he can be a little too logical for me at times he has helped me through a couple of situations. I think my pregnancy overloaded his logical mind. (**More tears**) Well its messing with my mind also. Man up, whatever that means. I do not like the idea that he was going to give up on me; his stated queen, his woman, his sweetie and those other names he would call me but what do they really mean if he was going to give up on me? Aww, I miss him so. I want my man back so badly, but cannot go back to him telling him how much I miss him. That would make me look weak wouldn't it? Sometimes I just do not know what to do. I know that I could have been wrong. I might have jumped the gun but then again I could be right, shoot. I cannot keep crying about not being with Boswell. I'm pregnant, and I read that emotional stress can have a negative effect on the baby… So, for the baby's future well-being I have to get it together. I am going to be a mother, a mother. I thought I had it together but I don't. I'm scared. I do not know what people are thinking about me. I am so freaking concerned about being accepted. A single 35 year old mother of an interracial child, now that's a novel concept. Everyday my body, the body I thought I knew, looks and feels different. What am I going to do…? I see colors more vividly and sounds*

In Search of a Good Feeling

are more alive now. All of these changes on how I perceive my surroundings is overwhelming. Everything is changing right in front of me. I need some consistency back into my life.

I do need Boswell, but not because I'm a weak woman, or that I'm lonesome, no I need him because together we are good. I miss his calls, his touch, his ability to make me feel special and appreciated. When I realized that all the pregnancy tests were correct I was truly elated. I was going to have a baby by the man I loved…oops did I say that. It's true, I do love Boswell. I delight in his presence in my life and the idea of having our baby together is a wonderful thing, although I have yet to express my feelings about our soon to be born baby in that way with him. Initially I wanted to feel him out, just to see where he was about us, the relationship, really to see if he was going to run. He didn't run. Boswell embraced me even more which scared me. Until yesterday I have been at his apartment for the last 4 months, and he has yet to tell me to go home. I just barged into his personal space and made it into ours. He has waited on me 24/7 since I made myself a resident in his apartment. Yes, a little anxiety can screw up a good thing very quickly. I was scared to trust that it was real, always somewhere in the back of my mind waiting for it to end I was making my mind think something that reality was not telling me. The voices in my head kept making the doubt in my relationship with Boswell grow, until it had me seeing things that were not true. So I listened to the voices because I was scared, fear makes you do some crazy things. Now I sit here alone not knowing how to get back what I had and it's not good.

After another restless night, Boswell wakes up at 3:00am and just rocks himself back to sleep. In the morning he pens the following letter and emails it to Michelle:

Note to my Queen

Good morning... I woke up this morning with you on my mind. How that is possible I do not know, but I did. I have come to realize that maybe we do not fit together like well grooved puzzle pieces, but with a little push and pull we do fit well much better than most. So that's what I want and desire to return to the fit that allows us to interact independently and interdependent with each other. I understand that I do not need you. I existed before I met you but I do want you in my life because since we met my life has been that much better and I know it is because of what you bring into my life. Yes, I am scared about our future which is not easy to admit. I do not know how you will accept my expression of this feeling but I am scared. I need you to understand that behind this laid back attitude is man who has the ability to express a zillion of emotions and one of them is being scared. I have never been in this space before. This is all new to me, feeling my feelings, but being scared has made me look at life quite differently. It has allowed me to ponder and to feel deeply which are good things. That is what I want you to know. And by the way I love you so much...which is a very good feeling.

Boswell

After sending the email Boswell smiles nervously, he never before has revealed such deep emotional feelings

In Search of a Good Feeling

to someone else. He feels quite vulnerable and begins to second guess himself. The early morning cup of coffee suddenly tastes bitter and the voices of doom begin to play havoc with his mind. He really told someone that he wants them in his life and on top of that he used the words scared and I love you in the same message. The voices were gaining power.

Boswell thinks back to a couple of former relationships and the manner in which he projected himself to significant others. How sometimes he was unwilling to open up in fear of what the other person might find and not like. *I do not talk sometimes because I fear that the words I have said will be used against me or brought back to my attention because I have not done what I said. I do not say things instead I display my feelings in actions by treating the person well. One thing that I have learned is that you are judged by what you have done in the present not in the past. The glory that you received in the past quickly disappears if you screw up in the present. There is nothing in the bank. That individual's mind goes blank about what good times you shared with them in the past.*

Boswell has never been able to verbally express what he felt. He has been very conscious of what the other person wanted to hear. He can remember times of saying the words, "I love you", only to be able to continue to play the game but already knowing inside that the game was over. It was never about love, it was all about continuing playing the game. Boswell suddenly realizes that he was not as good at this relationship thing as he pretends to be. How can I be me without giving me up? He recalls his discussion with Bill yesterday at the Wired Bean about his situation. Needing to get some air, Boswell decided to go to the coffee shop. As he was just sitting down with his ginger lemon tea in walks Bill with that mischief smile on his face. He orders a double chocolate something, waltzed over to Boswell's table and sat down without being asked.

"Hey Professor...you alone?"

Shaking his head slowly Boswell answers, "What? Do you see anyone here? Yea man I'm alone."

"Yo, calm down you are never in here alone, so what's the matter? Your girl coming late as usual or she has found another?"

"Can't a man be alone? And if she has found another I pity him. I'm sorry we are just having some issues at the moment, and so we are just slowing down, spending some time separate. Anyway before you ask I did not do anything."

Bill lifted his coffee cup and slowly finished his drink, he wiped his mouth looks Boswell in the eye saying, "Mm that was good, but maybe that's the problem."

"What?"

"That you have not done anything man. That woman is the best thing that ever happened to you, and I have known you awhile. I can remember Laural, Ada, and Carol and what was that redhead one that like ice coffee? Yeah, Vickie. For some reason none of them stayed around. I do not know if it was you or what, but they are gone. I really do not know what Michelle sees in you. I would have left your laid back sorry butt a while ago."

"Bill."

"It might even be begging time."

"Begging time, what are you talking about?"

In Search of a Good Feeling

"Begging for what you lost. It is more than the person that you have lost. You lost that good feeling that the person brings and that's what you are begging for my brother."

"Bill!"

"I'm not finished. Do something that you do not do well. Just listen for a change. Like I was saying this woman makes you feel good. I can see that when it she comes in here. Your eyes light up, and a smile comes your face. The signs of a good feeling. Not every woman can do that to a brother. I should know, I too have had my share. Whatever you have to do to get her back, do it. It's not time for pride it's time to get real with your true feelings, macho man is dead, and tell her how you feel. And yes that may make you uncomfortable. But that's life my brother. It's time to reveal. Stand strong but do something… good feelings are sometime hard to come by."

"Thanks for the advice Bill but…."

Suddenly Bill stood up and excused himself, "Boswell sorry to talk and run, but I just remembered I am supposed to be somewhere soon. Just think about what we just discussed. It's all about how a person makes you feel and if it's a good feeling try to keep it. Later player."

With that he was gone. Off to probably charm the pants off some innocent young lady. Why did that old fool give me advice like I do not know what to do? This is not my fault she left me.

That afternoon when Boswell comes home from work Michelle is sitting on the couch with a cup of tea. Without saying a word she comes towards him, hands him a sheet of paper and waits. The paper contains the following handwritten poem.

The Beginning

As swiftly as a summer's breeze
He walked into my life
No announcement or warning that
He was coming
How was I to know all the
Changes I would be going through
Not aware that I was about to fall
For him, I was captured
Helpless
As a baby crying, wanting to be fed
I reach out to be held, he took hold
And I was lost in the sweet rapture of
Long awaiting love
I am sorry, I was scared,
I love you....but still scared

They kiss and held each other as tears flow down both of their faces, it was the beginning of another good feeling.

CHAPTER 6

In search of two seats is Boswell's mission at the moment. He enters into one of the busiest food places in Philly, the Reading Terminal, at lunchtime. Boswell believes the Reading Terminal is one of the best jewels of Philadelphia. It's a building filled with food vendors who tempt every passerby with aroma, after aroma, layer on layer. Yes, the market does sells other goods like books and jewelry, but the main attraction is food; fresh, raw or cooked. In the center of the Reading Terminal is where the masses gather to inspect their tasty purchases and devour them. This area is full with tables and chairs. Even at 2:30 in the afternoon this area is full with no seat in sight. So the task of finding two seats can be a challenging one, especially when you are carrying two cups of hot tea, a salad, a turkey sandwich and two oatmeal cookies, but Boswell is good at reading people's behaviors. So it all of this chow down food chaos with eagle eye quickness, Boswell has spied out his objective, moves quickly, and victory is at hand. He smiles at the two young ladies as they arises from their seats, he says, "Thank you," and brushes off the table to wait for his queen.

Boswell spies her as soon as she enters the eating section. She just finish haggling with the vendor at the fresh fruit counter before obtaining her purchase. Her body although still slim is beginning show sign of her pregnancy. Her belly has emerged from it's previously flat hiding place to become a visible presence in her life. With a yoga mat holder swung over her shoulder, she sways effortlessly through the crowd of people. Boswell thinks, *"Aw my woman is having a baby, our baby. She is so beautiful."* But he notices something in her face that signals alarm inside of him. *"Damnit she is pissed about whatever happen between her the fruit vendor,"* he thinks. Boswell prepares himself as he slowly stands to get her attention and waves her over to their table. With a big smile on his face, Boswell awaits his queen.

"Good afternoon, my queen how are you feeling?" Boswell states as he quickly pulls out her chair as she approaches. Her tighten face loosens up, and a smile appears as Michelle leans forward to give Boswell a peck on the lips.

"Your queen is fine, but there are assholes everywhere. Did you know that fool attempted to overcharge me for my plantains? Like I do not know the difference between a plantain and a darn banana. He did not know that I spent three freaking years in the Central American tropical rain forest. I probably know more about tropical fruit that he does. But because I am more aware of things around I sensed something was wrong, and caught the mistake. He tried to apologize, but that fool just lost a customer. Remember I told you that this pregnancy thing is not all that bad? I just feel more in tuned to what is happening in my life. What do you have to say about that Boswell?"

In Search of a Good Feeling

Michelle believes that her pregnancy has caused her to see the world differently by enhancing her visual and auditory capabilities resulting in a higher sensitivity to colors, sounds and movements around her. Boswell thinks she is delusional as she listens for the sound of a bumble bee flying or examines the brilliance of the red stop sign at the corner. Michelle brushes off his statements as psych babble unrelated to her reality. She knows that pregnancy has changed her and how she looks at the world. She begins every day with yoga and recently changed from Asante's yoga to yin yoga, a more relaxed method. Michelle also attends a weekly relaxed yoga class with her friend Deb. She supplements her vegetarian diet with a weekend serving of chicken and fish. Michelle has even joined Boswell on some of his long weekend bike rides, although the biking shorts are becoming tight around her belly. Not really wanting to pick a fight, but knowing whatever he thinks does not matter, Boswell replies.

"I am glad that your super powers have granted you power to detect fools, but you are going to be quite busy, because as you say they are everywhere."

"Yes, I guess you are right because I am detecting I'm sitting across from one right now." Michelle laughs. After a long swig of lemon herbal tea with a dash of honey, Michelle states, "Thank you for the tea, just like I like it. Oops, let me not forget the wonderful salad and the oatmeal cookies were so yummy. My favorite. Sometimes you can be so thoughtful. So darling what are you planning to do for the summer?"

"Nothing, I am doing nothing. For the last 186 days I participated in combat with a well-equipped immovable force, some days they won and sometimes I did, but in the end victory was mine, and the spoils of the win is to do nothing over the summer. Always remember in my world doing nothing is doing something, therefore I will be really busy."

"Ok I did forget your doing nothing is doing something theory of illogic. Cool that means you will be available to go with me to visit my grandparents."

"Hahaha," laughs Boswell. "Who is available to do what and go where"? Let's slow down Michelle, you know I will go anywhere you want to go, but your grandparents, don't they live in South Carolina?"

"Yes they do."

"But South Carolina is quite hot in the summer and they have very big mosquitoes."

"Now how would you know?"

"Well, my father's people are from South Carolina and we used to visit them every summer until I was in junior high. We kids complained so much about the heat and bugs daddy stop taking us, which was fine with us."

"So, when was the last time you visited your southern relatives?"

"Hmmm about 20 years ago. I still have one uncle, three aunts and a zillion of cousins down there."

"Ok it's settled. Go buy yourself some bug spray and sun block. Oops, I forgot, you do not have any need for that. Meet me at my grandparent's place. By the way my grandparents do have indoor plumbing."

Boswell ponders for a minute *Their place*? Boswell knew very little about Michelle's Grandparents other than she grew up under their care in a place which Michelle called

In Search of a Good Feeling

the plantation that was located outside of Charleston, but that's about all.

"Oh you have jokes. Slow down. Since you said I will meet you in South Carolina when are you leaving? And their place? You expect me to stay with you at your grandparent's place, Are you crazy? Michelle are you listening to me?"

She smiles, "Yes Boswell I'm listening. It appears that you have some concerns. To be honest about it I had been planning to go visit my grandparents for a while."

Boswell looks Michelle squarely in her eyes saying,

"Question one my Queen? Do your grandparents know that you are with child?"

"Well yes, I talked to them about it about a week ago."

"Question two. Do they know that their great grandbaby will be bi-racial?"

"Yes silly man, I told them that, also. They seems to accept that fact, ands was very happy to have a great grandchild in the works. Yes I told them all about you with your Ph.D. and teaching job. I even sent them a pic of you."

"A picture are you serious? So you are telling me that you told your southern grandparents that you are pregnant, and the father of the baby is a black with a Ph.D. and you sent them my picture? Why are you just telling me this information?"

Michelle slowly wipes her mouth with the napkins. She notices that Boswell is becoming more irritated as the conversation goes on. His eyes have become bigger and his intonation has changed. She needs to end it as soon as possible. Maybe today was not a good day. So Michelle proceeds to give Boswell an offer that she knew Boswell could not refuse.

"Well Boswell, it's like this. I am going to see my grandparents and I would like you to go with me. Either you are going with me or not. That's up to you, ok?"

Boswell is taken back by Michelle's stand. *What gave her the right to make such a choice for the both of them?*

"Hmmm, I will ponder your wonderful proposal and get back with you."

There is a moment of silence between them with each person deep in their own thoughts. Michelle knows that Boswell does not like conflict and that he would probably agree on the visit. That is one of his strengths and weaknesses. "*So it's just a matter of time*", Michelle thought. "*Ponder all you want my dear, but you know and I know that you are coming to South Carolina with me this summer.*" Michelle was thinking about visiting her grandparents before she got pregnant, but there was never enough internal motivation within her to see the thought through to completion.

She cannot explain her desire to spend some time with her grandparents. The thought of going back down south after several years in self-exile frightens yet calms Michelle. The south that Michelle recalls is poetic, punctuated with rhyming verse along with perfect rhythm. The part that scares her is that she has changed and returning to the place of childhood memories with new eyes may change the rhythm of things.

Growing up on the estate among the large pecan trees has its privileges. Being in a certain social class insulated Michelle from the south of the common folks as her grandmother called them. Although Michelle grew up with maids, cooks and a prep school education, her grandparents did not doddle over her. It was the Waterman's way or no

In Search of a Good Feeling

way. Responses to her grandparent inquiries were limited to no sir, yes sir, no ma'am and yes ma'am. Michelle's indoctrination into the Southern way of life as presented by her grandparents was swift, deep, and through. Michelle passively accepted whatever was told to her while at the same time strategizing her escape.

Having to suddenly have the responsibility to raise a 10 year old in a place where a child had not roamed in over 25 years was a change, but a delight in Grandma Lizzie's eyes. It allowed her to surround her granddaughter with the social niceties that she did not have in her childhood. It was general knowledge that Grandma Lizzie's folks were from the other side of the tracks and that is how she got hooked up with rich kid Jed Waterman which is still the talk of the county.

Jed Waterman on the other hand is the only surviving son who was raised in the Waterman tradition of buying cheap and selling high. The Waterman family was viewed in awe by many people in the county. They were well to do, well-educated and well connected. It was said that Waterman menfolk never discriminated due to the color of someone's skin or social–economic status.

If there was a deal to be made, Jed Waterman would find a way to do it. Jake's views on race relations was simple. "There is only one race-the human race, God made all of us, just treat people well." His belief was the combination of good economic sense and the Golden Rule. Rumors had it that he was quite a character especially with the womenfolk of the county and did not discriminated because of class, race or size. Although those rumors were heard by Ms. Waterman she never questioned the validity of them or Mr. Waterman's faithfulness to her. It was the Waterman way.

Michele never had second thoughts about asking Boswell to accompany her. She needs him with her because he makes her feel good. She liked the attention, the affirmation and the assurance that he shows her. The feeling is quite different than before even with her former husbands. She has never felt this good about another human being... ever. So her reasons have little to do with showing him off to her Grandparents but more to do with being without her good feeling, which she has yet express to Boswell. Michelle smiles at Boswell as she reaches over to take his hand.

As Boswell smiles back at Michelle. He is under attack by forces within him. Michelle's request causes the voices in his head to come alive shouting in unison, *No, has she lost her mind?* These voices are not new to Boswell; he has heard these voices in his head before. He named them Fear, Doubt and Shame. The joy- sucking voices of life that resides in his head. They appeared suddenly when he started dating Michelle. They tried to convince him that dating someone outside his race was just plan crazy, but Boswell was able to silence them. The voices went away quietly, bruised but not defeated, just waiting. They appeared briefly when Michelle announced she was pregnant, but they were quickly defeated by Boswell's desire to become a father.

The voices had learned that if Boswell is not in agreement with the situation that they had much more influence over his decision. So they knew that a new situation would arise which would question the stability of the relationship and then they would attack again in full force. The voices quickly began to list reasons why the trip was wrong on so many levels such as going down south in the summer when it is much too hot. Secondly, going down south with a white

In Search of a Good Feeling

woman is just plain silly and staying at her relatives home on a plantation who may own guns. Is she nuts?

Boswell feels the warmth of Michelle's hand on his hand. There was something about her touch that was reassuring to him. He knew that she had no idea of the confusion in his mind about this issue, but it did not seem to matter. That touch meant it was going to be ok. Reassurance from someone else is a great weapon against the voices...the voices forces you to look at self with all of your frailties with questions about self. Today Michelle's touch was enough to force the voices to disband and go back into hiding. Boswell leans over to Michelle to give her a kiss.

"Sure Sweetie, you truly mean something to me. I believe I can trust you have my best interest in mind, so let's go visit your Grandparents. You are my Queen and I will go hand and hand with you anywhere you desire."

"Wow!, where did that come from?" blushes Michele.

"Within Michelle, within," as Boswell points to his heart. "You think that I am an individual without deep passionate feeling, I'm not. I believe also, but I am not always able to express what I feel. Sometimes language is not a good medium to express how you feel about someone. We are limited by the words we use to express a feeling so uniquely personal that to describe the feeling with words sometimes lessen its true meaning. So forgive me sometimes for not telling you how you make me feel in words that would truly express those feelings. I have simplified it to you. You are a good feeling my Queen."

"So that's what just a good feeling mean. Let me get this right. Because of the limited nature of the English language you have reduced your verbal expression of how you feel towards me to I am a good feeling? Wow," Michelle chuckles.

"Yes ma'am, that's my story and I am sticking with it."

They kiss again as a voice somewhere behind them yells out "Get a room, we are eating here and someone else needs that table". The couple laugh, quickly throw away their empty containers and walk hand in hand out of Reading Terminal. The lunchtime crowd had dispersed but since Philadelphia is a tourist destination, they were plenty of people milling around aimlessly in search of the Liberty Bell and other stuff.

"Well sweetie," said Michelle. "I'm off to my yoga class. What are you going to do?"

"Since it such a beautiful day, I'm going to sit outside of the Bean and do some reading until your class is over. Meet me there after class and we can decide if we're going to hang out down here or going home."

"It's a plan, later"

"Later, my Queen."

Boswell watches Michelle as she walk away and thinks, *For a white girl she does have a nice ass and for that I'm a very lucky man.*

After a short walk down to 5th and Cherry Street, Michelle enters in a building with a large sign hanging outside that says Yoga Time. It's a roomy place, with a lounge, conference room, small locker room, two studios and four wellness rooms for massage, reiki, and other healing arts. The lounge can also be arrange as a presentation area with stage and movable lights. One studio is larger than the other but both have beautiful hardwood floors and a stereo with iPod hookup. Yoga Time is described in their advertisements

In Search of a Good Feeling

as friendly and flexible. She began going to the studio last year and that's where she met Deb.

Recently she switched to a more relaxed type of yoga called yin yoga. Michelle believes that since yin yoga is focused on stretching the large muscle groups that it will help when the baby is due. The class is taught by Lisa, the goddess of yoga, one of those bony flexible types of women. Instead of using recorded meditation music, Lisa creates relaxing sounds with her voice. The class today has 10 members, all female. The ages range from 23 to about 50 but it's hard to tell. The class begins with a simple exercise of removing all negative thoughts from your mind while getting in a comfortable position.

Lisa starts off by speaking in a very surreal voice. "Let's get grounded snuggly down to our core. Drop back the shoulders, relax the hands on your lap, and close your eyes, become aware of each breath." Lisa begins to hum slowly as each person attempts to become more aware of their breathing.

As Michelle attempts to get centered she notices that it is taking longer than usual. *Something is wrong, she thought. Why can't I get comfortable?* Then it comes to her, it's her stomach. She cannot sit in her usual position because it's causing too much pressure on her stomach. Although Michelle has noticed that her stomach was growing, she never gave much thought of what that truly meant. Instead of eliminating stressful thoughts and becoming more in tune with the moment, the opposite occurs.

Michelle's mind becomes flooded with negative possibilities, while her body slowly tightens up. The thought that her body is about to place some great limitations on her movements and behavior attacks her mind throughout the whole yoga session. Her mood changes causing the normal five minute long positions to become an endurance test for her. While doing the butterfly, a position where a person sits on a pillow with their leg in a diamond shape as they bring their head as close to their feet as possible, Michelle notices that she could not get as low as she could previously which causes her to become distraught.

All the time Michelle is getting upset more with Boswell because his body is not going through the same changes as hers. She feels lousy. Four months into their partnership, Michelle believes that she is getting the raw end of the deal. Her distress did not evade the watchful eyes of Lisa especially when she starts crying during the final position. Her crying is interpreted as a stress releaser moment by the class igniting an emotional chain reaction as one by one each member begins to connect with Michelle's emotional state. The session ends with a lot of wet eyes and hugs, but very little talking. Each woman seems too linked to the moment with her own individual struggle or victory. Michelle sits still as the women mill out of the yoga room, one or two offering a hug. Deb motions to Michelle that she will be waiting outside. Lisa comes over and smiles at Michelle.

"How are you feeling?" asks Lisa.

"Oh I'm Ok I think. Well no, I was dealing with some negative thoughts. I'm sorry to have upset the class."

"Upset? I do not think that you upset the class."

"What? Everyone was crying."

"I think you help to free the class. For the first time in a while I think individuals were really in the moment and expressed emotionally what they felt. I want to thank you

In Search of a Good Feeling

for being so brave and honest with your expression," said Lisa as she walks away smiling.

Michelle just stood there speechless. She does not know what came over her. The tears, the moodiness, the anger towards Boswell, it was not her. She just knows that she is still mad with Boswell because it's his fault and he is going to hear about it. Michelle walks out of the yoga room and there was Deb waiting for her.

Deb hugs her while whispering in her ear, "It's going to be alright."

"What's going to be alright?" states Michelle as she pulls away looking Deb right in the face.

"You Michelle, the same thing happened to me during my pregnancy. I was moody, I cried about everything, and I thought I was ugly and fat."

"Moody and fat, that not my issue. I do believe that pregnancy has made me hypersensitive to things around me, even Boswell sees that, but I'm not moody. Fat? Do I look fat?" Michelle instinctively rubs her belly as she looks in a mirror.

"Girl you still look fine, but you must admit that your belly is beginning to establish itself as the major sightseeing item on your body."

Tears reappears in Michelle's eyes. "I don't know what just occurred, I do not mean to be so sensitive. I got to go Deb, Boswell is waiting for me at the Bean." With a good bye hug from Deb, Michelle moves quickly out of the door before someone else says something to make her begin crying again. Once outside the warmth of the sun has a calming effect on her. Michelle feels bad that she left Deb so abruptly.

She is my best friend, thought Michelle, *But I had to change the setting, it was too much for me. Now people think that I am fat, overly emotional and I have a boyfriend that does not care. Life sucks.*

Two blocks away, Boswell sits down with a large iced tea in one hand and a twice read New York Times in the other. Not attempting to become a sun worshipper, he finds refuge on a shaded area on the Bean's outside deck. The sun and Boswell has never had a close relationship mainly based on what his mother told him one day after coming in the house dripping with sweat. "Boy look how black you are getting, keep your butt out of the sun before you faint and burn up like them white folks." It was a message that most black parents told their children. With those words chiseled in his self-conscience Boswell did like most of his peers do, always to look for shaded walkways, never to sit, walk or lie in the sun and to shake your head at those who do. Boswell observes a couple individuals sitting in the sunny part of the deck and his head slowly shakes in wonderment.

He ponders his recent conversation with Michelle. He is not really overwhelmed by the idea of visiting her family, but he does believe that Michelle would not ask him if it was not important to her. Too often in past relationships, Boswell relied on his own judgment, and came up short, so this time he is going against his better judgment. But he thinks he understands Michelle and her world quite well based on what he called the System.

The System is Boswell's way of understanding other folk's worlds. It's based on discovering what things influence a person's world. Things such as family, children, grandchildren, church, jobs, and friends are seen as units

In Search of a Good Feeling

in the system. Units may have influence on how a person operates or see the world. Most individuals try to please the units in their system, which increases the units influence on them. The more units a person has the more units that he/she may have to please. The effort of pleasing the units may pull a person in such a way that they lose their self. Conversely, the pulls of the units on the individual may shape that person quite positively by tapping something inside the them that causes them to engage in situations that are; prosocial, enriching and benefits self.

Boswell came by this type of thinking by accident. He noticed a difference between women with kids and the women without kids that he dated. When he was with the women with kids, but the kids were not around, one type of persona was displayed by the woman. When the kids were around another persona was evident. Women without children did not display the mother's persona which made them easier to understand. But another side of them could appear from not only the presence of kids, but family, friends, and any other unit that the individual desires to please.

A couple of rules or absolutes that Boswell has established are the following: 1) The unit that the individual talks about the most generally has the most influences over their behavior. 2) Never talk negatively about those units because the individual will not hear you. 3) A person's system is to be understood but not to be criticized.

Boswell believes that Michelle's world is void of many units so her system is small and easy to understand. Her units are her grandparents, her friends and the baby now, with the baby gaining in influence every day. Michelle seems to be influenced more by her moral compass that was really developed during her time in the Peace Corp than units.

Boswell gazes at his watch and notices that Michelle is doing her late thing again. *It should have taken her only 15 minutes to walk from the yoga studio, she is 20 minutes late already am I'm getting hungry, thought Boswell.* Ten minutes pass and still no Michelle. Just as Boswell's anxiety begins to rise he receives the following text.

'I am not coming to the Bean, I going home and I'm not fat!'

Not knowing what the reason for the text, Boswell just replies, "Thanks for the heads up, I will see you at home. I'm going to grab some take-out and I do not think that you are getting fat. I see our baby getting bigger."

When Boswell arrives at the apartment Michelle is sitting on the couch reading a magazine. She slides the magazine down to her lap and Boswell can see that she has been crying. Before he can say something Michelle motion him not to speak.

She looks at him with her redden eyes saying, "Sweetie when you see that I have been crying, I need you to get me a cup of herbal tea and two oatmeal cookies, and then quietly back out of the room."

Boswell immediately goes into the kitchen and returns with a cup of peppermint tea. He places the hot tea and the cookies next to her on the table and disappears into the bedroom with his takeout meal where he remains until Michelle calls for him about 30 minutes later.

"Boswell will you come here please?"

"Yes, Michelle I will be right there."

Boswell enters the room and Michelle motions him to come sit next to her on the couch. He notices that Michelle's

In Search of a Good Feeling

eyes are no longer red, and it seems that she has applied a little make up to her face. Her body language is softer than earlier, and there appears to be a glow about her.

Michelle speaks, "Thanks for everything you have done, but I thank you more for allowing me to be me."

Boswell sits there quietly just grinning and staring at Michelle.

"What are you grinning about?"

"Do you know that you are glowing?"

"Glowing? I am not glowing silly man. I put some of your shea butter on my face. I like how it makes my skin feels. Glowing, ha ha ha you are funny. Anyway I just wanted to say thanks."

"You are welcome. I brought you back a salad and some cookies, but I do not know if you are eating or not."

"I'm eating, but my body and moods are changing. I crave oatmeal cookies all the time. So make sure we have some here at all times. Sometimes the baby makes her presence known to me like today in yoga class."

"Hmmm I am just pondering that last statement. Maybe baby does not like yoga and you are feeling its anger inside of you."

Michelle immediately growls at him about that suggestion. "First of all our baby is not an it, she is a she, secondly not only does the baby enjoy yoga," Michelle says smiling as she rubs her stomach, "She does yoga with me and she loves the caterpillar position."

Boswell responds "I have been corrected, but I truly believe she is not a she but he is a he." They sit quietly together as thoughts of who's gene set with be dominant in their child's expression of self entertains both of their minds.

CHAPTER 7

Its 3:05pm on a Friday, "*controlled chaos*" thought Michelle as she observes the movement of people around her. Today is her doctor's appointment and Boswell surprisingly is running late. Her doctor's office is located in downtown Philadelphia or Center City and people are everywhere. Michelle's obstetrician/gynecologist is Dr. Sharon Story who she met one day at an art show. After a brief conversation about not understanding what they were viewing, some laughs and a glass of wine, the two of them exchanged information and promised to keep in touch. The keeping in touch turned out to be Michelle becoming a patient of Sharon professionally and close friend socially.

From the beginning of her pregnancy Boswell insisted on accompanying Michelle to her doctor visits which to his credit he has yet to miss one. Unknown to Michelle, Boswell has difficulty finding his role in the birth of the baby process. He feels obligated to do something but is very confused as to what that is. Boswell believes that it is his role to be there with her, to hear about the progress of their unborn infant and to better understand what Michelle is going through during her pregnancy. Since finding out

In Search of a Good Feeling

that Michelle was pregnant, Boswell has secretly devoured as much information as possible about the birth of a child. So it's not unusual that during the doctor visits, he displays his newly obtained knowledge by asking a couple questions to impress Dr. Story. His behavior in the doctor's office amuses Michelle. *Look at him, Mr. Know it all, asking questions like he's pregnant too. My baby is something else.*

After the doctor visit the couple generally hangs out in Center city for dinner or shopping before heading back to Boswell's apartment. Since he was late, Michelle decides to wait outside the doctor's office on a bench to engage in one of her favorite pastimes which is to people watch. Today she has made the following observations. Good looking white men only exist in movies, women think that black is a color that should be worn frequently, and the use of the steam iron is a thing of the past.

Boswell looks at his watch. He is going to be late and there is nothing that he can do about it. He thought that his plan for leaving early today would work but now he has been delayed by some unknown source. *The subway god is not smiling on me today*, thought Boswell. When the news of Michelle's pregnancy finally stopped scaring him, Boswell had a meeting with his dean, Dr. Denise Brooker to ask her for time off to attend Michelle's doctor visits. Surprisingly, his request was granted with certain stipulations, like two weeks' notice, no more than one request in a month, and missing only one class a month. Since the initial conversation, their relationship has changed. Dr. Brooker confided in Boswell that her husband also attended doctor visits with her before their child, so she supported his effort to be there for Michelle.

Boswell catches the subway at the Temple University stop, but the subway car is not moving. The doors remain open with a lot of angry people inside. Finally five minutes later an announcement from the conductor, "Sorry for the inconvenience, the train is experiencing system problems. The train will resume service in the next five minutes. Again, sorry for the inconvenience." Shortly after the announcement the train doors shut and lurched forward towards the next stop. *All is well*, thought Boswell until the train doors opened at the Spring Garden stop to a massive number of school children; the black plague for any public transportation adult rider. Boswell silently curses his situation, *Freaking delay, freaking kids. I thought I would miss them.*

Although Boswell teaches the masses he does not enjoy riding public transportation with school age children especially at the end of the school day. By the end of school they are alert, loud and can be quite disrespectful. He cannot figure out if its hormones, mob mentality or what, but a group of under supervised school age kids is a problem. The Spring Garden stop is particularly troublesome because of the number of schools in the vicinity of the subway stop. They enter the subway car with body language suggesting they have no regard to anything but themselves. The car is suddenly turned in an atmosphere of adolescent verbatim attitudes and behaviors. With kids yelling and pushing to get on the car, Boswell braces for the worst. He listens in on a nearby conversation of five teen ager girls wearing a white and marron school uniform jackets with some sort of crest on them.

"Yo, look, Elijah is with his new girlfriend."

"She ugly, look at her shoes,"

In Search of a Good Feeling

"She must think that she cute the way she wears her hair."

"Girl, that isn't hers it's a weave."

"A bad one at that….Hahaha……"

Boswell's saving grace is that he is two stops from his destination, but suddenly he decides to get off at the next stop. That decision was reinforced when one of the female students sat down beside Boswell with her back towards him while she talk nonstop to her friends. It was a good decision because Elijah's girlfriend overheard the group of girls talking about her and she was making noise that it was going to be on when they get off the subway as the "b" word began to fly throughout the car. Leaving the subway train quickly Boswell runs up the stairs of the exit stopping when he gets outside to assess his situation. He quickly estimates he will be about 10 minutes late, so he begins to walk towards the doctor's office feeling good that he has evaded one potential negative situation without knowing that another far worst situation is yet to occur.

With no Boswell insight Michelle regrettably enters in to the doctor's office for her appointment. She notices a new receptionist at the front desk. Michelle signs in and when her name is called for her appointment she gives her the following instructions. "Hi my name is Michelle Waterman, and my significant other, whose name is Boswell, is running late. When he arrives let him know that I here and I am back with the doctor. So its fine that he comes backs and joins us. Any other time, nothing would have occurred and this would have been a normal doctor visit, but not today. Unfortunately there was another patient named Michelle at doctor's office who happen to be black.

When Boswell introduced himself to the receptionist and said that he was there for Michelle, the receptionist directed him to the wrong Michelle's waiting room which was a problem because the black Michelle was not fully dressed. From an outside observer the situation would have seemed quite comical.

Boswell walks into one room and a couple seconds later runs out saying," I'm, sorry wrong the Michelle." Immediately his Michelle comes out of the office when she hears his voice asking, "What's the matter baby?" The receptionist already red with embarrassment says, "I did not know, I did not know!" Later questioned by both Michelle's, Boswell and the doctor, the receptionist stated that she just assumed that Boswell's significant other was black and not white.

When ask why she assumed that particular thought about Boswell, the receptionist remarks, "That is how things used to be," and left work crying.

Boswell and Michelle quickly departed the doctor's office without talking much. The situation stuns Michelle and Boswell for a moment, causing them to become quiet during their five minute walk to Keith Lucas, their favorite restaurant in center city. The restaurant is named for the chef and owner Keith Lucas, a friend of Boswell. They met when Boswell volunteered at "Good Men Cook too" event sponsored by a local food bank. Keith, a chef helped supervised the charity event featuring about 60 amateur male cooks. He was impressed with Boswell's entry of double chocolate chip cookies, and from this event their friendship was born.

It's happy hour at Keith Lucas so the place was noisy, but the couple was able to find a table in a less crowded part of

In Search of a Good Feeling

the restaurant. After the dinner orders were place, Boswell asks Michelle "How does it feel to date a black man?"

"What?"

"How does it feel to date a black man?"

"Huh, you do not talk to me for 15 minutes and then this is the first thing that you say to me. Not you look beautiful today or how is the mother of your baby feeling? Why do you ask me such a weird question?"

"It's not a weird question, it's just something I'd like to know. We never talked about race before. I don't know why but we never haven't. With today's event still fresh in my mind I would like to know an answer to the question."

"We probably have never talked about race because it never has been an issue in our relationship and it's still not Ok. I'm willing to answer the question just as long as you answer a question about race for me."

"It's a deal."

"Hmm, how does it feel to date a black man? I can remember the first black guy I dated. I was a sophomore in college and was in this study group with a black guy named Derrick Smith. I think that was his name. Well one thing led to another and we decide to start dating, but he was somewhat self-conscious of being with me, so we did not appear many times in public together. I was ok with it, so we just crept around, if you know what I mean. It was exciting and thrilling. I wanted to know how he smelled, how it felt when he touched me, how a person with a different skin color tasted. His lips were very soft and the skin was so strong with not many wrinkles. I was so excited when he kissed and made love to me. It was a sensation that I had never experienced before in my life. I felt revolutionary, because I had a black partner, which was against the mainstream. I was curious to see if our cultural differences would allow for a relationship to last. Well I found out quickly that we were not strong enough to make it long term, but it was fun trying. But I can remember being out a couple of times with him thinking that people were staring at us which made me somewhat uncomfortable. Now I see a man whom I share common interests who strengthens who I am. Your blackness is a bonus for me, it allows me to see things through your eyes and your filters, which broadens my understanding of the world from another point of view much different than my own. That's my story ok it's your turn."

"Hmmm interesting. So let me get this right my blackness is a bonus? I have never heard it stated like that before. I will ponder that So, you want me to answer the question what it feel like to date a white woman?"

"Yes sir I do."

Their food arrives before Boswell can answer. Michelle's order of black bean hummus came with oven baked pita bread while Boswell ordered his favorite food item in the world, chicken wings. One reason Boswell always ordered chicken wings at Keith Lucas' was because they are well seasoned. Nice size whole wings, not pieces of wings that the other places serve. With five varieties of wings to choose from, today's selection is Jamaican Jerked wings and the spicier the better. Boswell just sits and stares at the chicken wings then turns to Michelle saying, 'Umm they look so good, would you like one?"

Michelle smiles, "Naw, Baby, I'm good and you know I do not eat meat during the week."

In Search of a Good Feeling

"It's the weekend dear, c'mon take a wing. They look nice and spicy."

Michelle shakes her head and says, "I'm spicy enough for you and me; enjoy your wings dear."

After a very quick blessing of the food Boswell immediately begins to chow down on the wings and Michelle notices a smile appear on his face. She just sits a for a minute or so watching him thinking, *That man loves his chicken wings, I wonder if that's a Black thing?* She giggles aloud, which takes Boswell's attention away from chicken wings.

He looks up, wipes his mouth with the napkins and looks across the table at Michelle asking, "So what's so funny, you don't like the way I eat or something?"

Michelle looks at Boswell's plate and continues to laugh but louder.

"What's the matter with you Michelle?"

She points to the mound of bones on Boswell's plate.

"You baby you do not eat, you suck the meat off the bones without stopping…there is nothing left on them."

Boswell smiles saying, "That's how you know that the wings are good, and that's how we do it where I come from Sweetie. When we suck the bones clean, it's our way of giving the chef the highest compliment." Boswell picks up a chicken bones from his stack. He slowly raise it in the air and smiles saying, "Keith, oh Keith, I present you with the highest honor, a sucked clean chicken bone."

Michelle smiles in embarrassment, as she pulls Boswell's arm down saying, "Shhh sweetie, you are disturbing the other diners. Why don't you place that bone right over here and tell me how it feels to date a white woman."

Boswell lets go of his grip on the chicken bone as it fell to the pile among the others. He grasped the napkin and wipes his mouth and then tears open a couple of the towelettes and wipes his fingers clean. After close inspection of his work Boswell repositions himself in front of Michelle.

"Well I never thought that I would date a white woman because that was not a need in my life. I grew up with the understanding that you date within your race, so I obliged until it did not work for me. One day I realized that if we were all God's children, I should be able to play with anyone that wanted to play with me. For me it really comes back to common interests. Some of the things that I enjoyed doing, my people or the people I was hanging out with had little interests in those activities. So I started to look for people who like doing the things that I like doing and surprisingly they did not look like me. I started hanging out with them, socialization led to acceptance, acceptance to dating. So what does it feel like to date a white woman? I would have to say that it can be exciting, yet hurtful at the same time due to the different possible interpretations of behavior or events. Like today's event."

"What about it?"

"I believe it's difficult for you to understand my anger about what happened and that it upsets me. The receptionist made an assumption that she should have not made. Why can't I have a girlfriend who happens to be white, who is the mother of my child, this is not the 50's."

"Yep, you are correct Boswell, I do not understand why you are still upset. Stuff happens but it's how you get over that stuff which is important. But the situation did make me closer to you. I saw a part of you that I had not seen expressed before. Not understanding it is not a bad thing for me. I'm ok with the idea that we have our own stuff, and that sometimes we will not understand each other no matter how hard the other person attempts to explain the situation. It's not a bad thing, Sweetie."

Boswell shakes his head and speaks the following words slowly touching Michelle's hand as he talks. "It is a bad thing. I do not want to always have to explain myself like I am something from outer space. I want you feel what I feel sometimes. I want to be able to share experiences with you. I do not just want you to hear my stories but be able to feel my joys and fears and to taste my salty moods and savor my sweet ones. I want you to experience me."

Michelle is quiet and excuses herself, rising slowly to go to the bathroom. Boswells watches her as she leaves wondering what she is pondering. Boswell leaned back in his chair while he sipped his ice tea thinking, *Michelle is a wonderful woman, and I am a very lucky man.* Suddenly he becomes panicky as dark thoughts enter his mind. *Why did she get in the middle of the meal to go to the bathroom I hope she is not getting sick…no silly that is supposed to occur in the morning, and it ain't morning. Should I go check on her*? Boswell takes another sip of his iced tea as he attempts to figure out what is occurring. Why *those thoughts?*

She returns shortly with a smile on her face, turns to Boswell saying, "Hello sweet man my name is Michelle Waterman and I have been looking for a man who fits your description. Will you propose to me?" The noisy restaurant becomes instantly quiet as the question ping pong around in Boswell's mind.

"What? Where did that comes from?"

"Well you stated that you want me to experience you, so what better way is there? Let's make a public commitment and by the way I need some security. Before the pregnancy happened, we were without a goal. We were just enjoying each other going from one good time to the next. I think I need more to be able to experience you. You do not have to marry me I just would like to be engaged."

"Again where is this coming from? Before you left we were discussing your inability to understand my anger and you come back from the bathroom wanting to be engaged? Did you stop at the bar in the back? Help me here!"

"You are right, this engagement thing sounds abrupt but really it is not. Frankly Boswell this and other things about us have been on my mind for a while now that my previous attempts at marriage failed. But as you know I am quite the hopeful person. Again, we do not have to actually get married, I just want to know that you will be there, so I can have some stability."

Boswell sat quietly trying again to understand what was occurring and why now. *Michelle looks sane and quite lovely but her thoughts are a little imbalanced. What to do? Engage?* Boswell's inner voices return to give their opinion on the matter. *Engage? You have never been married... what does that mean? She is already living with you why does she want to get I engage? Security? You are the one who needs security. Remember she is a runner, not you. She runs in and out of someone's arms; not a good sign. You are the one who should be running. What do you get out of the deal?*

Boswell finishes off his iced tea and slowly moves his chair closer to Michelle. They are almost sitting on top of each other. If you did not know any better a person would think that they were connected at the hip.

But before Boswell can respond to Michelle a voice came of nowhere to change the mood momentarily saying, "How was everything? Hmmm it looks like someone enjoyed the wings, am I correct?"

Boswell and Michelle looks towards the waiter and smile. "Yes he did enjoyed them a lot," Michelle stated, pointing at Boswell.

"Would you like some dessert?" asks the waiter as he begins to clear the table.

"Do you have oatmeal cookies?" asks Michelle.

"No ma'am we do not have any oatmeal cookies".

"Well no oatmeal cookies. Hmm ok, bring us a slice of sweet potato cheese cake, a cup of black coffee, a cup of lemon herbal tea and two spoon," replies Boswell.

The waiter moves quickly to clear the table and within minutes he was back with their order. After a sampling of the cheesecake both agreed that is was good but a bit too sweet for either of them.

Michelle brings Boswell back to the issue, "So before the waiter came were you going to say something to me?"

"Yes, I am overwhelmed with your offer. It has made me speechless, but I need time me to ponder what has been asked of me. It's a wonderful offer, thank you".

"Well I would advise you not ponder too long, those who snoozes sometimes lose."

"I have been advised."

Michelle starts squirming in the chair rubbing her back against the chair, "Boswell when we get home can you rub my back, please?"

"Sure it will be my pleasure."

After paying the check, the couple decides to take a cab home, avoiding the after work crowd. While in the cab holding hands, Boswell wonders what it would be like to be married, as Michelle smiles all the way home.

"Finally home in my apartment," states Boswell as he closes the door.

Michelle describes Boswell's apartment as Thrift store classic or affordably homely. It's a large two bedroom apartment with an enclosed sun porch in the heart of Germantown. At the moment it's their shared living space with Michelle loving every minute of it. Michelle announces that she is going to go take a shower as Boswell plods down on the sofa. "Hey I know how you like long showers…leave some water for me."

"Well you could join me."

"Naw, that's a little too freaky for me."

"Whatever."

Michelle makes a face at Boswell as she goes into the bathroom. As soon as he hears the shower comes on Boswell quickly undresses and waits for a moment before entering the bathroom. The noise of the shower allows him to enter undetected. He notices the fuzzy silhouette of her body through the shower glass. Michelle still unaware of Boswell's presence has her head under the shower head allowing the water to flow through her hair. He slides in to the shower behind her and softly kisses her neck.

Michelle replies, "What took you so long?"

"Hmmm, I wish I was a soap suds on your body, but I cannot figure a good location."

She laughs, "Silly man all over, be bold."

In Search of a Good Feeling

He reaches in front of her and feels the fullness of her breasts. He continues to touch her body, moving his hands around her rounding belly. He begins to massage her upper body as she arches it slowly towards the wall. Boswell slides his hands down to Michelle's waist while leaning forward. She braces herself against the shower wall while pushing herself towards him. He grasps her hips as she willingly spreads her legs feeling his nakedness press slowly into her. The sound of the shower cancels out their moans as water continues to flow down their interconnected bodies while their good feelings keep multiplying.

CHAPTER 8

Part of their vacation plan is for Michelle to leave before Boswell, and he would meet her in Charleston a week later. This gives Michelle some personal time with her grandparents, old neighbors and friends while getting back in rhythm to the southern way of life again. Boswell is interested in re-connecting with his family members in the area so the trip is beginning to looks like a series of mini family reunions. Together they are planning to stay a week before flying back to Philadelphia. It was decided while they are apart there was to be limited communication between them. You can text to tell the other person that you have arrived at your destination and you could call only if there was a change in travel plans, otherwise no communication, unless someone died. The limited communication is Michelle's idea. She is interested to see if this type of arrangement would strengthen the relationship. Boswell is on board with the idea thinking this may be the break from constant communication with each other that he needs. He is a quiet person by nature. The constant daily questioning of how are you feeling, and how is your day going are killing him. He sees the week vacation from his queen as a time to re-discover himself.

Michelle elects to take Amtrak to Charleston SC from Philadelphia. Although the train ride takes much longer than flying, Michelle is not in a hurry and the train has plusses that the plane does not. Michelle likes the train's comfortable seats, its café car, the changing landscape and a sense of informality. The crowded hyper-security, conscious narrow minded unfriendly atmosphere of air travel kind of turns Michelle off.

She decides to take the 4:35 am train to Washington DC with a later connection to Charleston. She desires to spend some time in the nation's capital sightseeing before continuing to her final destination. Her decision on the early morning departure did not come without objections from Boswell. When told the departure time of her trip Boswell raised a minor protest knowing that it really did not matter what he thought. He knew from past situations when Michelle makes up her mind it was a done deal with little chance of him influencing the outcome.

Lately, Boswell has noticed a change in Michelle that sometimes makes him shake his head in disbelief. He has observed her crying and five minutes later wearing a happy face. This has concerned him because being emotionally stable is one of the reasons that he is attracted to Michelle. He believes that the pregnancy must have some bearing on her changed emotional state, so he is ok with it for the time being.

At 3:30 am Michelle leans over Boswell awaking him with a kiss whispering to him that it's almost time for her to leave. Boswell cannot believe that Michelle is up, dressed and ready to go since waking up early is one of her least enjoyable things to do.

Unknown to Boswell it's not that Michelle has awaken early but the anxiety about going home had kept her from sleeping. So instead of sleeping soundly, the last couple of hours consisted of mini-naps accented by looking at the clock every 30 minutes brought on by the fear of missing her train. Fifteen minutes later a cab is waiting for Michelle outside the apartment to go to the train station.

Boswell has quickly dressed to accompany her to the station but she kindly refuses his offer. She reminds him that he is giving a final at 8:00 am today and he needs to prepare for his students. Confused and still sleepy Boswell humbly accepts her reasoning with little protest. He walks her to the cab, they kiss and hold each other as the driver places her things in the trunk.

After a round of, "I love you", Michelle kisses him again on the cheek and says, "Good bye." Boswell waves as the cab moves away from the curb, then just stood there for moment trying to figure out what had just occurred.

The 15 minute cab ride is uneventful yet during the whole trip Michelle rubs her stomach unknowingly. Upon arriving at the train station Michelle was immediately struck by the station's size and emptiness which triggers a sense of loneliness within her. Generally, the 30th Street train station is a busy place full of people and sounds, but at 3:30 a.m. it's the opposite. A couple of birds are flying around in the vast space area above the passenger's' benches keeping each other company while forms of humanity are sitting around Dunkin Doughnuts drinking dark brown hot liquids and eating sweet sticky things.

In Search of a Good Feeling

Michelle quietly sits on an unoccupied bench not wanting to socialize with anyone as the realization of how much she misses Boswell continues to bombard her consciousness. Suddenly, her loneliness is interrupted by movements in her belly which Michelle automatically responds to by rubbing her stomach. The idea of being physically responsible for two individuals instead of one awakens Michelle to her present situation of being pregnant. It took her awhile to become comfortable with the idea of being a future parent, but what's ~~is~~ more scary for Michelle is the idea that over a nine month period of time someone will gain more and more control of her body. She fights daily with her demons about losing control of her life, the loss of her freedom, feeling excited and guilty at the same time.

Michelle finds herself emotionally unglued. Crying, laughing, happy and even very sad, more and more. The feeling of the baby moving inside of her is a good feeling which centers Michelle, stopping her emotional~~ly~~ spiral. A tear rolls down her cheek while a smile awaits its turn. What *have I gotten myself into this time*, thinks Michelle as she continues to rub her belly while wishing for the presence of Boswell.

As the departure time approaches the station becomes more populated and noisy. At the gate for Washington DC a line begins to form. Reluctantly, Michelle strolls over to the gate to join her fellow travelers, looking over her shoulder along the way half hoping to see Boswell running towards her but no Boswell appears. Michelle is struck by how small and weak she feels this morning without his presence.

The Amtrak 56 left on time from Philadelphia with the usual mix of business travelers and summer time vacationers.

The two groups are easily distinguish by behavior, dress and conversation. The business traveler generally has no luggage and travels with a cypher companion via cell phone or laptop. The vacationing travelers are 180 degrees different, they travel in packs of 4 to 5, they dress colorfully, and their conversation is loud with expansive qualities. Michelle carefully navigates between the two groups as she boards the train attempting to avoid the loud and colorful and at the same time staying away from the cell phone addicts. She heads straight to the last car of the train, the quiet car, little talking, no cellphones, and no kids...*a paradise on wheels,* thinks Michelle. She locates an unoccupied seat, gives her ticket to the conductor and quickly finds herself asleep dreaming.

Not known as a dreamer, Michelle's dream consisted of an illogical enactment of familiar places and people which leaves her troubled when she awakes. With no good explanation for her dream, she gathers herself, walks into the café car and orders a lemon tea and blueberry muffin. She sits in the café car behind a group of first time train vacationers and gazes out of the window as they comment on the wonders of train travel. Suddenly she realizes that being away from Boswell for a week is their longest separation since they started dating. Michelle and the vacationers parted company in DC. In the train station she sees a young lady with a crying baby in a stroller. The scene causes her mental demons to have a party inside her mind prompting Michelle to automatically begin to rub her stomach and walk quickly to find an exit to get out of the station.

She emerges out of Union station in a huff and looks around. Its 6:30 am and Washington DC is just waking

In Search of a Good Feeling

up. A number of grey and white Metro buses awaits their early morning passengers. The sun peaks out accompanied by a warm summer breeze causing the flags around Union Station to wave to each other in unison. The demons have settled down now. Red and white cabs swoop up fares awaiting passage to their destinations.

A lone voice blurs out about the injustices in America as he collects donations for his struggle. Tour buses are parked on the left side of the station with their motors off, just waiting for the time to hawk the day tripper to DC. "*The breeze feels great*", thinks Michele as she wanders over to the lone voice to contribute to his struggle. There is something about his eyes that made him softer than the violent language that was coming out of his mouth. He says, "Thanks for the donation. God Bless."

Michelle smiles, but her mind is miles away. She is surprise how much of Boswell she sees in this man. His explosive protective external and soft underbelly is similar to Boswell. She wonders what he is protecting the same way she sometimes wonders about Boswell. Michelle ponders often why Boswell is so protective, what are his fears and will he ever reveal them to her. Her minds goes back to the conversation in the restaurant. She waves goodbye to the lone voice as her mind drifts back to her love. She wants to grasp his hand and stroll throughout DC exclaiming nonverbally that Boswell is her man. Michelle finds the act of holding hands one of the most powerful love acts two people can do. She was once told that there are people who you will sleep with and yet never desire to hold their hands, but there is no one whose hand you will hold whom you do will not have the desire to sleep with.

She catches the 520 train to Miami via Charleston while an unfamiliar voice from her dream continues to speak to her. The train quickly leaves the greater Washington DC area behind with the landscape changing from cityscape to farm land. Michelle drifts back to sleep only to be awaken by the train stopping in the quiet town of Rocky Mount, North Carolina.

The conductor calls out the destination causing movement in the car as a couple of college looking individuals pulled down their green duffle bags from the overhead rack and scurries off the train. Michelle looks out her window to observe the coming and going of the passengers. A certain familiarity came over her about the town. The college looking individuals were met by an older couple and their dog. They walk cheerfully to a red pickup truck. An African American couple comes on to replace them in the quiet car. Before the couple could place their luggage in the overhead the conductor yells, "All abroad", and the train took off to its next destination. Michelle's attention flips through the Amtrak magazine as the conductor comes through to check tickets.

Suddenly, she realized why the town seemed so familiar to her. It reminded her of the town of Rheine where her maternal grandparents use to lived. It was the place where she spent every summer until the death of her mother. Michelle accompanied by her mother and sometimes her father would fly into Amsterdam and take the train to Rheine where her grandparents would meet them. Rheine is located in the northwest part of Germany. It's a small country town with a big town feel especially on market day. It is surrounded by small farms and horse stables. It was not unusual for Michelle to wake up to sound of a

In Search of a Good Feeling

rooster crowing or to the sweet smell of cow mature flowing through the air. Michelle's grandparents owned neither cow nor rooster. They were city folks from Muster who decided to spend their retirement in a smaller less hurried country town. After Michelle's parents moved to the states, her mother, Cordelia Waterman, promised her parents that they would spend the summer with them in Germany. Cordelia was an only child the pride in joy of her parents. Tall, fair skinned, dark hair Cordelia was a striking beauty. Some men described her as a haunting beauty. She had a strong connection to her country. That is why it was so surprising when Cordelia started to date an American man. In the past Cordelia was known to fancy French and Swiss men and even dated an English man for a couple of months, but never an American. She was once heard saying, that German men were boring and only concerned with their football team. Being romantic with a woman was their most important interest which made her sad.

She sought a man who was more interested in her than who scored for the German's National team. She had her eye on Howard Waterman. In him she saw her American dream husband, tall, well liked, intelligent and very available. Howard on the other hand had sought a companion for a while, but his out of country assignments made it difficult for him to have a meaningful relationship with American women. His work assignments forced him to enlarge his pool of possible prospective to include European female. Their courtship seemed to many a hurried affair but actually it was the ideal relationship. He disliked like football both American and German, had few friends in Germany and found her to be a delightful woman. She sought a different experience than her Germany one and enjoyed the attention that he gave her.

Nevertheless after a six month courtship, they were married in a church in Augsburg Germany. Michelle's parent's marriage never went over well with her paternal grandparents. They wondered why their beloved son had to go all the way to Germany to marry someone whom they have never met. Although stung by the suddenness of the marriage, they were glad it happened and looked forward to the new addition to the family. The happy married couple continued to live in in Germany for the next three years. In the first year of marriage Michelle was born and by the age of three she was on a plane headed to America.

Living in America had always been a dream for Cordelia. She like the possibility of all the things that you could do in America and could not do in Germany. Although she had dreamed about coming to the states since she was a teenager, the transition was a rough one for Cordelia. With no friends or family for social support her world revolved around two people, inquisitive baby and a noncommittal husband. Michelle on the other hand transitioned well into her new country. By the time she entered kindergarten, she was fluent in both languages. Mr. Waterman adored his daughter but attempted not to pamper her. He turned over most of the parenting duties to his wife.

The couple's marriage would be viewed as a good one with the presence of love, commitment and a knowledge to learn about each other. Mr. Waterman showered his wife with love and affection when he had time. He initially did not want Cordelia to work but to transition into the America way slowly as a stay at home wife.

In Search of a Good Feeling

This arrangement worked out fine until Michele entered school. The solitude of being home alone was too much for Cordelia. She became restless as a housewife. She desired to experience more of her newly adopted country than what could be seen from watching television in her suburban home. She proposed to her husband about getting a job. He replied, "No wife of mine needs to work." Her counter proposal was that she understood that she needed to be home, but a couple hours out of the house would do her good. Her husband wavered but after a back massage along with a night of intimacy he agreed to her proposal.

In Germany, Cordelia worked as a claim adjuster at an insurance firm. It was a well-paying job by German standards, but boring. She did have a university degree in art which she had never used. The insurance job was the first employment offering and she took it. The job provided her with a steady income and allowed her to dap in art on the side. This arrangement was fine with her parents since they had visions that their only child would be a starving artist living with them the rest of her life.

She scanned the newspaper want ads daily until one day she saw a part time position at an advertising firm as an administrative assistant/layout person. Not surprisingly, Cordelia interviewed for the job at YnotCreations and received a call the next day from the boss, Mr. Wendell, that the job was hers. She started out working 10-2 pm four days a week. Her job responsibilities included layout work, answering the phone, copying, getting lunches and editing copies. YnotCreations was located not far from Michelle's school. Small in size, the company consisted of 5 employees and Mr. Wendell.

Every day when Cordelia picked up Michelle from school, she would tell her what she did at work, who ordered what for lunch and all of the office gossip. This was their routine for the next five years until one day Cordelia did not come to pick up Michelle from school. Michelle never saw her mother again. Cordelia was hit by a drunk driver while on her way to pick up lunch for the company. She died in the ambulance on the way to the hospital. A week after her death, Michelle was sent to live with her grandparents, and life moved on a little bit slower pace.

CHAPTER 9

It's 9:00 am in Germantown, a neighborhood in the northwest section of the city. Germantown has quite a historic background. It was founded by German Quakers and Mennonite in 1683. It is the birth place of the anti-slavery movement, the first commercial bank, and the site of a Revolutionary War battle. Although the Revolutionary War is over, a battle continues for the souls of the Germantown residents. That battle is played out daily on the streets of Germantown seen and unseen.

The street cleaners have appeared to attack the overnight litter that seems to multiply profusely on the streets of Philadelphia. The early morning hustlers are standing out on their corners attempting to sale their services. Surprisingly, this group of hustlers are not so young, Boswell estimates their age to be in the mid-40's and above. Most are "Hacks" or in other cities they are called jitney drivers. In short, unlicensed car drivers. They huddled together in the corner small talking until a perspective client appears, then they call out "Hack here, Hack here, anyone needs a hack?" It's slow this morning and hacking seems to be a dying business.

Boswell sits waiting to order his breakfast at Just Delicious, a new breakfast spot in the neighborhood located on the corner of Germantown and Chelten one of the major intersections in the neighborhood. From where Boswell sits he is able to observe the movement of the people from all four corners of the street. Another crowd of people wait on the corners for the 23, K and or J buses to take them to their appointed destinations. A man comes in from outside asking Boswell and other patrons for some change. Boswell fusses at the man for disturbing his peace of mind, but gives him the change in his pocket.

While waiting to have his order taken Boswell ponders his present life situation. It's been almost a week into his Michelle withdrawal and the results have been bitter sweet. He finds out that coffee, food and TV are poor substitutes for his queen. Boswell realizes that he is in deeper emotionally than he ever thought and it was causing him to feel an imbalance. On the other hand, Boswell believes that he needs this vacation from Michelle.

After being with Michelle on a daily basis for the last four months, he realizes how different living together with someone can be as compared to living by one's self. Initially, the only person Boswell had to think about was himself, but now each day is fill with thoughts of what are we doing instead of what I am doing. With Michelle being pregnant this change in thinking some days mentally exhausts Boswell. Although they had dated for a year, total time spent together was limited to dates, overnights and weekend trips which gave Boswell time to regroup and find himself after time spent with Michelle. But now when they go out to an event, and come home, she is still there causing

In Search of a Good Feeling

him to be "on". Now, this little time to regroup, resulting in Boswell's self-time to decrease while his "we" time with Michelle dramatically increases.

On the plus side, Michelle does have her own life. This change in his time allocation has left Boswell imbalance and confused as to what to do. The living with each other is not anything that he would had proposed, but as Boswell put to Bill, "Hey, I thought she was going to leave one day so I thought it would be cool, but after four months Michelle is still with me with no signs of going anywhere." He understands that he needs to find himself again, but at times feels guilty when he does not involve Michelle in his activities. This time spent away from Michelle is supposed to be used by Boswell to find himself but instead it has been used to realize how much he misses her.

A waitress named Betty comes over to take his order. She is an older lady attempting to act younger and pulling it off well. Her mannerisms are playful but professional and she understands the value of establishing a good relationship with the customer. The better the relationship the better the tip. She could teach a psychologist a thing or two about reading the body language of people.

"Good morning young man, what can Ms. Betty do for you?"

Boswell looks up and smiles. "What's that smile for?" They both laugh, and slowly Boswell begins to feel better.

"I will have a black coffee, two biscuits and a side of bacon Ms. Betty."

"Is that all?" Boswell ponders. He really wants some grits, but most places makes them too watery for him so he declines.

"Yes ma'am"

"Who you calling ma'am? I'm Ms. Betty."

"Yes ma'am...but this is the manner I was taught to address women, it's no disrespect to you Ms. Betty."

"I know,. I'm just messing with you. Your parents brought you up right, but just call me Ms. Betty, no ma'am. I'll get your coffee right way. No milk or sugar correct?"

"Yes Ms. Betty I like it black just like my women," Boswell laughs.

Ms. Betty smiles as she switches away. Boswell opens up the Philadelphia Inquirer, the daily newspaper. Reading was one of Boswell's favorite things to do while eating or traveling on public transportation. Not a fan of TV news, Boswell limits his viewing to CBS's 60 minutes program on Sunday night. He believes his enjoyment of reading comes from observing his parents reading the newspaper. There was an unspoken rule in the house that no one reads the papers until their parents are finished reading the paper. One day one of the twins attempted to read a section of the paper that his father had yet to read. It did not end well for her. Reading was never openly stated that it was important, it was demonstrated. So Boswell believed that if it was good for his parents it's even better for him.

Before he could find out who won last night in the world of baseball Ms. Betty is back with his order. She smiles and asks if there would be anything else. Boswell, attempting to avoid her flirting eyes keeps his eyes on his plate and replies, "Everything looks good."

"Are you talking about your meal or me," she laughs as she walks away switching.

In Search of a Good Feeling

The café has a constant flow of customers ushering in and out. Most stop for a cup of coffee and the local patrons like their coffee sweet with a donut. They sometimes combine their love for coffee with their love for sweets or as one person simply put it "Give me the Germantown special, sugar with milk and a little coffee."

Boswell notices a familiar face ordering the special. It's Smoke from Sister Juanita's café. Smoke is a character. He is a constant informational source of everything from trivia to world news. He seems to possess a photographic memory of everyday in his life. Unfortunately, he is ready and willing to share them with you. It generally goes something like this, "Hey I can remember …" With those words Smoke can bring back memories from any time in his life. "The summer of 69, it was hot and I was dating a yellow girl named Toni. She was so fine and she lived up in Mt. Airy and had big..." A man who has eaten too many donuts and not spent enough time on the treadmill Smoke is a man who just needs an audience. Boswell motions Smoke over to join him at his table. He wobbles slowly towards Boswell with a silly grin on his face.

"I see that you are walking a little stiff."

"Yea man I had knee surgery recently and its slowing me down."

"Yes, I can see. So why are you here and not at Nita's?"

"Well I am here to check out the competition. It's like I am a spy for Sister Nita. I can tell her that they make a good cup of Germantown special here, very sweet and smooth," said Smoke as he gulps down the last mouthful of his coffee with a look of contentment on his face.

Smoke leans back and places both hands on his head. He looks up in the air like he is pondering something and begins, "Yep, I can remember when places started to sell the Germantown special. I was 8 years old. Hmmm, that must have been around 1962, a good year as I remember." So for the next ten minutes Boswell learns about the history of the Germantown Special as his thoughts drift towards what Michelle is doing down South. Smoke finally finish the history lesson. "Young'un, that's enough talking about that. I need to get out of here before I am spotted by the enemy and report back to Sister Nita the goings on over here. She will not be pleased, but I will not say I saw you over here."

Boswell smiles, "Thanks Smoke. Yeah, you go do you and I will continue to do me." Smoke looks, "What… I do what?"

"You do…never mind have a great day."

With those parting words, Smoke is off, but not before ordering another Germantown Special to go. He looks towards Boswell whispering as he points at his order, "I need it for evidence," smiling as he leaves out. As soon as Smoke departs Ms. Betty reappears bending down low to give Boswell a bird's eye view of her tempting cleavage.

"Are you finish here or do you have a taste for anything else."

"I'm good thanks," looking down at his empty place as much as possible.

"I have no doubt about that. Well ok here's your bill. Pay as you go out, but if you need anything else from Ms. Betty let me know, do not be a stranger."

"Yes ma'am, I mean Ms. Betty."

In Search of a Good Feeling

Boswell grins. *Wow she is something else. Assertive, confident and has a walk that makes you go MM, MMM, MMMM, what is a man to do? She is a poor lonely man's kryptonite. I feel so nervous around her, Was it my need for attention or my lust for her? She was very nicely put together. I need to get out of here before she comes back asking me if I have changed my mind for having a taste for something sweet.* He quickly jumps up and pays the cashier but not before leaving Ms. Betty a generous tip. *Well she worked for this tip, the hussy.*

Back on the street after his two hour breakfast the neighborhood is finally coming alive. People were out on the street sucking up the sunshine. The sight of a couple walking hand in hand makes Boswell realizes how much he misses Michelle. He hurries back to the apartment to work on the following poem for her which took the rest of the day

The River

Because of you
Feelings are emerging
from within
o v e r f l o w
i
n
g
the protective border
of self
a collection of hues
waiting to color
my day

**bursting forth
leaping beyond my own
willingness to suppress
them
to become a
permanent expression
of my landscape
…I miss you**

Not to be caught up in his self-made pity party Boswell quickly places the poem in a folder on his desk with the intentions of giving it to Michelle when he next sees her. Across from the folder is a letter that Boswell received yesterday from his Auntie Nannette Story, his father's sister, someone Boswell had not seem since he was a child. The letter is an invitation to a family reunion scheduled next weekend in a small town outside of Charleston during the same time Michele and he will be in South Carolina. It appeared from information on the envelope that his Auntie Nannette did not have his updated address, causing the letter to go his old address somewhere on Brown Street, then back to the post office, then to his old Wayne Avenue address, then back to the post office and surprisingly to his present address.

Yesterday, Boswell called Auntie Nannette, the only name on the organizing committee that he recognized to get more information about the family reunion. She was very glad to hear from him, and apologizes for not having his correct address, but in the same breath scolded him for not keeping in touch with his family. The call went something like this:

"Hi may I speak to Auntie Nannette?"

In Search of a Good Feeling

"Speaking."

"Hi, I do not know if you remember me I'm your nephew. I'm Thomas' son."

"Thomas my brother?"

"Yes ma'am, I'm Boswell."

"Hmm that's a funny name. Oh yea I remember you. I had to give you a spanking that time you opened up the chicken coop and all my chickens got loose. I still think we were missing two or three of them.

"You remembered that?"

"You would remember it too if you lost three of your good egg laying chickens. Shoot I can remember your father's first girlfriend. Her name was Betty Jean Crockett. She lived down around the bend and the last time I hear anything about her she was living in Livingston North Carolina with her kids."

That is how their conversation went for the next 45 minutes, Auntie Nannette displaying an uncanny memory of places, people and events. They eventually talked about the reunion and what would be occurring next weekend. The more they discussed the reunion the more interested Boswell became in meeting his family. His father had always been his connection to his southern relatives. When he passed, Boswell lost his connection. Although his memories of the south's scorching heat and big mosquitos were not pleasant ones, he did enjoy being around his many cousins, aunts and uncles when he visited. They displayed a different sense of family and of rhythm that was very dear to him. Not being raised around a bunch of relatives, Boswell was always amazed about the sheer number of family members and the slow methodical beat that life was conducted by in the south.

"So will we see you next week?"

"Yes ma'am you will."

"That's good, are you bringing your wife and kids?"

"Well Auntie Nannette, I am not married but I do have a girlfriend and she will be with me."

"Well that's good but no children hey?"

"No ma'am not yet but soon. But one more thing Auntie Nannette…it's about my girlfriend."

"Yes, Is she sickly?"

"No ma'am she is quite well but she isn't black she's white. Really she is a German- American because she was born in Germany but had an American father."

Auntie Nannette laughs, "Well white is a just a color, it looks good on some people."

"I just wanted you to know. I did not want to surprise you."

"Its fine child. I guess you have to be some color, she just white. See you next week with your girlfriend. What's her name any way?"

"Michelle, her name is Michelle Waterman. She is down there in Charleston now visiting her grandparents."

"Did you say Waterman in Charleston…hmm, I think I knew some Waterman's a while back. Well, I will see you and Michelle next week. Nice talking to you nephew."

"Bye Auntie Nannette I will see you soon."

That was yesterday, and reconnecting with his people made it a good day for Boswell. Today is Friday that means it's time to loosen up because its Rumba night.

The faint sounds of drums could be heard as Boswell turned the corner towards the Green Street Art Gallery. Bambambam…bam…bam babababababamm. The call of the drums echoed through the neighborhood. It is rumba

In Search of a Good Feeling

time at the gallery! Musicians, regulars and onlookers alike are making their way towards the rhythmic beats of the drums. The Gallery as Michelle likes to call it is the home to a regular scheduled Friday night rumba session. A group of men of various ages, hues and nationalities sit in a semi-circular fashion around an assortment of Congo drums, shakeres, palitos and other percussion instruments taking turns in producing soul stimulating music. While the group plays a driving beat, a singer may join in singing songs of musica negroide in Spanish. Boswell later found out that musica negroide means the music of the blacks. It's the music that the African slaves brought to the island of Puerto Rica and Cuba.

Foot tapping and head bobbing increases as the crowd begins to connect with the music. Initially, an onlooker Boswell is swept into the beat of the drums like the rest of the crowd. Tapping his foot, the bobbing of his head and finally the movement of his hips to the beat of the rhythm links Boswell spiritually with his century old ancestors. He has entered in the world of the funk and there was no coming back. He dances with anyone and everyone until the spirit of the boogie wears him out.

While seeking momentary relief from an unoccupied chair Boswell notices an older gentleman who walks in the gallery as the musicians are playing. Each musician comes forth to greet him. He stiffly sits down and slowly begins to tape his fingers. When there is a break in the music he slides in a chair in front of a conga and suddenly something magical occurs. Boswell watches in amazement as the man plays the conga like his fingers are on fire, bringing forth incredible beats and textures from the stretched skins. The conga begins to talk to him …calling for him to dance, yes dance the spirt of the boogie is again upon him and Boswell unconsciously moves to the beat of the congas. After two hours of dancing, he is tired but feelings so connected to everyone and everything.

A warm glow and a smile accompanies him as he says goodbye to musicians, dance partners and onlookers. He is feeling good and cannot wait to go home to tell Michelle what a good time she missed. But suddenly he realizes that Michelle is not home, but in South Carolina. Consequently, there will be no talking about anything with her tonight. Boswell can barely walk down the hall to his apartment as he steps off the 4th floor elevator. He reaches for his apartment keys while mumbling under his breath that he is too old for this, *They got the butter from the duck tonight... Yes sir they did.*

He stumbles into the apartment tossing off clothes and he heads straight to the bathroom. His tired body seeks the relief that only comes from a hot bath with mango scented soap. His mind deals with disappointment since Michelle is not at home to share his good times with him. As quickly as he can Boswell fills the tub with hot water. While undressing his cell phone slips onto the floor. Picking it up, he notices that Michelle had sent a text a couple of hours ago.

The text reads, Sorry about not texting sooner, got here ok…everything is wonderful, but I know that you should be at the rumba by now. Enjoy but don't dance too much without me…. Really miss you.

Love always, Michelle.

He smiles while slipping down into a bathtub of mango scented bubbles thinking, *My baby loves me.*

CHAPTER 10

Michelle looks out of the window as the rain falls from the sky. *"Summer rains can be so refreshing,"* she thinks. Unable to wait until the rain shower is over, Michelle runs out in the back yard without shoes or umbrella. The wet grass feels comfortably cool on her feet while her slightly sun tanned skin glistens in the rain. She stops at the big mahogany tree to hide from the rain. It suddenly stops giving way to the sun allowing the water vapors to make colors in the sky. It's Friday morning and Boswell is scheduled to arrive in the evening. It's been a long six days without him. Last Friday her train arrived in the station at 6:55pm, just five minutes late.

The Charleston train station is not a thing of beauty or history. *"It looks like something out of the 50's",* thought Michelle as she stepped down onto the platform. She detrained and went looking for her grandparents. There in 93 degree weather with the humidity rising stood her grandparents, Jake and Lizzie Waterman, a little grayer than before in their starch white outfits with a small sign that said, "Welcome Home." Grandma Waterman, a petite woman wore a white blouse over a white skirt which complimented Mr. Waterman's white shirt, blue polka dot bow tie and white pleated pants. They stared at each other for a moment before Michelle let out a holler and ran into their arms. After all the hugs, kisses and stares from onlookers, they moved joyfully to the car. The Waterman Plantation is located a good hour drive outside of Charleston. During the ride back to the plantation the discussion was mostly centered on what used to be and is not now. The Waterman's were like a well-rehearsed duet, Grandpa Jed attempted to fill Michelle in on the latest developments in the area as Grandpa Lizzie Waterman finished each of his thoughts.

"Remember the Old Glisten Mill general store, where they had the coldest soda and best ice cream around?" asked Grandpa Jed.

"It's gone, replaced with a darn 7-11, "said Grandma Lizzie.

"Sure miss that ice cream," said Grandpa Jed.

"The cold Pepsi Cola and the big pickle barrel, those were the days Jed," said Grandma Lizzie and that is how the conversation flowed.

As her granddad turned off of I-17 and on to state road 10, Michelle began to be slowly transform back to a stage in her life which she escaped long time ago. Everything started to seem familiar and memories were retrieving bits of information that had been dormant but not lost. A smile appeared on Michelle's face as she thought, *There is old man Bray's place way in the back. I wonder if he is still around? Wow, there's the old weeping willow tree! I can remember the first time I saw it I thought it was haunted with all that weird Spanish moss hanging from it, ugh.* One memory triggered another reopening. A concealed past with renewed energy.

In Search of a Good Feeling

Finally, they arrived at the plantation,. The house seemed much smaller than Michelle remembered it. The grounds were still well trimmed, but as she viewed it from the car Michelle thought, *Its grandeur is gone, but its familiarity has remained.*

The Plantation is 600 acres of property that the Waterman have owned since the early 1800's. Today some of the acreage is leased out to local farmers with about 300 acres remaining wooded and wild. In the woods lives deer, rabbits, turkey, wild pigs and all kinds of wild life. During hunting season, Grandpa Jed allow hunters on to his property for a fee. The house is located back off the state road connected to civilization by a long winding driveway. It's a three stories high castle with four bedrooms, three baths, a dining room, living room, large kitchen, an attic, cellar, a small office/library and a room Grandma Lizzie called her sewing room.

It has a long wide covered porch in the front and back of the house where you can enjoy the blessings of the sun without getting burnt. The front porch had always been Michelle's favorite place. The porch is where as a 10 year old child she met and talked to the sun and even attempted to do the same with the moon, but she found the moon's attitude varied, sometimes not showing up at all. "That was no way to have a relationship," she told the moon one night. So she stayed with the sun because even on cloudy rainy days she could still feel its presence. The sun became Michelle's playmate and confident due to the fact she did not have a lot of friends.

The kids at her school called her names like Nazi girl and foreigner saying that she talked funny so no one would play with her, but the sun. She took her luggage out of the car and placed it on the porch. Michelle just stood there and began to hear the soft voices of the gathering spirits. "Welcome Home," they whispered to her, "Welcome Home." She was overwhelmed by the reception. A deep believer in the role of spirits in the lives of people Michelle became misty eyed.

She must have looked quite strange because Grandpa hollered out, "C'mon Chellie, why you just standing there smiling, you waiting on something? You home now child." Michelle smiled in his direction knowing that he would not understand if she tried to explain to him.

"I'm coming I was just greeting some old friends."

"You must be tired little girl, I do not see anybody out here but us and a couple cats."

"I told you he would not understand," she mumbled to the spirits.

When Michelle finally walked into the house memories, sounds, and smells like old friends meet her at the door to usher her inside. Once inside she stood in the big hallway and began to softly cry.

Grandma asked" What's the matter baby, you sad?"

"No Grandma I'm happy, I'm so happy to be home," Michelle replied.

"CHEEEEELLLLLLLLLLLLIE is that you?" Suddenly out of nowhere two big black arms picked Michelle high in the air scaring her close to death.

"Martha, Martha, yes this is me, now put me down," laughs Michelle. Martha Mae Waters has been around the Waterman Plantation as long as Michelle could remember. A tall strong dark skinned lady, Martha was 6' ft. with

In Search of a Good Feeling

no fat on her. She wore hair like she has always has in a short afro, and took no stuff from anyone, not even Mr. Waterman. On those rainy days when the sun could not be her playmate Michelle would venture into Martha's kitchen and spend time with her. During her time in the kitchen Martha taught Michelle about life from her perspective.

"Girl, have you put on any weight since the last time I seen you? Let me look at you." Martha twirled Michelle around in the middle of the kitchen like a top. "Hmm you look a little porky in the belly. Have you been eating too many cheese steaks up there in Philly or are you having a baby Chellie?"

Immediately, Michelle's face turned a bright red but before she could answer, Grandma Waterman stepped in,

"Now, Martha ain't that a bit personal?"

"Well, I I been around the barn a couple of times myself Mrs. Waterman. You know I had 3 chiltens, most as grown as you Chellie, and I know it ain't no cheese steaks because cheese always upset your stomach. Well, I'm going to let it be for now. It's real nice to see you again, real nice. Now give Mrs. Martha another hug."

After another bear hug, Martha disappeared to the cellar to get some vegetables for dinner tomorrow, but not before she whispered something into Michelle's ear. Grandma Waterman moves quickly towards Michelle saying, "Pay her no mind child, Martha is always saying something that she should not be saying. I do not know why we have not let her go by now. I know that she is up to something, I saw her whisper something to you. Do not believe anything she says."

"Grandma everything is fine and you know the reason why Mrs. Martha is still here because you don't cook, nor clean. Anyway she just whispered to me that there was some newly baked cookies in the cookie jar. Oatmeal raisin, my favorite."

Grandma Waterman took Michelle's hand. "Well Chellie, let's put your stuff in your room so you can get comfortable and all. I know you must be a little tired from all of that traveling. I know I would be. And where is your grand pappy with the suitcases?"

"What do you mean where am I at? I am doing all the work as usual."

Both of them turned around and there was Grandpa Jed's red faced with Michelle's bags coming towards the stairs. "What are you two waiting for, Christmas?" he stated as he struggled with the bags. Both women laughed hugging each other as they did.

"Wow granddad are you ok?" asked Michelle as she reached down to lend a hand to him.

"I'm fine just these bags are a might heavy. Thanks for the hand little girl."

It was a peculiar sight the three of them bracing each other from falling as they went up the steps with Michelle's bags. Thankfully her bedroom was right off the stairwell or the three of them would have never made it standing up. Grandma Lizzie opened the door to the bedroom then turns to Michelle.

"Well here is your room. Just like you left it with a few minor improvements. We always thought that you would be back so we kept it up just for that day, and that thank God that day is today."

Michelle was speechless as she viewed her bedroom, just as she left it. Memories flooded her consciousness while tears

In Search of a Good Feeling

flowed down her face. She hugged her wet eyed grandmother and kissed her grandfather saying "Thank you."

"Well it's getting late so we are going to let you be. If you are hungry, Martha left you something in the icebox. Get some rest now baby. We will sit and talk in the morning."

After another exchange of kisses, Michelle was left alone in her bedroom with Tommy her teddy bear, her rocking chair and her books. She sat in the rocking chair. It was one of the many presents from her father that she kept. Rocking in the chair has always had a positive effect on Michelle's mood. She leaned back in the chair and began to rock slowly with Tommy in her arms. It felt good and familiar. Michelle closed her eyes in an attempt to center herself. Extreme exhaustion immediately came over Michelle causing her to quickly undress and slide into the shower. Michelle emerged ten minutes later with wet hair, refreshed and a little hungry. During that passage of time, someone had left a ham sandwich, a scoop of potato salad and some lemonade for her.

Michelle briefly pondered her situation. She is now vegetarian, but she is also the granddaughter to the best hog farmer around. The decision came quickly, and soon Michelle along with the ham sandwich, potato salad and lemonade were having a great old time. Soon after her last sip of lemonade Michelle fell asleep awakening 6 hours later to movement in her belly and with a salty taste in her mouth as the fowls of the county began their early morning serenade. She slowly looked around in the bedroom attempting to figure out whose bed she is in and how did she get here. Michelle rubbed her belly to sooth the wild beast inside of her. She quickly glanced at the clock. It's 5:37am and far too early for this city girl to be awake Slowly, Michelle put the pieces together and fell back off to sleep wondering what Boswell was doing in Philly.

Two hours later, Michelle awaken to the smell of bacon, coffee, homemade biscuits and voices, some familiar some not. The beast within Michelle had the same reaction as she had. *Yum, that smells good. But who can be visiting her Grandparents so early in the morning* thought Michelle, *and why are they talking so loud?*

Michelle threw on one of Boswell's t-shirts and pair of yoga pants to wear downstairs. She pretended like she did when she was a child to be a secret agent attempting to be as quiet as possible going down the steps to check out the happenings in the kitchen. Unfortunately, the house's aged steps gave her away, creaking loudly as she went down them.

"Chellie is that you?" Michelle froze in place on the last step like a dear in the headlight of a car not knowing what to do. Realizing that her secret surveillance plan was exposed, Michelle directly replied, "Yes ma'am, it's me Chellie."

"I know you are not trying to sneak up on us like you use to do as a kid. Boy some things never change. Come on around that corner girl, breakfast is ready."

"Yes Ma'am I'm coming."

Michelle turned the corner and there around the kitchen was Grandpa, Grandma, Ms. Bracey a grey haired lovable friend of her grandmother, Billie Jean Smith, her high school get high buddy, Willie MacBean, the only boy around here that she allowed to kiss her, two little unknown kids and Grandpa's asshole brother and sister- in-law Uncle Jesse and Auntie Debra. Everyone had their plate piled up with food. There was bacon, eggs, potatoes and coffee in

In Search of a Good Feeling

plain sight while Martha was at the stove bringing out some freshly baked biscuits.

Michelle smiled, "Well good morning everyone. It looks like you guys started without me."

"Good morning," replied the crowd in unison. Grandma Lizzie comes over and takes Michelle by the hand saying, "Well since we all were going to the Festival today I thought it would be a good idea to kill two birds with one stone so I invited everyone over for breakfast to surprise you and then we can all go over to the Kissing Pig Festival to see your Grandpa's pigs win the blue ribbon again.

"Well it's a surprise, a noisy one but a surprise." remarked Michelle.

"Well, Well, Well, it seems that the German princess has awaken," said Uncle Jesse.

"A wise man once said the more things change, the more they stay the same." Michelle muttered under here breath. *"Although my uncle is older he is still an asshole."* She smiled in his direction and goes over to greet Ms. Bracey with a hug.

"My child I have not seen you in a month of Sundays," says Ms. Bracey.

"Ms. Bracey you know that I was always a busy person even as a child…going here and there…but very glad to be finally home."

"Well I am glad you are too. Hummm, you gaining weight? I remember you to be on the small size last time I can recollect."

"Well yes ma'am I have, but remember it's been ten years since you have seen me. I'm a woman now."

"Yes you are and a mighty fine one at that."

Michelle turned in the direction of the comment and there sat Willie MacBean smiling like a Cheshire cat.

"Shut up Willie Mac. You a married man now. You married to me," beams in Billy Jean. She playfully punches Willie Mac in the side of his head then kisses the spot.

"I'm just playing, you know you are my one and only," smiled Willie Mac. Michele does not know whether to cry or to laugh. Billy Jean and Willie Mac were the last two people she ever thought would get married and too each other. Billy Jean and Michelle used to smoke weed in high school behind grandfather hogs pens. That was a great location because no one would smell them smoking weed because the hogs smelled so bad. Last time they talked Billy Jean was talking about going to the army. Willie Mac on the other hand never drank or did drugs. He was raised by very strict Bible believing parents. He had a crush on Michelle and one day after school they kissed behind the gym. The next time she saw Willie Mac he apologized for kissing her because he thought he had sinned. He said although he enjoyed it, it was not the Christian thing to do until two people got married and since he did not want to go to hell, we could not kiss anymore. Michelle was fine with his decision because he was not a good kisser and she could not see them doing it again.

"What, you two are married? Oh my gosh, when did that happened? Said Michelle.

"Well about five years ago. He was the last one standing...them our kids over there." Billy Jean pointed to the two children sitting at the end of the table. "That's Betty Mae she is the oldest and Willie Mac Jr." Both kids smiled at Michelle but quickly turn their attention back to eating their breakfast.

In Search of a Good Feeling

Michelle turned to Willie Mac, "Willie Mac, I am proud of you being married and a father too. Who knew?"

She turned to Billy Jean, "They look like some fine kids Billy Jean. Wow, you have been busy."

Billy Jean smiled while nodding her head. "Yea, but how about you? It's been ten years. We have a lot of catching up to do."

"But first let me catch up with you guys food wise because I'm hungry. Martha, may I have two of those biscuits, oops I mean catheads you just brought out of the oven?"

Immediately, Martha got a plate from the cupboard and began filling it with food. "Yes you can. Let me have the pleasure of fixing your plate." She hands Michelle a plate with two biscuits, three thick pieces of bacon, grits and scrambled eggs.

"Like I said the princess is home," remarked Uncle Jesse as he sops up the last of his syrup with a biscuit.

"Yes Uncle Jesse, it's good to be home, but by the way I am not a princess any more, I am a queen."

CHAPTER 11

Boswell awakens Saturday morning with a bad case of Michelle on the mind. He will be flying out in early evening to meet up with her. It had been a long week for him. He will be able to see his queen again, but questions do remain about meeting the rest of the family. What do you say to set of grandparents who knows you got their granddaughter pregnant, and coincidentally is Black? Boswell just shakes his head trying not to think about his future interactions with Michelle's family.

It was time for Boswell to do his morning walk around the neighborhood to see the happenings. Germantown on Saturdays in the summer is like a village market place made up of different hues, patterns, and textures of people. One of the entrepreneurial models that is quite common to Philadelphia that is closely associated with a village market concept is vending. A street vendor in Philadelphia is defined by the following ordinance:

> Any person travelling by foot, wagon, motor vehicle or any other type of conveyance from place to place, house to house or street to street or on property

In Search of a Good Feeling

owned or controlled by the City of Philadelphia carrying, conveying, or transporting goods, wares or merchandise and offering and exposing them for sale, or making sales and delivering articles to purchasers; or who without travelling from place to place, sells or offers for sale products from a wagon, handcart, pushcart, motor vehicle, stand, conveyance or from his person who submits orders, and as a separate transaction, makes deliveries to purchasers. A "street vendor" shall include any "vendor," "peddler," "hawker," "huckster," "itinerant merchant" or "transient vendor" but shall exclude any vendor licensed under Section 9-201; [17]

Everyone is in the vending business or knows someone who vends in some form or another. The examples runs from selling fried chicken dinners for the church's building fund to hawking those tasteless Girl Scout cookies so that some girl can attend camp in the summer. Vending is alive and well in Philadelphia. Today outside of the apartment building where Boswell lives, one of the more common type of vending is occurring in the form of a garage sale. But this was not just any type of garage sale, it was a street wide sale with multi-families displaying their saleable used wares on tables in front of their residence for strangers to gawk at, inspect and hopefully purchase.

He moves slowly through the crowd looking, smiling and sometimes touching but not buying anything. This behavior is somewhat unusual for Boswell because he does like buying other people's used items. His friends sees him as being cheap. Boswell does not disagree about not liking to spend money but he sees himself as a resaler helping society to rid itself of stuff that would probably end up in a land fill.

Boswell reaches Germantown Avenue without spending a cent of his money when suddenly he hears music. Marching down the street is a parade celebrating Juneteenth, a celebration commemorating the passing of the 13th Amendment that ended slavery in the United States. According to the brochure that a young lady hands him the parade is called the "Freedom Walk". The parade commenced where the first protest against slavery happened in 1688 where Germantown Avenue and Wister Street ends. The Johnson House, located on the corner of Washington lane and Germantown is a National Historic landmark that's significant for its role as a safe house in the antislavery movement and the Underground Railroad. Although the participants in the parade are small in number the visual is quite powerful as traffic piles up behind the parade delaying some from their destination.

Boswell shakes his head in amazement because this history occurred just a brief distance from where he lives. As life on the festive-like day continues a siren fills the air, not an uncommon sound in the neighborhood that sometimes is met with a sense of indifference. The hair stylists at the Perfectly Beautiful Hair Salon on the corner of Chelten and Brown are busy doing what they do best. Through personal testimonies, magazine articles and friendly advice they are attempting to convince women that a new hair style will change their lives for the best. Not by reading a book or obtaining a new set of skills... nope. But by getting their hair processed, adding extensions, colored, curled or even twisted can make her feel like a queen for a day. By the looks

In Search of a Good Feeling

of the number of women going in and out of the salon they must be very good at what they do.

Not far away a man pushes a red shopping cart down the street filled with rags and a bucket. It is the equipment he needs to service his clients. His hustle is to wash women's cars as they wait to get their hair done and certainly his business will be good today. A group of young black girls walk by the car washer each wearing store bought waist length hair masking their uniqueness with the sameness of a designated style. During his Saturday morning stroll Boswell notes that white headphones and wires gangling out of ears passes for fashion these days. What are these people listening to he ponders?

Boswell ducks in to Just Delicious to get a cup of coffee while reflecting on his own situation. He looks around as he enters and determines that Ms. Betty must be off. He breathes a sigh of relief because he did not need that type of temptation at this moment. He finds a seat at the counter and orders a black coffee and blueberry muffin. He has a pleasant verbal exchange with the waitress resulting in quick service with a smile. While sipping his coffee, Boswell realizes that he has to pack for a week's trip to South Carolina where he will meet Michelle's family who he does not know and his father's people that are mostly strangers to him, also. In the middle of meeting new people that he does not know and who may not like him, he has to deal with mosquitos, the heat and strange food. All of these thoughts are swirling around his head causing him to question his decision to go south. He checks his watch and sees it's 11:30. The morning is moving quickly and based on the number of people that are lining up inside the door waiting to eat at the restaurant, Germantown is truly alive now. Boswell pays his bill and slides pass waiting prospective customers onto Chelten Avenue. He looks to the left and right before proceeding down the street back to his apartment to pack his clothes.

He arrives at the airport early, and discovers that his flight has been delayed 6 hours causing the flight to arrive in Charleston at 4:30 am in the morning. Instantly he calls Michelle to relay the bad news. Its appears the Michelle is more shaken about the long delay than Boswell.

She asks, "So what's the plan now?"

"Well, instead of you picking me up, I will just rent a car and drive to your grandparents' place in the morning, no big deal. We have to rent a car anyway."

"So let me get this right, you are going to rent a car and drive tomorrow morning to my folks' place, correct?"

"Yes ma'am, I am, because it does not make any sense for you to wait for me in the middle of the night at the airport when we do not know for sure when the plane is going to arrive. Baby, it's going to be fine."

"Ok, Ok, I cannot say that I am happy about the new developments but since I am powerless on this end to change anything I guess I will see you in the morning. I know my grandparents will be also disappointed because they cannot wait to meet you."

"Well tell your folks that I am looking forward to their southern hospitality, although it will be somewhat delayed. By the way we have been invited to my family's reunion next week in Summerville, a little town outside of Charleston."

"What! When did you find out about your family's reunion?"

Sensing something in her voice Boswell knew he had to get off the phone in a hurry. Michelle does not like surprises,

In Search of a Good Feeling

and since she had been on him to get in touch with his folks Boswell realizes that she wants much more details than he wants to talk about at the moment. The 6 hour delay has put a damper on his spirit so he just wants to tell Michelle about the delay and get off the phone, so he creates a lie.

"Well sweetie, it's a long story. I will tell you more about the details when I see you in the morning, and hey I have to go…they are announcing something about the flight."

"Ok, I miss you, and so does the baby. See you in the morning. I will be waiting."

"Bye."

Minutes turn to hours as Boswell finds himself in a prone position on a bench watching the workers as they put the airport to sleep. At 2 am Boswell finally boards the airplane headed for Charleston. As he enters the plane cabin he hears the flight attendant announce that it is a full flight. *Damn it*! thought Boswell, *I need a break*. There in seat 24e sat a large individual whose body seemed to flow over the seat's arm rest into his seat. Resigned to the real possibility of being fleshy with a very large man for the next two hours Boswell smiles at the guy and bucks up.

The next two hours go quickly as Boswell discovers that his seatmate's name is Bruce and he has a deep knowledge of gardening, a subject of great interest to him. They talk the entire flight and exchange business cards at the end of the flight. The plane finally lands to the applauds of the weary passengers. Immediately, Boswell has two things on his mind… getting his bags and finding the rental car area. He deplanes to an almost empty airport, absent of any type of personnel with the exception of a couple of bored TSA workers and a ground crew whose job it is to unload the baggage. Boswell makes his way to the baggage area where he waits with a bunch of other fellow sleepy passengers for about 15 minutes before he gets his two bags. Due to the 4:00 am arrival, Boswell reaches a rental car counter area that would not be open for another hour.

The sounds of the vacuum cleaner awakens Boswell from his early morning slumber. It should be known that driving a car is not one of Boswell nor Michelle favorite activities. Since both determined that car ownership is not an urban necessity, public transportation, walking, biking or a cab are their chosen modes of transportation. When someone ask Michelle why she does not drive, she goes into her smaller solar footprint rant, while Boswell just states, "I can, but I choose not to, end of story." Recently he had a conversation with Bill about car ownership over at the Wired Bean. Boswell had just told Bill that he was going to be a father. Bill congratulates Boswell and to celebrate the occasion, Bill buys Boswell a coffee.

Boswell said, "I know that you have some advice for me, so Ok I'm listening."

Bill rubs his scurry beard and says, "Buy yourself a car for you and your woman. You are going to be a father soon and you got to start acting more responsible. It's not just going to be you anymore frugal man, things are about to change," he laughs.

Boswell replied, "Frugal me? Bill you do not even know how to spell the word let alone use it in a proper sentence."

"Be a man."

"Bill, what the heck does be a man mean?"

"Men are providers, they take care of their people."

In Search of a Good Feeling

"What cave have you been living in Bill? The statement be a man is a sexist statement and what does being a man have to do with car ownership?"

Bill smiles while he rises, "My brother if you do not know I cannot tell you. Have a good night and ponder… isn't that your word? Yea, ponder on what I just told you. Later player." Bill waves good bye and hurries out of the coffee shop.

Boswell sits in silence as he repeats the statement, *Be a man* in his mind. He concluded that Bill must be projecting some of his faults on to him therefore being a man is Bill's issue and not his. He chuckles and ask himself, *so what does that have to do with car ownership*?

Boswell approaches the car rental area and obtains a vehicle with no problem. Although the customer service attendant is cooperative, she has little knowledge about the area so she gives Boswell a map of the area and wishes him well. He did require some luck but after a little misdirection, Boswell finally finds route I-17 then he turns off onto State Road 10 just like the service station person told him. He passes the old willow tree and Mr. Bray's old barn. The morning dew interacting with sunrise causes the summer corn fields to glisten before Boswell's eyes. After a number of corns fields Boswell passes a horse farm with several horses feeding in the pasture. He pulls off to the side of the road for a better view of the horses. As he exits the car he watches as a red fox approaches the herd intently before being scared away by their movement. Boswell is in wonder for a moment looking around at nature's creation of hues, patterns and colors. The color combination of the orange clay roads winding through the green pine tree forests amazes him.

Suddenly the voices begin to yell at him, "Remember where you are, this is not Amish country fool, this is the South, the home of slavery, lynching and the KKK!" Boswell quickly jumps back into the car emotionally shaken and unable to beat back the message of the voices. He sits silently for a moment attempting to get his wits together. The voices are quiet for now, they did their job well. They brought deep hidden feelings about the south back to his awareness. Boswell is emotionally changed, he is now on edge. The bright sunny morning does not seem so innocent to him now.

He quickly merges back on to County Road 33, a changed man. A gentle breeze stirs the pine trees causing Boswell to shiver as thoughts of the KKK begin to reemerge. Remembering his father's words that a scared man cannot do anything, Boswell calms himself again and proceeds on to his destination.

Ten minutes later he passes a sign stating the Waterman Plantation was just ahead. He finds himself at the border of the Waterman's property. *Oh my Gosh,* Boswell thinks to himself, *The Waterman's large white house with it's well maintained lawn looks like it should be on the cover of Southern Living magazine.* As he turns in to the long driveway a lone crow in a nearby tree announces his arrival. Boswell realizes that he is scared, less about who he is about to meet but more about the uncertainties of the future. He pulls up to the house and remains in the rental car for a minute not knowing what to do. Then he sees her sitting in one of those rocking chairs on the porch just looking at him smiling and rubbing her stomach. Boswell jumps out of the car and runs towards Michelle. The good feelings have return. As he runs up on the porch Boswell thinks that he hears the sound of many voices cheering.

CHAPTER 12

Michelle awakens early attempting to beat the sunrise but her childhood friend is waiting in the window for her. She exchanges pleasantries with the sun and dresses quickly trying not to make any noise. The house is quiet, the only sound coming from the hallway ceiling fan humming in the background. Michelle attempts to walk silently down the stairs without waking up her grandparents. But like on a previous attempt, she miscalculate which step was the squeaky one and the creaking sound seem to reverberate throughout the whole house. Michelle freezes afraid to move an inch, however, the next sound she hears is, "Chellie is that you?" There is momentary silence. Michelle quickly ponders her next move. When she realizes that not acknowledging her Grandma may cause her Grandpa to get up with his shotgun and come down stairs looking for intruders.

Michelle answers, "Yes Ma'am."

"What's the matter you can't sleep?"

"No ma'am I slept fine just getting up to meet Boswell when he gets here."

"Oh that's right he is coming this morning. Let me get up and fix some coffee and warm up some vittles from yesterday."

Before she can speak Michelle hears, "Jed get up, that boy is going to be here soon."

"What boy?"

"Michelle's boyfriend, I guess. The only thing she told me is that they are dating, so I gather that that's her boyfriend."

"I reckon."

Michelle shakes her head as she begins to rub her stomach like there is a genie inside of her. The thought of her grandmother preparing food for someone is a scary thought for her. "But maybe, thought Michelle, she has gotten better at it." Nope smiles Michelle, "It's not possible." She can remember her Grandpa fussing at her grandma for burning up a pot. He said, "Darn Lizzie how the heck can you burn water?" So based on that incident and others like it Grandma Lizzie is banned from the kitchen by her husband to the delight of Michelle and Martha who had to clean up her mistakes. The noise over her head increases as it appears that her Grandparents will be part of Boswell's early morning welcoming party. This new development is just typical of her week at her Grandparent's house. After the surprise breakfast with family and friends they all went over to the Kissing the Pig Festival where the sounds and smells of country life quickly returned for Michelle. With her pregnancy induced sensory abilities heighten by the animal's odors, sights and sounds at the festival, Michelle concluded that some memories should not be re-visited. Everyone seemed to have a great time at the event.

In Search of a Good Feeling

The Kissing Pig Festival is an annual event that is supposed to emphasize the importance of pork to the region. Fifty years ago, pork production was one of the main industries in the area. But over the years most of the pork farmers have either died, retired or were forced out of business by the large pork producers. There are only a handful of old timers left, and Grandpa Jed is one of them. He maintains a small drove of Yorkshire hogs that he butchers for meat for the house and sells the rest to his neighbors. So in comparison to other fairs around, The Kissing Pig Festival is a small time gathering of the community that lends its self to fellowship, good food and bragging rights. There are a couple of highlights at the festival such as the BBQ cook off, the Best Hog competition and the crowd favorite, the Kissing the Pig Contest which the festival is named after. It's a fundraiser done by the local elementary school where Michelle attended. The school employee who receives the most 25 cent votes has to agree to kiss the pig. During Michelle's tenure at Lawrence Kershaw Elementary school the winner was generally the principal Mr. Doaty.

It was about 10 am when the group got to the festival where they split into two groups based on age. They all agreed to meet back up at noon to watch the hog judging contest in the red barn. Surprisingly, Michelle was quiet, lost in her thoughts at the festival. But it did not seem to stop her friends from keeping the conversation alive. Billy Jean talked about the kids and life in rural South Carolina, while Billy who tagged along attempted to impress Michelle with what he knew about livestock. The kids, well they were kids, Betty Mae and Willie Mac Jr. rode anything and everything, ate cotton candy and had a good old time just like Michelle had when she was their age.

Of course, Grandpa Jed's pigs won their 20th blue ribbon although there was some talk that one of the judges Ms. Stengel, a little senior citizen cougar with grey hair, had the hots for Grandpa, so that's the reason he won again. To celebrate his victory Grandpa Jed took the group to Red Lobster for their shrimp special. While at the restaurant the conversation was light as the group reviewed the happenings at the festival. Everyone was having a good time with the exception of Uncle Jesse who seemed to be upset about something. He sent back his order twice while talking negatively about the service.

Two days later Michelle and Billie Jean are sitting on the back porch sipping lemonade while watching the kids try to climb the mahogany tree with little success. It was late afternoon and the sun is attempting to get Michelle's attention, but she would have none of it. Saturday's good time at the festival had left her red and sunburned, so for the moment interacting with her childhood friend is not in her plans. A lone mosquito makes its presence known to Michelle. *It does appear that Boswell is correct,* thought Michelle. "*The mosquitos down here are quite big, but that makes them easier to kill,*" as she successfully smashes one against her leg. After laughing at Michelle's antics, Billy Jean takes a sip of lemonade and asks, "How is your Uncle Jesse? Is he still fussing about black folks?"

The question took Michelle by surprise, "What are you talking about?" she replied turning curiously towards Billy Jean.

From Michelle's reaction, Billy Jean figured out that Michelle is clueless about what she is asking about. She takes another sip of lemonade before saying, "Hmmm, I guess you do not know that Uncle Jesse became upset when he found out that a black man owned and managed the Red lobster franchise where we had eaten dinner."

"What?"

"Yep you know when you come into the restaurant there is a picture of the owner and it happens to be a Black man. When Uncle Jesse saw that picture he became red in the face. You had gone to the ladies room when he went on a tyrant about black this and black that and mumbled he did not want to eat in a nigger restaurant. By the time you had gotten back your Grandpa had silence him, but he still acted a butt."

"Wow...he said that!"

"Yea. Did you know that your Uncle Jesse has always been part KKK in disguise. He is a just a big talker though slow with action and very confused in thought."

"What does he have against Black people?"

"I do not really know, maybe your Uncle Jesse just wants those old days to come back, the days when the white man controlled all of the south. Well there has always been rumor that your folks back in the day owned slaves. Some folks, those left who can remember, believes that is how your family obtained all the land around here."

Michelle becomes momentarily silent not really believing what she has just heard, but not wanting Billy Jean to know that she is upset. She said, "You know you may be right about Uncle Jesse. Either that or he is just an asshole."

Billy Jean looks at her watch. "Darn it Michelle," she says, "It's 5 o'clock and Willie Mac will be home soon looking for his darn dinner. You know sometimes marriage is not all it's made up to be." She quickly stood up and hollers out in the directions of her children. "Betty Mae you and Junior come on now it's time for supper and your daddy will be home shortly."

Both of them came running yelling, "Yes Ma'am," in unison.

Billy Jean hugs Michelle. "Well Chellie, thanks for the lemonade. Tell your grandparents goodbye for me. We'll will talk soon. Hey how about going to the mall with me on Wednesday? Belk's is having a one day sale."

"Hey, you are welcome," says Michelle, "I will let you know about Wednesday."

Billy Jean runs off the porch, corrals her children into the car and speeds off down the long driveway.

Michelle continues to wave at the car until it was out of sight. She returns back to the rocker to ponder her conversation with Billy Jean. *Is Uncle Jesse a racist, and did my family own slaves?* Those are the two questions that are on Michelle's mind. Her perception of Uncle Jesse has always been a negative one ever since that time she saw him kick a stray dog for nothing. From that day on she thought that he was the evilest man she had ever known. So he disliking blacks did not surprise Michelle because he probably did not like himself that much. But she did not want him to cause any ruckus while Boswell is visiting therefore she had to figure out a way to neutralize him. The possibility of her ancestors owning slaves was a thought that had never crossed Michelle's mind until today. She attempts to remember what has been told to her about her family's history by her father. It was known throughout the family that the Waterman's plantation began back in the early 1800's as a small plot of land bought by James Waterman, an Englishman, the first American descendent. James had traveled to America in 1807 after a successful shipping business in Liverpool England. With his shipping fortune James bought the land that is now called the Waterman Plantation sometime before he dies in 1842.

Suddenly Michelle stops and lets out a silent scream. Simultaneously, the baby kicks as a nauseous feeling came over her. She runs past her grandmother into the upstairs bathroom, closed the door and throws up. Grandma Lizzie and Martha gather outside of the bathroom asking her if she's alright.

Michelle replies groggily, "Yes, I'm OK. Must have gotten sick by being in the sun too much. Not use to this much sun. I'm going to take a cool bath. I will be out soon."

"Do you need anything?" asked Grandma Lizzie.

"No I feel better, I'm just going to take a long bath. I will be down for something light to eat later," said Michelle.

"Ok then, if you need something just holler. I hope you be feeling better soon" said Martha.

"Me too Martha, thanks."

Michelle hears Martha say to her grandmother as they walk down the steps, "If the sun made her sick hmm, that sun must be heap powerful."

Michelle smiles and leans her head against the porcelain toilet. The coolest of its surface felt good touching her skin. Tears slowly appeared as she attempted to figure out what just occurred. Michelle stands up to get a wash cloth and washes her face as the water runs in the tub. In her nakedness, she notices her recent maternal development which in its own way initiates tears once again. Her slender body had become a little rounded in a certain area. Michelle rubs that area wondering if she is adequately prepared for what is to come. She slides in a bath tub of lavender scented bubbles. Soaking in a tub has always been therapeutic for Michelle and being in water has always put her mind on ease. She desperately needed this type of comfort now. The tubs at her grandparent's home were the type with the claw foot made out of cast iron. As her Grandpa Jed said, "Tubs are like miniature ponds to be enjoyed like you were royalty." Since she is someone's queen that means that it is time to her to enjoy the good life.

The cool water along with the lavender scent does the trick and soon Michelle enters into a very relax state. Her present concern over past family deeds have been stored away. A lone nightingale song filled the air as Michelle drifted to sleep until an unresolved dream or the cooling temperature of the water caused her to awaken. Refreshed from her bath, Michelle dresses quickly and proceeds down into the kitchen to get something to eat. A stillness filled the house. Her grandparents were nowhere to be found and Martha must had left for the day. In the icebox, there was a dish covered with aluminum foil with a note on it saying, *'I hope you feelin better Chellie. You need to eat something because you will need your strength, Martha.'*

Martha is such a sweet heart, thinks Michelle as she uncovered a plate filled with two pieces of fried chicken, potato salad, macaroni salad and a biscuit. She pours herself a glass of iced tea and began her feast in the quietness of the kitchen with her only companion being the tick tock of the grandfather clock in the hall way. With her dinner half devoured Michelle begins to think what it might have been

In Search of a Good Feeling

like living here 150 years ago; the sounds, smells and sights of the old south. Before getting too deep in her thoughts Michelle's grandparents reappeared through the back door of the kitchen. After an exchange of pleasantries, the three of them agreed to retire to the living room for dessert. Grandma Lizzie serves the group a slice of pound cake with a scoop of homemade black walnut ice cream.

"Mmmmmm," said Grandpa Jed with a smile on his face and an empty dish in his lap, "Martha truly put her foot into that dessert. "Pound cake and ice cream too."

"Jed Waterman you're just one hungry old fool with one large sweet tooth," laughs Grandma Lizzie.

When all the dishes had been collected and Grandma Lizzie had returned from the kitchen Michelle looked toward her grandfather and asked, "Grandpa, Why doesn't Uncle Jesse like black people?"

Grandpa Jed glances at his wife, back at his granddaughter then he replied, "Chellie there are a couple things that you need to know about your Uncle Jesse. First, he is not your true blood uncle but a close friend of mine. Second, his father was a black man. Unfortunately in those days the community did not look kindly on one of their precious vessels being impregnated by a black man, so they hung him. Surprisingly, his mother raised him but she died when he was seven. During the time she was alive, although he looked white like everyone else he was teased and ridiculed by his peers for having a black daddy. At the age of fifteen he came to live with us and my father, bless his heart, raised him like he was his own. But Jesse has always blamed blacks for his struggles in life. Strange isn't it?"

"No Grandpa, it is sad," said Michelle shaking her head.

Grandpa Jed ponders for moment before he said, "One lesson that my daddy taught me was not to ask questions that you do not want answers to because once you receive the answer you are now responsible for it. Little girl you will learn that there are things about the past that should stay in the past. Do you have any more questions Chellie?"

"No sir, not at this moment."

"Good, I'm going to sit on the porch until the mosquitos tell me to come in. Anyone brave enough to join me?"

Not surprisingly there were no takers, so Michelle and her grandmother spend the rest of the night engaging in small talk and watching television while Grandpa rocks himself to sleep on the porch as mosquitos buzz over his head.

The rest of the week can be described as uneven. Grandpa appeared to be in his own world after his talk with Michelle. Pleasant, but distant at times. He spent a lot of the time in his den going over old papers, mumbling about something and began having a shot of whiskey at night.

Billy Jean and Michelle did go to the mall on Wednesday as planned and had lunch at Friday's but not surprisingly, Uncle Jesse's name did not come up in their conversation ever again. Willie Mac Jr. fell down out of a tree and strained his ankle. He had to be rushed to the hospital on Thursday afternoon. Michelle hung out with Billy Jean at the hospital until Willie Mac Jr. was ready to be taken home. Billy Jean's parenting skills impressed Michelle.

After closely watching Billy Jean she became concern about her own ability to show empathy, compassion and love to her yet to be born child. This mothering thing is something she never thought about. With no mother to

In Search of a Good Feeling

guide her, Michelle felt doomed. She realizes that a hug from Boswell is needed to assure her that it would be alright. How she longs for his presence. Boswell's flight delay did not help matters any. The voices of doubt were beginning their attack on Michelle's self-esteem. So as she waits now on the front porch in her rocking chair in the early morning, Michelle can feel a change coming over her mental state believing that a good feeling was on its way. Hope has a way of defeating the forces of doubt, and as she looked down the driveway, hope was on its way in the form of Boswell.

CHAPTER 13

They seem to meet in midair holding and hugging each other. Using their lips as means of communication, Boswell and Michelle begin to convey how much they hurt, missed and needed each other. Time has a way of returning good feelings for those who wait. Remaining patient, Grandpa Jed and Grandma Lizzie look on at this reunion of lovers waiting for their chance to be introduce. Michelle finally realizing where she was, stops the lip communication with Boswell, and just smothers her head in his chest.

After a while she slowly looks up and both of their eyes meet, Michelle says, "Hi Boswell I missed you." Before Boswell can reply he feels something move inside of Michelle.

He asks, "What was that? Do you have the hiccups?"

"No silly man," laughs Michelle, "That's the baby, she missed you too."

Boswell holds Michelle closer, "Wow, what a cool feeling, our baby moving inside of you and I felt him." He twirls her in his arms, their closeness produce the good feeling that reminds them why they are still on this journey together. Boswell looks down in her eyes, lightly kisses her lip while

In Search of a Good Feeling

saying, "Hi Michelle, I missed you too, I guess those are your grandparents over there smiling in our direction?"

Michelle turns in the direction of where Boswell is pointing and there stood her grandparents smiling and waving to them. A little red faced from her release of emotions, she straightens her hair and smooths out her top while saying, "Boswell let me introduce you the two people who raised me, Grandpa Jed and Grandma Lizzie."

Like on cue, both of them put out their hand out to shake Boswell's, but Boswell says, "I have come too far for just a handshake, c'mon show me some that southern hospitality I heard so much about and give me a big hug." So there on the front porch of the Waterman plantation at 6:30 am on a Saturday morning in July, three individuals were embracing like they were old friends. Michelle just stands there in amazement while the baby responds with kicks of joy.

While wrap up in Boswell's arms Grandma Lizzie asks, "Well Boswell you hungry?"

"Yes Ma'am I reckon I am."

"Well good, Jed and I fixed you breakfast, so come on in and wash up, Michelle will show you where to go …leave your suitcase in the car for now, it's time to eat."

Michelle stands in shock when Boswell and her enters the kitchen. There on table is a fully prepared breakfast smelling and looking good. Grandma Lizzie winks at Michelle with her white apron on and says, "I told you could cook, but around here I just do not have to. Boswell just sit right down and make yourself at home, it's time to eat."

An hour later after a breakfast of ham, bacon, eggs, biscuits, grits and orange juice Michelle and Boswell find themselves on the porch as comfortable as two pigs in the slop. They slowly rock in their chairs relishing the early morning coolness, and silently enjoying the company of one another.

Then it happens, Michelle desires to talk. "So Boswell," Michelle says as she shakes him, "What did you miss about me?"

Boswell knowing Michelle like he does is not caught unprepared for the question. He pretends to ponder to give the moment some drama then he takes her hand saying, "Well, I miss the feeling that I have when you are around me…you make me feel good."

There is silence. Again Michelle is speechless due to Boswell's expression of emotion. "What happened to you…I go away for a week and you find your feelings?"

Boswell smiles while saying "I told you once before that I am a man of many emotions silly woman, and sometimes language is not the best communication medium, so what is the plan for today?"

"Well we need you get you settled, and maybe you would like to take a shower or just sit a spell. If we are going to do something outside we need to move quickly, the sun does not play down here." Not desiring to deal with a jealous lover, Michelle made sure that before Boswell's visit she explained to the sun his place in her life. Despite the discussion, the sun indicated disapproval of the presence of Boswell by blasting the south with high record temperatures everyday he was there.

"Ok…..I will get my stuff out of the car, take a shower, and be ready in about 30 minutes to see what trouble we can get in to." Boswell leaves Michelle on the porch with the intention of retrieving his belongings from the rental car. He suddenly stops when he starts down the stairs and quickly turns towards Michelle with a frighten look on his face.

"Did you hear that?"

"What sweetie?"

"I thought I heard someone say good morning."

"You probably did."

"Who?"

"It's whom...the spirits."

"Oh shoot Michelle, do not start up with that hearing and seeing thing stuff... what spirits? I do not want to hear about how you can sense supernatural beings now also."

"Well I know that your logical scientific mind will find it hard to believe about the existence of spirits, so let's just say when the wind blows through the tree branches around here, it sometimes sounds like voices are talking to you... it's a southern thing Sweetie."

Boswell just shakes his head, but before continuing down the steps and he looks around to see if any spirits or anything are around.

Since Michelle is unable to determine if Boswell is being serious or sarcastic, she just shakes her head in response to him. Boswell gets his bags from the car and Michelle shows him the guest bedroom. "Boswell I am sorry that we cannot sleep together, my grandparents are a little old fashion so we are going to have separate sleeping arrangements, and I hope you are not mad."

He looks at Michelle with a disappointed face. "It's cool, I figured that would be the arrangement. Anyway, I do not know how I would feel sleeping with you in your grandparent's house, so I am going to take a shower and be with you in about 15 minutes."

They kiss and Michelle leaves Boswell at the bedroom door. He enters the room and closes the door behind him smiling. There before him was a queen size bed with goose filled pillows with matching blue curtain on the window. *Yes*, thinks Boswell, *My week of sleeping solo continues.* In the last 4 months, Boswell found that the act of sleeping together in his opinion is overrated. The first two weeks it was cute and romantic but Boswell soon discovered that someone did not learn sharing in kindergarten causing him to sleep on the edge the bed. So the news of them not sleeping together makes him a very happy man. He looks around and concludes that the room does not get much use, but it is clean with an adjoining bathroom. On the wall are a couple of framed photos of individuals, some that seem quite old. Not surprisingly, there is an oversized rocking chair in the room with blue cushions. The morning sun is peeking thru the window blinds as if it's looking for someone. Boswell undresses hurriedly and soon finds his body being pummeled by the cool water of the shower. He moans in delight while applying some flowery scent soap to his skin, another good feeling has returned. After a long shower, he emerges smelling like jasmine but tiredness begins to make itself evidence. The early morning flight paired with a breakfast of hots grits and biscuits is enough to make any man a little sleepy. He sits with the towel wrapped around himself in the rocking chair and soon finds himself asleep. Boswell awakens two hours later still in the same position with Michelle watching him.

"How long did I sleep" asks Boswell?

"I would say about two hours give or take, it was like you were in another world sitting in that chair wrapped up

In Search of a Good Feeling

in that towel. Grandma Lizzie is worried, she thought her food had gotten you sick or something. I had to come up here to reassure her that you were just sleep but not sick. Well how are you feeling?"

"Tell your grandma her food just made me a little sleepy but hardly sick…I am still a little tired, but otherwise I am fine."

"Good, well get dressed, Grandpa Jed is waiting to take you on a tour of the Waterman Plantation."

A tour of the Waterman plantation thinks Boswell…now that's an unseen pleasure…but I wonder what the old guy has planned…he seems likable enough. Maybe he thinks if Michelle gets married the place will be ours…so I need to know the lay of the land.

Boswell dresses quickly and goes downstairs to meet his tour guide. At the bottom of the steps Boswell feels a pair of eyes on him. He looks around and there stood Martha smiling at him. Unable to think Boswell unconsciously says, "Good morning ma'am my name is Boswell."

Martha just stands there looking at him not saying a word.

Boswell is confused and without a clue what to do or say next so he just stands on bottom step looking at Martha. Finally, Martha says "I think you are the first black person ever that has been invited to the spend the night at the Waterman Plantation for the except of slaves…and they had no other options…Michelle has done fine. … yes indeed."

Boswell's confusion heightens with the mention of slaves….what slaves? The voices scream out. "Well thank you for the compliment ma'am but what….."

Before Boswell can finish his sentence Martha butts in, "Its Martha…. just Martha and Boswell it's named the Waterman Plantation.

"Who works on a plantation?" But before Boswell can receive his answer, Michelle's enters into the hallway entrance looking for him. "There you go…Grandpa is waiting out back for you…so I see that you met marvelous Martha…world's greatest cook and the keeper of the Waterman secrets."

"Yes, we have met, says Boswell who is still in a state of confusion.

"Nice chatting with you, says Martha, turning to Michelle. "This time you have done well child…and he's black also…he's a keeper. Don't let your folks scare him off. I have my morning chores to finish up…see you guys soon." Martha disappears into another section of the house laughing as she goes.

"What did you two talk about?" asks Michelle."

"Just the weather…its mighty hot." replies Boswell not knowing if he is relieved that Martha did not answer the question or not. He moves quickly behind Michelle as she leads him to the back porch where Grandpa Jed is waiting. He is wearing a tan shirt, brown cotton pants with a straw hat and is sitting a World War Two vintage army green jeep. It appears to be in decent shape with the absence of a windshield and a roof.

Grandpa Jed waves at in his direction. "Good morning Boswell, I hope you had a good sleep…I thought since I was going to do my weekly tour of the grounds you may like to ride with me before it gets too hot to do anything."

"I would be honored Grandpa Jed," replies Boswell as he slides down next to him in the jeep.

In Search of a Good Feeling

"Well let's get to getting. I want to check on a group of wild hogs that have been destroying some of the farmers crops. I see you looking around for some seatbelts well there ain't any...just hold on tight, you will be fine."

Michelle laughs as Grandpa starts up the engine. She yells, "Grandpa be careful with Boswell! Remember he is from the city so take it easy on him. Here take this." Michelle hands Boswell a red checkered handkerchief. "You will need it, and Grandpa don't take him back by the swamp because the mosquitos are probably pretty bad now."

"Woman I will be fine," yells back Boswell as Grandpa heads out on a dirt road located behind the house. They pass Grandpa's award winning hogs in their pen while Grandpa slows the jeep down a bit and identifies the different hogs to Boswell. He points to the heavy gauge fence that surrounds the hog pen stating proudly. "It's to keep the wild pigs out, We had to dig down about 2 feet and cement the freaking fence in place so that the hogs would not dig under it."

Grandpa gives the jeep some juice and the two of them are on their way. The noisy engine and the lack of a roof on the jeep did not lent itself to hearable conversation which suits Boswell fine. His inner voices were causing enough commotion for him to contend with at the moment. They kept repeating the words, slavery, swamp and mosquitos over and over until Boswells yells out, "STOP!"

Grandpa immediately hits the brake causing Boswell to be thrown out of the jeep. Grandpa jumps out and runs over to him.

"You alright?"

"Yes sir, I am ok I guess"

"Hmmm, so why did you tell me to stop"

"I thought I saw a snake crossing the road, I did not want you to run over it."

"Ok...next time just point to it, you almost got both of us killed, and I thought something terrible had happened to you. I am too old for this."

"Yes Grandpa, will do and how about investing in some seat belts?" laughs Boswell.

Grandpa helps Boswell to his feet as he shakes his head, "Michelle told me to take it easy on you. If she finds out about this she might not let us play together again."

"No problem, what happens out in the field stays out in the field," replies Boswell brushing himself off. He rejoins Grandpa in the jeep keeping a secret from him. There was no snake in the road. He learned that one way to stop anxious thoughts is to yell out the word, 'Stop!' and the thoughts generally stop. So that is what he did and it worked. However, Boswell wonders if Grandpa believes his story about the snake.

They continue on the dirt road and enter into carefully tilled farm land. Grandpa stops sand points out to the left of the jeep. "This here is some of the land we lease to the area farmers for a small fee. Back when my ancestors bought this here land they would flood it and grow rice in these fields."

The morning sun is doing its thing on Boswell, causing sweat to pour down his face. He takes the handkerchief that Michelle gave him and wipes his face.

"Hot enough for you Boswell?"

"Yes sir plenty, it ain't been this hot in Philly yet."

With his unanswered question still on his mind Boswell launches down a Path that will change him forever.

"Mr. Waterman"...

In Search of a Good Feeling

"You can call me Grandpa like everyone else around here."

"OK Grandpa, how long has your family owned this land?"

"Since the first Waterman came to America in 1807 from Liverpool England. And yes, Boswell that means that the family owned slaves at one time.

In the background a lone crow calls out as the wind becomes still. The aroma of mint from the nearby field accents the air as it clashes with the smell of Grandpa's hog pens. Neither says anything for a while. Grandpa cranks the jeep's engine up and heads off down the road as inner voices beginning to play havoc on Boswell's mind. Grandpa turns off the road and drives towards a grove of trees. He stops the jeep under the shade of the trees and says, "Boswell you mighty quiet...what's on your mind?" Boswell continues to look out at the grove of trees enjoying the shade.

"Well Grandpa...the idea of Michelle's family owning slaves is not something easily swallowed."

"Well I am sorry that I told you in the matter in which I told you but Michelle told us that you are quite intelligent so it would be only a matter of time that you put 2 and 2 together."

"I thank you for sharing your family history with me. It's not a revelation that one's hears everyday, so excuse me for my quietness."

"No problem. You might be wondering why I stopped here under these trees other than to get out of the sun. Well this here is one of them apple orchards on the plantation. All wild hogs love apples. Look over there." Grandpa points to an area in the middle of the grove where it looks like something has been digging holes. "They go over there and root in that soil after their meal of apples...destroying the soil. If you are up to it tomorrow morning me and Jesse is going wild hog hunting. You are invited to come along."

"Well I have never shot anything before... being a city boy."

"We do not shoot ...we trap them...then slaughter them...I will bait some traps this afternoon ...and tomorrow we will reap the benefits."

"Well Grandpa...I will ponder your wonderful offer and get back with you."

Whatever else is being said to Boswell by Grandpa Jed during the rest of the tour was lost to him. They rode for half hour or so with Grandpa Jed pointing out different things about the land and telling stories about their significance.

While Grandpa Jed is discussing the nuances of the Little Snake River that flows thru the property, Boswell's voices are attending to his newest dilemma. *Did he really say that the family has as history of owning slaves or is he pulling my leg attempting to scare me off his granddaughter? Martha mentioned something about not letting Michelle's folks scare me off, but she was the first one to mention slavery to me...maybe it a conspiracy and Martha is in on it. More importantly ...does Michelle know? Is this the reason she had me to come down to this hot ass mosquito biting side of hell?*

Before he knew it, Grandpa is pulling the jeep into the back of the house. There on the porch sits Michelle looking like a love struck lover waiting to greet her warrior returning from battle. From the sight of Boswell it looks like he was in a fight and lost. His freshly pressed bright orange polo shirt is now a dark orange due to perspiration. Some places of the shirt are mud smeared creating a funky collage of his today's

In Search of a Good Feeling

adventures. His brand-new sandals and feet are coated with dried mud while his pants looks like he has been sitting in a puddle. A later examination of his skin will reveal numerous mosquito, gnat's and horse fly bites.

Boswell slowly removes himself from the jeep like he is an old man. He turns to Grandpa who remains in the jeep. "Thanks for the tour, it was quite informative. I will let you know about tomorrow." With those words Boswell slowly marches pass Michelle saying, "We have to talk. I am going to go take a bath and get out of these dirty clothes." He goes into the back door which opens into the kitchen and sees a young lady leaving out. There seated peeling apples for dinner is Martha.

She takes one look at Boswell and burst out in laughter "Did he hitch you to a plow...I told you to remember where you are at."

Boswell did not look in Martha's direction nor did he verbally respond to her question walking up the steps to his bedroom as fast as he can.

"Darn it," yells Martha at Boswell. "You could have the courtesy to knock the mud off your sandals...you have ruined a beautifully clean floor...tracking mud in here like they have not taught you any manner up there in Philly. A woman's work is never done...where isthat freaking mop... like I do not have anything else to do than to clean up after a grown man...Chellie!"

Although Michelle hears Martha calling her name, she is too busy with Grandpa to answer her now. Michelle, still dealing with the shock of Boswell's return and walks quickly over to Grandpa, who seems to be sitting in the jeep waiting for her.

"So what happened to Boswell, why is he all muddy? Didn't I tell you not to take him down to that swamp Grandpa? He probably got eaten alive by bugs…poor Boswell."

Grandpa just looks at her as he attempts to figure out what to say. He takes off his hat, wipes his brow and says, "Chellie, I did not take him to the swamp. He's muddy because when he told me to stop, I hit the brake and he flew out the jeep into a little mud puddle. It's just some mud. A little soap and water and he will be fine."

"That's all…a little mud? No Grandpa, something else happened while you guys were out in the back. He is upset about something. I saw the look in his eyes, and his mind is pondering something."

Yea maybe. First, could you go get me a glass of ice water… then we will talk."

Yes sir, one glass of ice water coming up, and Grandpa I want the truth."

Grandpa is quiet now. Michelle enters the kitchen and Martha is standing in the middle of the room waiting for her with a tray containing two glasses and a pitcher of ice water on it.

Before she gives the tray to Michelle, Martha asks, "Didn't you hear me calling your name Chellie?"

"Yes Martha, but I was busy with Grandpa trying to figure out why Boswell came back so muddy and upset."

"Muddy indeed. I had to re-mop the floor because of him, and you need to tell your Mr. Boswell that people in the south have manners and we expect the same from him."

"Sorry Martha about Boswell. He is just not himself… maybe it's the sun, the bugs or whatever happened between him and Grandpa on their little adventure but I am going to get to the bottom this. Again sorry about Boswell, he will apologize to you, and thanks for getting the water. Martha…?"

"Yes Chellie…."

"Well I have a taste for some oatmeal cookies. I was going to go out and buy some but I prefer your homemade ones…..so if you get some time I would die for some."

"Don't be dying around here silly girl. This house is for the living. Ha, ha. Well, I will see what I can do."

Michelle heads out to the back porch for her discussion with Grandpa, more determined than ever to find out what happened. As soon as she leaves out Martha pulls her chair a mite closer to the back door to be sure that she does not miss a word of their conversation.

While Grandpa sits waiting for Michelle to return he notices an unnatural movement of a flock of crows that were nesting in the mahogany tree. They flew away suddenly as though they were spooked by something. Grandpa quickly looks around attempting to locate the intruder in the tree but he sees nothing. A breeze picks up causing the tree branches to sway and make a sound like someone is moaning. The sound spooks Grandpa but just as soon as the sound began it ends and Michelle reappears with the tray of cold beverages.

Michelle's notices that Grandpa looks a little flush but disregards it as anything serious since he is sitting in the sun. As the words begin to come out of Grandpa's mouth Michelle enters into a state of shock. She can hear the words coming out of Grandpa's mouth but logically based on everything she knew it could not be true. Her mind is processing the information much quicker than she can speak. She says nothing for a moment as the words 'slave owner' ring back and forth in her mind. Finally, she could not hold it. Her logical mind requires answers that she did not have so Michelle in an effort to fully understand what was just said asked the following question as unemotional as possible.

"You told him what? I thought those rumors were not true. I remember asking you about them when I was in school. You told me that people have been spreading rumors about the Waterman family for years...they were just jealous of what we had. Why did you lie to me?"

"For the same reason any parent would, to protect you from yourself. If I told you the truth I was fearful on how it would affect you. After that day you never asked again so I thought it was all over. I cannot say I felt bad about not telling you the truth. The truth can be hard to swallow and live with year after year. I thought when you went away and disappeared that the family secret would go to the grave with me. Your father knew but he died before he could tell you. It's not a subject that comes up in daily conversation. So I did not tell you...but now you know...what does it change? That was in our regretful past not unlike most southern families. If the past has taught us anything it's that a man can change and the Waterman Family has changed. Until you can be honest about your past you cannot move on to your future. I am sorry that you had to find out this way but the truth is out now. I hope this news does not affect your relationship with Boswell. He seems like a wonderful man. Well I am going down to the lodge. Tell Martha to put away a plate for me because I may be late for dinner."

In Search of a Good Feeling

Grandpa stands and makes his way to the jeep leaving Michelle alone on the porch to deal with what was just said. There are no parting words to each other, no good byes or waves. Both individuals slide into their own world attempting to face the demons of today.

Grandpa turns down an orange clay road headed for his chill out place. After picking up a can of soda pop, a bag of chips and bologna sandwich on white bread from the 7-11 he decides to find some me time. He drives to the river to sit under the large oak where he learned how to fish when he was young. Grandpa turns off the jeep, sits for a moment and starts crying.

Michelle does not move from the porch all afternoon. She just sits quietly calling to the sun for companionship not unlike what she did as a child. Anytime life found a way to discourage, disappoint or hurt her as a child Michelle would call on the sun. So, she sits with the sun as company rubbing her stomach as her mind slows down to where she can process today's events.

Slaves…we owned slaves? My family were slave owners? And because of what the slaves did for my ancestors I have benefitted…so what does that make me???...how are I suppose to feel about the revelation…yes it happened a long time ago…and yes it was legal then…yes I know…but it is not morally right to own someone like they are property…oh my God…and stupid me did not know…why not ….I was raised a freaking place called the Waterman plantation…I never asked why it was called by that name…I just assumed that it was a name…now I learned it was more than a name …its represented a way of life…I must be the biggest fool in the world…we the Waterman

Anthony Webb

have reaped the benefits from the toil of black slaves...that we purchase as one would buy a mule ...and we worked them until they died ...just like a mule...how can I face Boswell ...what do I say to him...how can I look him in the eye...and what is he thinking about me...I wonder if he thinks that I lied to him...or that I hid something about my past from him....how is he feeling knowing that the mother of his child comes from a lineage of slave owners.....and what about our child...what do I tell her about her ancestors...Oh God.. I do not know why I wanted to come home...but if was not what I expected...oh Sun I need you right now... am I a fraud...I have attempted to be a person who cares for their fellow man...but I have done it from a place of privilege... oh my God so I am one of them...descendant of slavery owners...raised on a freaking plantation...where slaves uses to tend to needs of my family.... Slaves....we owned slaves...human beings which we attempted to makes less than human for the soul purpose of doing our bidding.....like we could not make up or own beds...or work in the fields like them....yes the sins of my forefather does affect me...my existence is the product of their sins....yes, their sins against humanity...for their own good and the good of future generations like me....they did it so that descendants like me can live the good life...I grew up on a freaking plantation not in a housing unit...a plantation.....am I losing my mind.... truth can hurt....Betty Sue was right all the time ...we were slave owners...I told her that we were not...and then punched her...I thought that she was just being her cruel self....but that freckled face pain in the ass was right...and I am the fool and she knew it... am I a fraud?... and again I have attempted to be a person who cares for their fellow man...but I have done it from a place of privilege oh my God so I am one of them...

descendant of slavery owners...raised on a freaking plantation... where slaves uses to tend to needs of my family....Slaves....we owned slaves...human beings which we attempted to make less than human.

Michelle's eyes begin to water and soon tears appeared. She weeps because of the sins of her fathers, she weeps because of lies told, and she weeps because she is sad and hurt. Her cries attract a flock of crows that are nesting nearby. Michelle watch them leave their perches and begin to fly over her. Soon she hears voices say, "Wipe your eyes cry no more...what's done is done...make it better." She looks around for the source of the message and the birds are gone but Martha is standing next to her with a wet face cloth in her hand.

"I thought that this might refresh yourself since it's a mite hot out here."

Michelle says, "Thank you Martha...did you see...never mind."

Martha looks motherly at Michelle. "Today I do not think the sun is your friend. Come on back in the house with me. Being in that sun so long may make you see or hear things that are not there.

Michelle stares at Martha for a moment before getting up to go inside the house. Before leaving the porch she searches the sky for the sight of a crow...she sees none, sighs and lets the door close behind her.

Boswell dumps his clothes in a heap on the floor. He has not decided on his next step. Even the voices have calmed down due to a lack of experience with this type of situation. He blasts the hot water making his bath as hot as possible attempting to punish himself for the situation that he is placed with at this moment. Maybe the sensation of the hot water will clear his mind of what he has to do. As he prepares to enter into the pool of hot water a crow in a tree outside the window makes known his presence. Boswell stops before his foot hits the water. He realizes that the situation is not his to fix. He was given some information that is unsettling but not unviable to work through.

CHAPTER 14

A noticeable scent of jasmine is in the air as the overhead fan supplies a constant light breeze. Boswell is sitting in the oversized rocking chair quietly rocking back and forth. During the majority of the last three hours he has been sitting in a tub of hot water attempting to make sense out of his last 24 hours. Philly, the delayed flight, the flight, the drive up, the horses, the voices, Michelle, Grandma, Grandpa, Martha and the revelation has all played a part in bringing him to this point in his life. It did not mean that he is overjoyed about what was told to him by Grandpa. His logical mind understands that no one in the present had anything to do with the past even though they might have benefited from it. But Boswell's emotional side cries out for justice for those who could not speak for themselves. Something inside of him seeks healing for the past hurts of his ancestors which he has carried with him since birth. He realizes that he hid those feeling deep inside of him where no one could touch them, somewhere that they could not erupt in violent action due to a misunderstanding during a human interaction. Now at this moment they have found their way into the present, uncovered by accident, an innocent human conversation with no intent but to tell the truth.

Boswell knew that those feelings must return to the hidden spaces as quick as possible until the time is right to release them. Although the feelings of rage have been hidden for a long time they still remain too raw, too sensitive and too hurtful for Boswell to deal with them in his present emotional state. He needs a cathartic moment or event to emancipate these feelings safely. So, he does what he has always done several times not unlike what his ancestors did before him, he acknowledges their pain and sends those feelings of past suffering back down in the hidden places of his soul before he hurts someone.

Exhausted from dealing with all of the mental variables, along with a sore body, and the warmth of the water Boswell falls asleep in the tub. As he wakes up in the jasmine scented bath something spiritual occurs that cause Boswell to rethink the past 24 hours. Boswell believes he heard the spirits of the plantation. He initially thought it was just the trees the wind or even birds playing with his mind but when he listens closer Boswell hears them.

Michelle is right. There are spirits here, they were moaning a low soulful moan that made me feel that they were hurting but still strong, that they had been through a lot, but they were nearing the end.

Despite being in the hot bath, a chill suddenly came over Boswell's body and tears slid down his face. *Wait a minute... spirits, did I actually hear spirits? I'm sounding like Michelle now...c'mon maybe it is because I am tired, confused and angry that caused me to hear something that is not here. I have read that people under severe stress can have auditory hallucinations. It's all the stress that I have been under since I have come here: being in the south, meeting new people, the bugs and the freaking heat can cause a person who is not use to these conditions to go crazy. So, yeah that's the reason. I'm stressed so it caused me to hear things and whatever happens in this bathroom stays in this bathroom, enough said. Time to get out of this tub.*

"I did not know," are the first words that come out of Michelle's mouth as she stands before Boswell. Wanting to hold and comfort him but unable to determine if that's what he desires Michelle just stands there waiting for a response from him. She looks away from him like she is a little child that's has disappointed a parent. The revelation brought initially shock, then disappointment and lastly shame for Michelle.

"I know that you did not know. I am not blaming anyone for anything…at the moment I seek comfort. I am in search of a good feeling."

Michelle softly touches Boswell's cheek and kisses it. The sensation of her kiss causes Boswell to close his eyes as Michelle continues her quest to make him feel good. First kissing his face then turning her attention to his lips she increases the intensity of her effort. Short pecks turns in a series of deep long kisses with the tongues gracefully dancing with each other as probing hands carefully unbuttons each other's clothing. Michelle slowly slides down on Boswell's lap causing the rocking chair to creak and the couple to moan in unison. Savoring the feel of this exquisite moment their rhythm begins slowly as their need for a deeper connection builds. Time becomes a blur as the creaking becomes louder and louder until it instantly stops and the only sounds are the ceiling fan and the heavy breathing from the two occupants in the room. They fall into each other's arm allowing the good feeling to wash the worries of the day away and reconnect them to each other. The couple remain in each other's arms for a moment until the realization of where they are at comes to them.

Boswell whispers in Michelle ear, "it's time."

She whispers back, "You need to know that the stimulation that you create by either touching me with your hands or mouth give rise to the desire of the ultimate bond." They slowly disengage still attempting to enjoy their sensuous connection as long as possible as warm hands continue to caress the other's body parts.

They embrace each other before separating. With bodies closely pressed together Boswell reaches down and rubs Michelle stomach which creates a good feeling for both of them.

"I hope the baby did not mind being rocked a little fast."

"I think she really enjoyed it," smiles Michelle. "She mentioned to me that she is looking forward to future rocky rides before it all over."

"Watch it naughty woman, I think that can be regularly arranged."

After a quick peck to the lips Michelle leaves Boswell to his solitude and goes to have another talk with the sun before he disappears.

Boswell feels whole again. His cognitive state has caught up with his emotional one leaving him no longer off balance. He takes a quick shower, then gathers up his muddy clothes, wraps them around his bath towel and proceeds downstairs.

In Search of a Good Feeling

There in the kitchen sits Martha working on a crossword puzzle. Her presence startles Boswell making him stop in his tracks.

"What's the matter with you?" asked Martha, looking up from up from her puzzle, "You look like you seen a ghost or have you never seen a black woman doing a crossword puzzle before?" Boswell's good feeling is slowly evaporating, he stands at attention pondering his next move. "Ms. Martha ma'am, I apologize for tracking mud on your clean floor earlier today. I was not in my right mind my mother would have been quite upset with my behavior."

"First of all Boswell, its Martha, not Miss Martha. I am not much older than you. Second, if you know it's going to rain get an umbrella cause down here it rains a lot."

"Rain, what rain? It has not rained today."

"It rained, Boswell but you just did not know It." smiles Martha

"Rained? OK if you say so Martha. And if it rains next time I'm going to be ready."

"Ha ha," laughs Martha, there is going to be a next time. There are a lot of truths back in them fields just waiting to be found out. Yes sir, yes sir."

Martha's voice had such a spiritual tone to it Boswell did not know if he should shout halleluiah or not. He just stands there a moment lost in his thoughts. *There is something spooky about Martha. It is like she is an old soul from another era and when she looks at me it feels like she is looking at my soul.*

"So Boswell what are you going to do with them there dirty clothes you holding?"

"Well Martha, I was going to ask you the same question. What can I do with them?"

"Well throw them over there in that there basket in the corner. I will have them washed in the morning. Michelle told me to tell you that she will be in the back with her granny sitting out on the porch."

"Well, thank you Martha for everything."

"You're welcome. One more thing. Next time you two desire to play husband and wife in the big rocking chair please place the rocking chair on a towel, that way it won't creak so much.

Boswell feels his face turning as red as his dark complexion will allow it. He quickly says, "Thank you," and marches straight out to the porch attempting not to trip nor look in Martha's direction. She smiles as Boswell jets out the door.

"Hmm there is a lot of truth in theses here walls...they can talk too...that what is done in the dark will in due time see the light I do believe."

An unspoken rule of silence and contemplation occurs for the rest of the day. All but Grandma Lizzie were deep in thought about the events of the day. Granny did not know nor care about the events especially since it had to do with the past. She realized in her life that the past has the power to keep you in the past if you allow it. So during Grandpa Jed courtship of her Lizzie was determine to reinvent herself so that her dirt farmer daughter past would have no power over her present and future. She romanced Grandpa as much as he romanced her after meeting one Sunday at a church social. Once they were introduced to each other by a common friend the chase was on for Granny. After a six month courtship, to the surprise of her friends and family she was married to Jed Whitman one the most eligible

In Search of a Good Feeling

bachelors. Around her wedding day, in her mind, Elizabeth Huckleberry lived no more and Elizabeth Whitman existed in her place. Every earthly possession that she owned she burned in the fireplace with the exception of a rag doll her mother gave to her when she was six and a couple of photos.

She had done her homework on Whitman so when she heard rumors around town about the family's wealth being built on the slaves it did not surprise her. It just confirmed what she knew. If you are white, from the south and your family well to do, there is probably slave ownership in your family. How stupid can people be? There is nothing out here but forest and farm land and who do you think picked the cotton, the tobacco and the rice in the field? Not anyone in the Whitman family that's for sure. Anyway that's the past and I live in the present.

After brief speaking with Michelle and grandmother Lizzie, Boswell sits down in the living room to escape into one of his book. But before he can read a word Boswell quickly falls asleep with the book laying on his lap. Boswell wakes up from his nap with crows on his mind. He goes into the bathroom to wash his hands and heads to the kitchen. There on the table is a platter of fried chicken, bowl of mashed potatoes, string beans with a plate of corn bread.

Michelle suddenly appears from another part of the house. They greet each other a big hug and a kiss and were on their way to making a long kiss until they hear Martha say, "Boswell what did I discuss with you earlier...this ain't no motel."

"Yes Martha you did," as the two of them separate from each other and sit down at the table. As soon as Martha turns her back

Michelle whispers to Boswell, "What is Martha talking about?"

"Never you mind just some words of wisdom from her."

For dinner only Michelle and Boswell are present, Grandpa Jed not returned home at dinner time and grandma had a dinner date with the church women that she could not break. The dinner is absent of actual words between Michelle and Boswell but they delight together in Martha's handiwork that creates a language of its own. The sounds of smacking lips accompany by moans of contentment fill the room. As soon as Boswell sucks the last piece of meat off his third chicken wing he declares" You know Michelle these here wings, as he waves a chicken bone in the air pointing it at her, they are better than any I have ever eaten, even Keith's comes into second against Marvelous Martha's chicken wings. It's truly amazing how good food can make a person feel."

"So how did dinner make you feel Boswell?"

"It made me feel good, and if I do not watch out I am going to be rubbing my belly like you. There is something about the feeling of fullness that you get when you've had a tasty meal that's makes you feel good.

The statement makes Michelle laugh.

"So did I say something funny?"

"Well some of us have the feeling of fullness for other reasons, as she rubs her protruding belly, and I think she likes fried chicken…a lot."

"Like daddy like son."

Both of them break into laughter as Grandpa Jed walks into the kitchen. He looks around and says, "What did I do that was so funny?"

In Search of a Good Feeling

"We are not laughing at you Grandpa. It's Boswell's fried chicken eating gene in his DNA that is causing all the laughter."

"I do not know anything about genes or DNK...just as long as I am not the butt of the joke I'm OK."

"Grandpa it's DNA not DNK, and no this time it is not you."

He looks at Boswell saying, "I guess I will see you in the morning. About 6...we will get some coffee...make some cold chicken sandwiches." Grandpa eyes the pile of bones on Boswell's plate. "If there's any chicken left. Then we go get them hogs."

Michelle says, "What hogs?"

"Me, Boswell and your Uncle Jesse are going hog hunting in the morning. I set the traps yesterday afternoon and tomorrow we go see what we got."

"Hog hunting? Boswell have you lost your mind? Grandpa talked you into this? Grandpa you should be ashamed of yourself!"

During their verbal exchange Michelle's face explodes first with surprise then anger towards her grandfather. Amazingly, it makes Boswell feel good that Michelle is attempting to protect him from possibly himself. The idea of someone on his side is a new one for him. Generally, Boswell is a person who seldom relies on the support of others. He is relishing this moment of support. He notices that Michelle is beginning to rub her stomach much quicker, a possible indication of stress, so he moves to clear up her misunderstanding...reluctantly.

"Yes sweetie, I am going with Grandpa in the morning and yeah maybe it's a little risky because I have never done it before but I trust Grandpa that he will not put me in harm's way. I see it as another adventure on my southern vacation."

"Don't sweetie me Boswell, I'm done with it," she mumbles leaving the kitchen heading to her bedroom. The bedroom door slams behinds her in a display of her emotion. Michelle finds herself tired from the day's events and figures that a shower and bed may be the best medicine for her tonight. Michelle feels the baby moving seeming to indicate that someone else is in agreement with her decision. After the door slam there is silence for the moment in the kitchen then people start moving in their separate directions. Grandpa heads out to the front porch to wait for Grandma Lizzie with his night cap, a glass of iced tea mixed with a shot of whiskey. Martha silently reappears to clean up the kitchen before heading home. Boswell remains there slowly sipping his iced tea really enjoying the peaceful moment.

As he leaves the kitchen to give Martha her space she stops him looks Boswell in his eyes and says slowly, "Them woods have many secrets that have been kept hidden for a long time. Be watchful Boswell… trust the spirits, they will lead you."

Not knowing how to respond to her cryptic message Boswell says "Yes Martha," and heads quickly up the steps to his bedroom as the voices in his head begin their bombardment.

CHAPTER 15

Boswell brings his luggage down the steps to the car where Michelle and her grandparents were waiting. It is time to leave Michelle's folks to connect with his folks. The last couple days have not been without some, as the people in Philly would say drama. On the night before the hog hunt, Boswell returned to his room to find Michelle in his bed. He closed the door quickly, undressed, set the alarm for 5am and slid into the bed next to her. Very little was said between their quiet kisses and silent hugs. Her presence silenced the voices and all was well in their world.

The next morning alarm rang too early for Boswell. He noticed that Michelle was no longer in bed with him suggesting sometime during the early morning that she had left or had he dreamed that Michelle was there? With no time to ponder about that puzzle, Boswell showered and dressed in an orange t-shirt, a pair of brown shorts and sneaks. By 5:30 am he was in the kitchen with Grandpa who was already drinking coffee while making sandwiches.

He looked at Boswell and said, "Son where you going with that bright shirt on? You are going to scare away the hogs." He reached down and tossed Boswell a green army style camouflage t-shirt saying, "Put that on. Remember we are going hog hunting and not to the beach," he laughed.

Grandma Lizzie and Michelle came creeping down the steps into the kitchen. They are whispering about something when they entered but took time from their conversation for a unison greeting of good morning.

Grandma Lizzie said "We come to see out menfolk off," as she greeted Boswell with a kiss on the cheek. The gesture made Boswell feel warm all over. He looked quickly over to Michelle to see her reaction and she is smiling at him. But before any other words are spoken there is a vehicle honking its horn outside.

Grandpa smiled, "That's Jesse right on time."

A couple of seconds later a raspy voice said," Where's my coffee?" and Uncle Jesse walked in the backdoor. A scrawny grey haired fellow with a bent over posture made Boswell wonder to himself, *How much help will he be when it comes to catching hogs?* Uncle Jesse came towards Boswell and shook his hand. His strong bony grip and body smell of old liquor took him by surprise,

"So you must be Boswell. I heard a lot of good things about....yep...I have."

Michelle smiled sarcastically at Uncle Jesse thinking, *I bet you have. You are probably thinking of ways to castrate Boswell back in the woods for defiling a white woman.*

"Yes I'm Boswell, nice to meet you Uncle Jesse."

"Now that we all know each other, interrupted Grandpa, it's time to get familiar with them hogs."

Uncle Jesse headed out to his truck with his coffee while Grandpa resumed gathering up the food supplies for the trip.

In Search of a Good Feeling

Michelle moved instinctively behind Boswell and whispered, "Be careful...those woods can be dangerous."

Boswell turned quickly facing Michelle and noticed concern in her eyes. But before he can say anything they hear a big collision outside. Uncle Jesse's flatbed truck with several cages on them had been parked directly across from Grandpa's jeep. In an attempt to display his driving skills Uncle Jesse accelerated on the damp clay drive way too quickly and rammed his truck right into the jeep. Everyone screamed and ran towards the collision to inspect the damage. Uncle Jesse was hanging out the driver side window with a stupid look on his face trying to explain what just occurred.

"I just hit the gas a little because on the way up the pedal was sticky...I guess it's still sticking."

So with one heavy foot of an alcoholic, the hog hunting expedition was temporarily is slowed to a halt. Grandpa angrily waved his fist at Jesse as he inspected the jeep. The collision caused the jeep to flip over and land upside down. Boswell stood around the confusion wondering what would have happened if he had ridden with Uncle Jesse. He was sorry for Grandpa for losing his beloved jeep. But glad that they did not go hog hunting because he was still sore from his fall yesterday and there is something about Uncle Jesse he does not like. So as Grandpa was calling around to find a tow truck and Grandma Lizzie was tending to Uncle Jesse's minor bruises Boswell led Michelle back into the house.

"That was the damnest thing." stated Boswell.

"Let's not talk about it. I'm just glad you did not go."

"I'm kind of glad myself. I know this is changing the subject but did we sleep together last night?"

"That's a strange question. If I did it means it was not memorable and if I didn't it means you really miss sleeping with me. Is that true?"

"Could you just answer the question? Yesterday is kind of a blur. Forget it, if you did you are quite a naughty one and if you did not thanks for the dream because you were fantastic. That rub the belly thing that you do as you swivel is just amazing," laughed Boswell as he gently smacked Michelle's backside.

"Funny man continue to have your dreams about me. I hope they serve their purpose," remarked Michelle.

They find themselves in the living room where they separated. Boswell decided to go back to bed while Michelle wandered over to the front porch to commune the with sun.

About three hours later Boswell returned back downstairs looking for Michelle. He ran into Martha in the hallway sweeping the floor.

"Good morning sleeping beauty how you feeling this morning?" But before he could answers she continued, "You better be glad the spirits were on your side this morning. That half- crazed man could have killed you....but they are looking out for you ...for some reason you have found favor in their eyes." Before Boswell responded, Martha immediately changed the subject. "Your breakfast is in there on the stove, so get in there and eat before its get cold. Hurry up boy, I got housework to do, you slowing me down getting up in the middle of the day like you the son of a king. This ain't the north you know. I will be in there in a minute to make you some fresh coffee as soon I am finish sweeping this here floor."

Learning from his past discussions with Martha, Boswell quickly responded, "Yes ma'am," and hurried off

In Search of a Good Feeling

feeling somewhat like a little boy who had just received a scolding but not understanding what he did. There on the stove was a covered platter that when Boswell sees what's in it just makes his eyes water. There were several country sausage patties, strips of bacon, hash browns with onions, scrambled eggs, and 4 large biscuits; a meal for a king. The breakfast triggered a memory of how his mother used to cook Saturday breakfast for the family. Saturday breakfast was a big deal in their home, and it was a welcome change from the daily issuance of oatmeal and toast the twins and he ate for breakfast on schooldays. Boswell's remembered the time that his mother made French toast for breakfast and he stated that he was going to marry a French woman so that she could make him toast like this every day.

His momentary flash back is interrupted by Martha saying, "Boswell you all right, what's that silly smile on your face for? My food is for eating and not fantasizing about, now eat before it gits cold. You want some milk in your coffee?"

Boswell returned back to reality but the smile remains as he partakes in his breakfast. He looked up from his plate, "I was just having a moment. This meal reminds me of how my mother used to cook. I just wonder if your biscuits are as good as hers. No milk or sugar for me."

Martha poured Boswell's coffee and placed it next to him. She sat at the table, looked him in the eye and said, "Boswell I cook from my soul. I have never tasted your mother's food and I have no doubt in her own way she is a fine cook but I reckon no northern bred woman's biscuits will be better than mine. But I will let you find out for yourself. When you are finish eating wash your dishes. They may think that I am the maid around here, but I'm not…"

With those words Martha took off her apron, patted Boswell on the head and disappeared to the front of the house. Not waiting for an invitation Boswell took a plate from the counter and filled it up with everything from the platter and then some. Not a religious man, but for some reason Boswell bowed his head and said a silent grace for the blessing of having a well cooked meal. He took the fork, scooped some potatoes into his mouth and just waited for his taste buds to explode in celebration. His food merriment last for a while, but soon he was down to his last biscuit which he must say were far better than his mother's. e

He cut it in half and filled it with grape jelly, just like he did when he was a child and devoured it. He balanced off the sweetness of the jelly with a gulp of black coffee and announced out loud for everyone to could hear him, "Now that's eating….southern style."

Unknown to him, Michelle was viewing his whole eating episode from the window on the porch. From her advantage point, she perceived some new things about him. Michelle observed, the way he ate, continuously without stopping until the end, which is quite different than when they are eating together where he stopped…chewed …talk…chewed. She watched his face as he ate the last biscuit; how he closed his eyes and his mouth turns upward in a sign of ultimate delight. She realized that there was a part of Boswell the she did not know….those little things that gave him pleasure which they have never shared together, like eating a flaky jelly filled biscuit. She began to hold her belly desiring in the same way to embrace Boswell with her whole being. Michelle smiled. To her he looked so childlike in his joy at this moment. A part of him that the ultra-serious Boswell had seldom revealed; he had found his good feeling place and it showed. Michel left her window view and entered into the kitchen, wondering to herself when will that little boy come out to play with her. She kissed Boswell's bald head and the baby moves. Oh there you go." stated Boswell. "I thought you had abandoned me for one of your lost lovers."

"Naw, the boy I kinda liked is married to my best friend so I guess for the moment we are stuck together."

"So where is everybody at?"

"Well soon after you went upstairs Willie Joe Jr. showed up with a tow truck and took Grandpa's jeep away. Grandpa and Uncle decided that it was still a good day for hog hunting so they got Willie's son Spider and his friend to go with them. Grandma went to visit her people...so baby it's just you and me."

"Cool."

"I want to go for a ride. I have not been here for a while and I am dying to revisit some of my old secret places on the farm."

Before he knew it, he was driving along a red clay road on the plantation with Michelle pointing out various landmark not unlike his previous tour with Grandpa but with Michelle giving her own version of their importance. For a while they were silent. All of a sudden Michelle told Boswell to stop the car as they began to cross over a dried up bed. Michele started to giggle.

Boswell asked, "What so funny?"

"I'm being naughty."

"Naughty...you...how?"

"Well as long as I lived on this property I was told never to go over the riverbed. Why I do not know. But Grandpa always told me not to do it because some animals wandered on this side the river. Whatever the reason I never did it... too scarred...so now I'm going to do it."

"Do what?"

She pointed somewhere in the distance. "We are going over there."

Boswell drove the rental car over the riverbed wondering to himself how he is going to get all that orange clay dust off the car before he turned it back to the rental agency. He maneuvered down the road and stopped. Boswell noticed that the road ends about 15 feet in front of them close to a grove of trees.

"I see why your Grandpa said what he said...there's no road."

"That's fine, Let's park the car under the trees and go on a hike."

"OK, as long as we stay out of your friend, the sun's direct sight."

The shade of the trees shelters the two city dwellers from the sun, but the 90 degree heat is a constant reminder of its presence. They found a path at the edge of the grove and agreed to take it, not knowing where it leads causing Boswell to quickly reminisce about some of his childhood misadventures that occurred using the same type of logic.

After obtaining some broken tree branches as walking sticks, Michelle took the lead. The path was free of much undergrowth indicating that someone has traveled this way before. Other than occasionally swatting at bugs flying around their head and a stumble by Boswell over a hidden log, the hike was without incident. About twenty minutes into the hike Michelle motioned to Boswell to stop and

In Search of a Good Feeling

listen. In the distance a group of crows were gossiping while the scent of evergreen fill the air. Michelle pointed out that they are in a forest of long leaf pine trees.

She said, "You can tell them by their long drooping needles. Grandpa used to take me on walks and tell me all about trees, bushes and plants in the forest. Pretty cool hey?"

"You never cease to amaze me my dear," as Boswell stole a kiss while rubbing Michelle's belly. The pine tree needles covered the forest floor giving it a soft cushiony feel as the couple walked, making Boswell feel like he was walking on a cloud. Suddenly, there was some rustling in the bushes before them and out of nowhere appeared a group of about five wild hogs. Michelle and Boswell froze in place but before Boswell can say anything to Michelle she lets out a loud banshee scream. Immediately the hogs ran in the opposite direction not knowing what evil spirit they have disturbed. Boswell stood in amazement over the events that just occurred.

He said, "I do not want to know, I really do not want to know the source of your super powers but baby haven't we gone far enough?"

"OK, let's walk over to that clearing and call it a day. You know that I spent two years in a Central American forest. Shoot, scaring wild hogs is just one of the skills that I possess."

"Watch it Michelle you are scaring the baby and me."

They walked to the clearing laughing but then the laughter turns to silence. The clearing opens to area enclosed by an old wooden fence.

"What the heck is this doing way out in the middle of nowhere?"

Boswell does not respond as he left the clearing and walked towards the gate in the fence like something is drawing him there. The voices in his head are quiet. It's like they are waiting to see what's going to occur.

"Where you going? Wait on me," said Michelle as she ran to catch Boswell. She grasped his hand which she found cold and damp. They moved as one towards the fence gate surveying the area as they walk. Upon arrival at the gate they stopped and gazed.

Michelle said, "Oh my God, its looks like a graveyard," as she points to an object. "That's a headstone. Hey we better not go in there I do not mess around with the dead."

Not waiting for an invitation or for Michelle's permission Boswell opened the gate and walks thru. *Yes it is a grave yard*," thought Boswell. He cannot remember the last time he was in one, then it comes to hi. It was his father's burial and after that ceremony he vowed never to attend another funeral. He did not like how it made him feel. It was as though he was on a stage. Nor did he like the crazy comments of the so called well-wishers. So until today he has avoided the whole death funeral grave yard scene. But at this moment he feels different. This graveyard back in the woods seems to be filled with more life than death and the death which is present is without airs or pretense.

He walked up to the first mound and saw a wooden block with a number and letter on it. He wiped his face with his hand as sweat from the summer heat drip down. Boswell is not tuned to Michelle's pleas to stop, but he heard voices around him applauding his arrival. He was struck by his calmness, the absence of fear in his movement and yet he was not able to understand why. It's like he is home among

In Search of a Good Feeling

his friends Willie, Rob and Max, but there is no one around but Michelle and the voices of the spirits. Boswell thought, *This place seems so familiar yet it cannot be since I have never been here before.* He counted ten rows neatly spaced with about twelve mounds of dirt in each row. Boswell looked closer at the mounds. He noticed there is a wooden square in front of every mound. Some look older than others but all of the mounds had some type of headstone.

After a quick inspection he notices a pattern. Each square has a number and letter on them. The mounds in the first row are labeled 1A, 1B 1C… and so on for the exception of the one mound with the headstone made out of stone. That headstone is grey and about one foot by two feet. It sits in front of the other mounds.

Michelle wandered over from her safe place at the end of the clearing to join Boswell. For some reason she felt safer being closer to him. The crows are no longer gossiping and even the bugs have stopped flying around their faces. There was a quietness in the air that even had Michelle breathing easily. Michelle asked, "What are you looking at?"

"The wooden markers. All of them are in alphabetical order with numbers."

"But why?"

"That's easy. Whatever or whoever is buried here, someone laid it out, probably based on some type of written plan. Writing letters and number is much easier than writing out someone's name."

Boswell kneeled down to inspect the headstone with Michelle beside him watching his back. "Hmm no names… so these are really graves but who is bury in them?" she asked aloud. The dust of the summer's red clay has covered some of the lettering up. Boswell brushes some soil off the headstone and suddenly Michelle points to it shouting, "Shed...look Boswell… the person's name is Shed. There on the granite tomb stone read the word SHED in capital letters. Michelle and Boswell just stared at the headstone for a moment attempting to connect the dots in their head. "Maybe Shed was somebody important and that's why their headstone is made out of stone and sits and fron.t"

"Or maybe Shed is an animal, like a dog, a good old dog and they buried him back here and just ran out of material for other headstones. So some started to use wooden blocks. Slowly the couple looked up and sense there was a change going out around them.

Michelle said, "I think I heard the voices of the spirits saying the name Shed over and over."

Boswell looked around him and said, "I do not hear no spirits but something is happening. Look at the clouds." The clouds began to swirl in the air accompanied by an unexpected wind gush. The big pine trees swayed back and forth communicating to the forest dwellers to be prepared for the worst. Suddenly the crows fly out of the trees. The sky quickly darken in the sky and in the distance thunder was heard. Not wanting to be caught in a summer storm in the middle of the nowhere, the couple hastened back down the path to the car.

Their flight and fear response flips in making their minds think swifter, and their bodies moved faster allowing the couple to make it back to the car much quicker than they came. Not much was said on the way home other than Michelle giving Boswell directions on where to turn. As the car pulled into the backyard, the heaven released buckets

In Search of a Good Feeling

of water from the sky. With no desire to get stupid wet as Boswell called it, the couple decided to stay in the car and wait out the storm.

Michele moved closer to Boswell and placed her moist forehead on his shoulder. She closed her eyes and smiled. Boswell took her hand causing the baby to move inside Michelle's belly. All was well in their world for the moment. As their minds wandered between the past, present and future they feel surprisingly safe in a rental car in the heart of the south in the summer as the rain pummels down on them. Their moments of safety did not last long because as soon as the storm came it went.

As Boswell and Michelle reluctantly left out of the car Martha appeared on the back porch. "Look at here, look at here what the storm brought in," she laughed. "And look what it left you. She pointed to the rainbow. It's mighty nice to be loved."

The water vapors and the sun had done their thing and produced a rainbow. Michelle and Boswell just gazed at it for a moment trying to understand if the rainbow has any significance to today's events. As soon as Boswell goes into the kitchen to get both of them some water, Michelle walked towards Martha.

"Martha do you know anything about a person named Shed we found this…."

Martha wagged her finger back and forth to stop Michelle from saying anything else. Once Michelle was silent she said, "Now Chellie, I have told you thousands of times I do not know anything unless I'm told and I have not been told. If you really want to find out about anything that goes on at this plantation ask your grandpa, but remember do not ask questions that you do not want answers to, because you're responsible for the answers once they are told to you. There are some things that should stay hidden. It's better that way. Your grandpa should be home soon, but do not forget what I just told you."

"*Damn you Martha,*" thought Michelle to herself, *That must be the motto around this freaking place.*

CHAPTER 16

By the time Grandpa and Grandma came home it was after 6 pm...the heat of the day had drained out much of the energy of anything living. On top of the heat, the little rain shower left behind humidity so unbearable that every movement of the body created a pool of sweat. Michelle and Boswell spent the afternoon poking around the old house trying to find a cool spot to escape the unbearable summer conditions. Although the bedrooms had air conditioning the rest of the house remained under the cooling control of slow moving ceiling fans stationed in every room. These very ceiling fans have been a fixture in the house since the time Michelle lived here. When asked why he had not installed air conditioning throughout the whole house Grandpa replied, "The motion of the fans remind me that you do not have to be in a hurry to get something done." They are on duty constantly during the summer months meeting the enemy in a daily battle. Some days they win, but most days they become unwilling partners with the heat as transporters of hot air.

After watching the couple move around the house like they were playing hide and go seek Martha remarked aloud,

"What the heck is the matter with you two? If you just sit your butts down in one place maybe your bodies will cool off...don't you both have college degrees?"

A lady of immense personal resources, some days Martha can be short on patience and today was one of those days. Not desiring to be on her bad side no more than necessary the couple decides after quick deliberation that the sitting room, a room adjacent to the living room, was the coolest room in the house. The sitting room, as Grandma Lizzie called it, had a love seat with a matching chair in it. Generally, not a heavily use room, but none of the other downstairs rooms of the house were frequently used either other than the kitchen and the porch.

The official meeting place for the house appeared to be the kitchen to Martha's dismay. She constantly complained about people in the kitchen while they have a whole house that no one ever goes in.

"How the heck can I get my work done with all you folks sitting in here like it's Sunday morning in church? This ain't no restaurant, bar or meeting place. Eat your food and leave and stop bringing folks in this here kitchen like it's the only room in the freaking house. And when you are finished eating scrape your plate and place it in the kitchen sink. I have told you before I ain't nobody's maid." Generally when Martha goes into one of her rants Mr. and Mrs. Waterman scatter to other rooms until she has cooled down.

The couple switched on the ceiling fan as they entered the sitting room. A cool breeze swirls around as they make a decision about sitting arrangements. It was a dilemma for both of them...if they decided to sit on the love seat...being close is wonderful but closeness creates heat...the one thing

In Search of a Good Feeling

they are trying to avoid. If they decided to sit in separate seats, it might appear they are estranged but their goal of being cooler would be achieved. In the end, the decision was to sit together in the love seat. Later Martha asked they chose to sit so close together.

Boswell answered, "Well you said if we sat still we would be cooler so we did not think it mattered how close we sat to each other."

Michelle heard the car as it pulled into the backyard and nudged Boswell but he was fast asleep. The day's adventures had taken a toll on him. She wiped the beads of sweat from his face and proceeded to the kitchen. She met her grandparents in the kitchen as they were inspecting the icebox for something to eat.

Michelle said, "Hi y'all. You guys been gone a while. Martha went home and she told me to tell you that there is some sliced ham, potato salad, coleslaw and lemonade in the icebox."

Grandma Lizzie brought her head out of the icebox. "Well, well if it's not the queen of the house. I am glad to be home dear. Your granddaddy had me out in all of this heat... got my hair all messed up. I'm just trying to cool off."

"Where is grandddaddy?" inquired Michelle.

"He went to look at his hogs. They do not do well in the heat because they do not have sweat glands like horses and dogs," said Grandma Lizzie as she wiped the sweat from her brow.

"You better watch it. One day he will have those hogs' pens air conditioned."

"You are probably right about that."

"Grandma, keep your head out of the ice box. Martha told us to just drink some water and sit still and you will cool off."

"Well I reckon that Martha does not know everything!"

"You are right Grandma…just most things…," said Michelle as she left out of the back door in search of her grandfather with a bottle of Pepsi-Cola in her hand.

At 6:30 pm, the presence of the sun was still evident especially on the orange clay back roads of South Carolina. The air was still with an occasionally gnat or horse fly buzzing pass Michelle's face. The mosquitoes had yet to gather for their endless quest for the arms and legs of humans. Maybe they were waiting for night to secretly ambush their prey.

Before coming outside, Michelle equipped herself against the flying foe by dressing in long pants and a light long sleeve shirt and sprayed any exposed part of her body with insect repellant. She knew that without putting on the insect repellent she would be a fool, and with it she might stand half a chance against them. She found Grandpa right where his loving wife stated he would be, at the hog pen spraying them with water. Michelle watches for a moment as grandpa tends and talks to his hogs.

"Hey Grandpa," yelled Michelle, "I brought you a Pepsi-Cola."

Grandpa turned away from his hogs and towards his granddaughter and saw something in her face that was familiar. It was that look and the offering. He had experienced it many times in Michelle's early life when she was attempting to understand something and did not have the answer. She would always offer him a Pepsi-Cola and then she would tell

In Search of a Good Feeling

her side of the self-imposed dilemma. One thing Grandpa knew was little kids have little dilemmas while big kids have big ones. He was mentally preparing for a big one.

"Thanks," said Grandpa. "It's might nice of you to think about your grandpa in such of a way. Not unlike I feel about these here hogs…you see their life is not a noble one because in the fall many of these gold medal winning hogs with be led to the slaughterhouse where they will be killed, butchered, packaged and placed in some lucky person's freezer for the winter. Many folks, you included, wonder why I spend so much time and energy with something like a hog. Well I tell you I cannot stop their destiny, nope I can't but I can make their journey a lot more pleasurable. Even those hogs we caught today which Boswell missed out on, I attempted to make their life a little better but sometimes it is not always easy. And by the way, I do not think that Boswell is made up for hunting hogs. It was probably best that he stayed home. Today was not a good day for a rookie."

"That's might noble of you Grandpa. Thanks for the different perspective of a life of a hog and for Boswell's future as a hog hunter. I agree with you that it is nonexistent and I'm glad he stayed home with me too," said Michelle laughing.

Grandpa raised the soda pop to his lips and proceeded to drain half of its contents. "Mm, that is good, but you know I really miss drinking them out of the glass bottles. These plastic bottles are not the same…but I guess I'm one of those dinosaurs who live in the present but long for the past. So Michelle what's on your mind?"

"Well Grandpa… I need to ask you a question," said Michelle.

"I hope it is not about slavery, I told you what I knew."

"Well Grandpa, it is about slavery and I do not believe you have told me everything you know. You admitted to me that we had slaves but when the slaves died where were they buried?"

Grandpa looked in Michelle's eyes and knew that she knew something that she was not supposed to know. After the last conversation he came to the realization that she was no longer a little girl from Germany unaware of the ways of her new country. His role as interpreter of the culture for her was over and had changed overnight to the unwilling teller of the truth but only if asked.

"Hmmmm, that's an interesting question."

"Grandpa, please stop stalling. Boswell and I found something that resembled a graveyard over there past the riverbed in a clearing in that area where you told me never to cross over to because some animal would attack me. No more tales to protect me Grandpa, remember I'm not a princess anymore."

Grandpa drank the last of Pepsi-Cola, licked his lips and looked at his granddaughter of 35 years. "Well," he said, "What you guys found was a graveyard where slaves were buried. What I am about to tell you was told to me by my father and told to him by his, and it's the same story I told your father who forgot to tell you. The graveyard was located in that far off part of the property because it was heavily wooded and it too much trouble to farm it. One day one of your ancestors found that clearing in the woods far away from the plantation house and begin to bury slaves there. He could have done like most of his neighbors and bury the slaves anywhere without much regard to them but

In Search of a Good Feeling

this relative saw things a little different. He had heard that a fellow slave owner had desecrated his slave burial grounds by allowing his cattle to trample through it. The spirits of the dead slaves sought retribution so they haunted that slave master plantation until his death. Your ancestor did not want to be on the wrong side of the spirits so despite being called foolish by his neighbors for wanting to a finding a burial place for his property, he did it anyway. It was more out of the fear of being haunted than moral dignity that drove his decision about the slave's burial ground."

"Fear has a way of being a catalyst to decision making Grandpa. The cemetery is laid out with number and letter combinations. What's all that about?" asked Michelle.

"Again it was done to be on the good side of the spirits and of God. Instead of just piling them in a nameless pit, the slaves were placed in wooden coffins and carried by horse and wagon until it got to the river bed. There the coffin was transported over the river by slaves and thru the woods until they reached the clearing. The slave was buried using a letter and number to establish where the body was buried. The ancestor believed that he was responsible for the souls of his slaves and when he got to the judgment and was asked by the Lord where a certain slave was buried, he could easily identify the location, unlike other slave owners."

"C'mon Grandpa, is this one of your tales again?"

"No Michelle, this is the truth. I could not even make this up."

"But the burial place seems to be well taken care of. Who's responsibility is that the spirits?"

"No silly girl! In the will to the property which had been handed down over the generations there is a stipulation about the care of the slave cemetery. I can show you a copy of it. I have it in the house. I hire a group of Mexican gardeners to take care of the area every month."

"Hmmm, but what happens if that part of the stipulation is not carried out?"

"I would not want to be one who does that because then you have to deal with the spirits."

"But wait a minute Grandpa, you are telling me that yes we owned slaves and yes we have a place set aside for their remains based on an ancestor's fear of being haunted and it's stipulated in a will? And location of their remains were know by the owner because of a letter number combination?" said Michelle in disbelief.

"Yes Michelle, that is what I am saying. I have documents to prove it."

"Wow you have papers? What type of papers?"

"Well, papers about the deed, the property, copies of the will and stuff like that. Your ancestors were a strange lot. They came from Liverpool England and made a fortune in the ship building trade. Once they came to the New World they were very careful to write everything down as a way to communicate with each other because they thought their American counterparts were an ignorant bunch of fools without much schooling. Their ability to read and write in their mind separated them from the others. So the tradition at the Waterman Plantation was to write first then talk," replied Grandpa. He turned off the hose and told the hogs good night.

Michelle waited patiently for him watching his every move. He locked the enclosure to make sure none of the wild hogs in the area get in and then waves goodbye. The hogs

In Search of a Good Feeling

replied with a series of grunts. It seems that he was correct about having a deep feeling of responsibility for those hogs. He was caretaker of someone's future Christmas ham.

The confirmation of the cemetery and revelation of historic papers about the property has Michelle hyped. "I cannot wait to see these papers…and tell Boswell," she said.

Grandpa looked in her direction as they walked back to the house. "Ok Michelle lets slow down. When you and Boswell return from visiting his folks we can sit down and view the family papers, until then no more talking about them. What will be will be." he replied.

An owl began to hoot from somewhere in a nearby tree causing a flock of crows to take to the air. Grandpa and Michelle watched as crows begin to circle the hog pen and then quickly flew away.

"That was strange," said Michelle. "Those birds must be following me around. There were a bunch of crows around the burial grounds this afternoon."

Grandpa was quiet, his mind was on more than a flock of birds. On the walk back home they were both lost in their own thoughts. As they approached the back porch Grandpa said, "You might ask your grandmother about those crows. You know she is part Native American and although she can be quiet Lizzie does know a lot about stuff like that."

"Will do," said Michelle as she wiped the sweat from her brow. "It is time for a shower now."

Grandpa stopped in the kitchen to retrieve his supper while Michelle went looking for Boswell. She found Grandma Lizzie and Boswell watching a rerun of "Seinfeld" together in the living room. The fan hummed overhead as iced tea in tall glasses was being consumed by both viewers.

As Michelle entered the room they both looked in her direction and smiled.

Michelle went over to Boswell, gave him a kiss on the head and sat next to him. "How was your nap, you can sleep anywhere?" asked Michelle jokingly.

Boswell yawned and hugged Michelle, "Well, my nap was fine but I woke up all sweaty so I took a shower, got clean, and started watching TV with Grandma Lizzie. Martha made us some iced tea before leaving so we are doing fine."

Grandma Lizzie smiled and sipped tea slowly. She seemed to enjoy Boswell's company and appeared to be somewhat upset with Michelle's arrival so Michelle sat in silence until the end of the show then turned to Grandma Lizzie.

"Grandma, do you know anything about the meaning of crows."

Grandma Lizzie face lit up and she looked straight in Michelle's direction. "I know a little about them being half native American. My mother was from the Catawba trib. My daddy married her and we lived around my mother's people until I was 8. So yea, I know little about animals and what they symbolize. Were they dead, flying, perching or what?"

"Well let me see.....earlier today when Boswell and I were in the woods they were perching then they all got up and flew away and about 30 minutes when I was with Grandpa they flew from their perch and circled around the hog pens and then flew away.

"Wow you are a popular person my dear," said Grandma Lizzie, "crows are funny animals and symbolically very

In Search of a Good Feeling

powerful. Unlike ravens, they always travel in groups. I was taught by my aunt that the presence of crows mean a change is coming. It is seen as a communication from the God."

Boswell was silent, listening to every word of their conversation and pondering it's meaning. *A possible message from God that a change is coming. Hmmm, now if I only believed in God the crow thing would have more meaning, thought Boswell.*

"So God's trying to communication something to me or us, me and Boswell?"

"I cannot say." All I know is that the presence of crows is a powerful indicator of change in the Native American world. Anyway, ok no more of this crow talk before it causes me to dreams about those birds tonight.

Grandpa walked into the room rubbing his belly.

"Hey grandpa, what's the matter, you with child?" laughed Boswell.

"No Boswell, sorry to disappoint you but just giving the ultimate compliment to a tasty dinner. Anyway you missed a good hunt today. We got 5 good size female hogs, some piglets and one big boar. Jesse was disappointed that you could not make it, maybe next time." Before Boswell can reply Grandpa said, "I'm tired. I know it's early but I'm tired and a little sore so I am going to bed. I'll see you folks in the morning before you leave. Good night." With a wave of the hand Grandpa walked up the stairs to his bedroom.

"I will be up there in a moment to rub you down dear," yelled Grandma Lizzie up the steps. She got up and took her glass into the kitchen. She returned shaking her head. "That man is crazy. He is too old to go running after some hogs with that half-wit alcoholic brother of his. Let me go take care of my man while I still have one. Remember Michelle, a wife's work is never done. Good night my loves, don't stay up too late."

"Good night grandma. Take care Grandpa. He has a good heart...but just a little stubborn."

A voice yelled back, "I can hear you down there, I am not deaf yet."

"Coming dear." With those words Grandma Lizzie disappeared up the steps to tend to the needs of her man. Another rerun of Seinfeld was about to begin on the television. Michelle traveled to the kitchen and returned with the pitcher of iced tea and her glass. She poured a glass of iced tea for her and topped Boswell's glass off. Taking the glass in her hand she raised it and motioned Boswell to do the same. "A toast to relationships, easy to find difficult to maintain." They touched glasses, sipped a gulp of tea, and kissed each other like there was no tomorrow.

"Didn't I say this ain't no motel?"

The couple stopped in mid-motion and looked at the living entrance. There stood Martha with a red bandana. They quickly separated and became like statues while casting their eyes down to the floor.

"You guys do not want to listen. Anyway I was half way home before the spirits reminded me that I did not say good bye or wish you safe travels.

Michelle was the first to speak, "That was sweet of you to come back to say good bye Martha."

"There ain't nothing sweet about me. I just do what I am told, unlike you two."

"Yes ma'am I have been corrected."

"So, be safe. Hopefully I will still be here when you return. The spirits say show compassion for those without and it will serve you well and stop worrying about those crows. What they are, are what they are."

"How did you know about the crows?"

"Michelle, what did I tell you about asking questions?"

"Yes ma'am I forgot."

Martha walks to the front door. "Take care of her Boswell. I will see you when I see you," and she was gone.

CHAPTER 17

Boswell pulls the rental car into 2510 Fish Road. There stands a brick ranch house with three cars and a pickup truck in the driveway. The garage door is open and Boswell can see in it various picnic items such as grills, tables, and chairs. "This must be the place," says Boswell.

Michelle nods in agreement but her thoughts are elsewhere as she rubs her stomach slowly. Boswell pulls in behind the pickup truck. Scared but determine, he kisses Michelle and says, "Let's do this."

The couple emerges from the car and immediately hold each other's hand like they were marching into the gates of hell. Boswell goes to the front door and rings the bell.

"Who's there?" A female voice rings out.

"It's me, Boswell and Michelle, we spoke on the phone earlier this morning."

"Comin." Suddenly there appears at the door a short salt and pepper headed woman with an apron around her waist. She opens the screen door. "Boswell. I assume?"

"Yes ma'am." Before he can introduce Michelle his aunt makes the following statement, "Boswell rule number one around here is that guests comes to the front door. That's

In Search of a Good Feeling

why we keep the screen door locked. Family comes thru the garage. That door is always open. Got that?"

"Yes ma'am."

"Now give me a hug...looking just like your daddy." Auntie Nannette releases Boswell and turns to Michelle. She holds out her hand causing Auntie Nannette to laugh. "I thought you were from the south baby. Down here we don't shake hands with family we squeeze them."

Before Michelle can move, all 5 feet of Auntie Nannette is hugging her. "Ok, you both know the secret greeting therefore you are now officially family." Everyone laughs. "C'mon in and let me introduce you to some good people."

They travel through a couple rooms before coming to the kitchen where two women of undetectable age are engaging in various meal preparation tasks. As soon as Auntie Nannette enters the kitchen they stop what they are doing and look in her direction.

"Boswell, Michelle, this is Peggy, my youngest sister, your aunt and this Sally her daughter, therefore your first cousin."

On an invisible cue both women open their arms as they approach Michelle and Boswell and proceed to give them hugs.

"You look just like your daddy," says Auntie Peggy. "I was his favorite sister. We did everything together while growing up. Times like this I really miss him, but I am so glad to see you again. I guess I have not seen you in over 25 year. Welcome home."

Boswell just smiles as Auntie Peggy talks, not really knowing what to say or do. Michelle is amused with all of the attention that he is receiving. She likes to observe how Boswell gets himself out of uncomfortable situations.

After Auntie Peggy finishes with her opening statement she says, "Oops I forgot my manners. Are you all hungry?" "You did all that driving so I know you must be hungry. There is some sausage, potatoes and biscuits on the stove. How about something to drink? I can make you some fresh coffee. We have soda pop and tea in the ice box.

"No ma'am, we just ate before we came here but thanks."

"Well before you leave we are going to have breakfast together."

"Yes ma'am."

"I see that you are preparing for the reunion. Do you need any help in the kitchen? Remember I'm not a guest, I'm family."

There is a moment of silence then Auntie Nannette says, "Sure go over there and wash your hands. There are some carrots and cabbage that needs shredding."

"No problem."

Auntie Nannette looks at Michelle, "You want to help?"

"Hmm," replies Michelle, "Sure, but something nonfood related like wrapping utensils with a napkin."

Auntie Peggy disappears into an adjoining room and returns with a tray with a box of forks, spoons and knives along with a pack of napkins.

"Well, Michelle, ask and it shall be yours."

"Yes ma'am," says Michelle as she takes the tray and retires to a table adjoining the kitchen which was a great advantage spot to watch Boswell perform.

Perform he did. With the kitchen being a place of good feelings for Boswell, he dazzles his newly met family members with his skill level. Michelle's watches as Boswell's anxiety level lowers while his comfort level with his family

In Search of a Good Feeling

rises. From his new level of confidence, Boswell is able to talk and joke freely.

From the initial introduction of his auntie and cousin begins an endless string of first time meeting with family members. With his Auntie Nannette by his side Boswell and Michelle meet cousins Travis, Pop, Cliff, Clover, Jean, Kimberley, Eighty Five, Debbie, Judy, Cooty Gal and so on as they pass thru the house dropping off food and other items for the reunion dinner. Intersperse between the kitchen tasks and introduction of family members are the stories about Boswell's family. Auntie Nannette seems to be the historian and is eager to displays her vast knowledge of the family's comings and goings. She recalls how when Boswell and his family would visit during the summer he would sometimes cry because of the heat and bugs. Michelle laughs thinking that nothing has changed much. Remembering what Martha said about asking questions Michelle takes on the role of listener until the questioning turns to her.

Auntie Nannette asks, "So where did you grow up?"

Michele replies, "I was born in Germany and moved to South Carolina to live with my grandparents when my mother died."

"Sorry to hear about your mother."

"Yes, she was a good mother. I miss her dearly. My grandparents have a place outside of Charleston and that's where I lived until I went to college. I guess I'm a German southern belle. Hahaha."

"So, what's your last name?"

"Waterman. I'm Michelle Elizabeth Waterman."

"Waterman hmm, that does not sound like a German last name."

"Well it is not. My father's ancestors came from England in the 1700s and landed in Charleston."

"Hmmmm, ok."

After about three hours of this constant high volume social interaction combined with kitchen tasks, Boswell and Michelle become worn and seek refuge to their hotel room. They say good bye to the family kitchen crew with hugs and kisses and promise that they will return for the dinner.

"I'm exhausted," states Michelle, Your people can really talk."

"You are correct on that but it was a good time. I liked it."

"Some strange names though, Eighty-Five and Cooty Gal. Where did they get those name from?" But before she could hear the answer Michelle closes her eyes and the next thing she knew they are pulling up to the hotel.

"I did not realize that I was so tired."

"I think that you forget that you are two instead of one."

"Yea I guess that could be it."

"Go take a nice hot shower. It may make you feel better. I'm going to put my feet up and relax some myself before tonight's affair."

"That's a good idea Boswell. Do you think there will be any dancing tonight?"

"Michelle this is a black family reunion. There will be dancing and lots and lots of eating. Well what did you think of them?"

"Your aunts and cousin? They were friendly enough although I was a little taken back when I was the one being questioned. It made me all tense."

"Well I tell you what. I will massage your neck to relieve some of your tension.

In Search of a Good Feeling

"Ok no funny stuff remember I'm with child."

"I promise," says Boswell grinning from ear to ear.

Michelle disappears into the bathroom as Boswell stretches out on the bed. Before Michelle can return back from her shower he is fast asleep. With the promise of a massage not met Michelle tucks herself under Boswell and commences to engaging in a couple sleep.

They arrive at Summer's Banquet Hall at 6:30, 30 minutes after the appointed time which did not set well with Boswell.

"You act blacker than me sometimes."

"What do you mean by that remark?" says Michelle as she looks at herself in the car's rear view mirror?

"Your unwilling desire to be late. Where I come from we call it "CP" time."

"CP time?"

"Yes, Colored People's Time."

"Colored, who's colored, me? I'm colored now?"

"Just forget it, and stop looking in the mirror. Anyway, you look great. Just remember who you came with," laughs Boswell.

Michelle blushes. "Sometimes you surprise me. And thank you, you handsome man you."

The reunion is being held at a hall located in the downtown section of the city. From its architecture the Summer's Banquet Hall must have been a thing of beauty in the past. It is a red brick two storied building with four big white columns in the front. It has a southern stately appeal, something that you might see on a post card from this region. Even with its central location there is very little foot traffic on a hot Saturday evening. The number of cars in the parking lot makes Boswell think that this side of his family are timely folk. Boswell parks the car and in a playful gesture goes around the car to open Michelle's door. As he opens the door Boswell announces to anyone in listening range, "The Queen has arrived."

Michelle emerges from the car laughing, wearing a loose light orange dress with spaghetti straps and speckled white and orange cloth brown flats. Boswell compliments her dress by sporting an orange Kente' cloth bowtie with a white shirt, black suspenders and black pants. They walk hand in hand into the banquet hall. Two members of the hospitality committee, cousin Barbara Norton and her younger sister Archie Mae Smith greet the couple at the entrance. After a pleasant exchange of, "What's your name, I remember your father, are you two married, this is the Meet and Greet part of the program, and welcome home," they escape towards the dining hall.

"Are you two married? What the heck did she mean by that?" whispers Michelle to Boswell as they walk into the hall holding hands.

Boswell quickly looks in her direction but before he can answer Auntie Nannette comes up from behind and takes his other hand.

"There you two are. I been waiting on you."

Michelle and Boswell quickly put smiles on their faces but not quick enough. "You guys look great, like a matched pair." Auntie Nannette is wearing a printed dress with a head piece, she reminds Boswell of an African queen.

"What is the matter, your smile is saying one thing but I feel your soul is saying something else."

In Search of a Good Feeling

"Well you are correct, when we were registering, Cousin Barbara asked if we were married. I thought it was a weird question."

"Hahaha. Cousin Barbara is at it again! Hey, well never you mind her, she was trying to see if Boswell was an eligible bachelor."

"Why?"

"Her daughter needs a husband and so does she."

"I'm her cousin."

"Not really she is a play cousin. Barbara has been around us since childhood so we just started introducing her as our cousin. So, Michelle keep your man close, there are some cougars among the family."

"Yes ma'am," said Michelle as she slides her hand momentarily around Boswell's waist.

They laugh and follow Auntie Nannette into the banquet hall. The hall is set up with large round tables in the middle surrounding a dance floor. There is a podium on the front with tables along the side of the hall with appetizers and drinks. Boswell recognizes one or two family members from this afternoon but everyone else is a stranger to him. With Auntie on one side and Michelle on the other, he slides through the gathering saying hi to everyone and anyone along the way to their table. After more introductions of family members, Michelle turns around in her seat and notices that the banquet hall is filling up. Surprisingly she is not feeling out of place or on display among Boswell's family. Michelle notes that there is a smattering of non-black individuals present at the reunion but she does not nod at any of them. With her extrovert personality in full bloom she is able to engage in small talk with any and every one.

Boswell admires Michelle for her way of conversing with a stranger like they are old friends. It's a skill set that he lacks therefore, a gathering of people where the focus is conversation can be uncomfortable for him.

Michelle believes Boswell's shyness in groups maybe due to years of living by himself where he did not have to talk to anyone. She has noticed that at times when they are home together, he seems to be in his own world, quiet and disconnected.

One day he realized that he could sit in a room with people talking all around him and be content with nobody talking to him. Whenever the subject comes up Boswell counters with the phrase, "Sometimes I do not have anything to say so I say nothing and that makes me feel good."

Over the last four months, Michelle's value of the touch of a person and their presence has grown while conveying feelings through verbal communication has lessen.

Boswell leans forward in his chair, positioning himself in a way that he is in contact with Michelle's body. He is close enough to smell her recently shampooed hair and feel the warmth of her body making both individuals feel good. Boswell's table includes Michelle, Auntie Nannette, Auntie Peggy, Cousin Sally, Sally's boyfriend George and himself. A number of family members come over to their table to reacquaint themselves with Boswell and to talk about his father. So in this setting Boswell smiles and just listens for his name. It seems that his family members know more about him than he knows about them. Their collective memory allows Auntie Nannette to become the central story teller tying together Boswell's past with his present. The story telling goes on for another couple minutes.

In Search of a Good Feeling

Suddenly there is an announcement from the podium saying that everyone should take their seats because the program is about to continue. The mistress of ceremonies is Mrs. Brenda Brown, who Boswell later finds out is his father's second cousin. She introduces Rev. Jamie Frazier the pastor of Mountain View AME church to bless the food.

Boswell has a negative reaction to preachers. He believes they talk too much while manipulating their flock to live righteous by guilt. He dreads the idea that a pastor will bless the food. *We will be here all day as he blesses everything but the food, thought* Boswell. Surprisingly Rev. Fraser's blessing lasts only about 20 seconds. He ends the blessing by saying, "I was told to say the following, 'Count Memories not Calories' is the motto for this reunion so let the feast begin. Now follow the instructions of the hostesses."

With those words, a group of women dressed in white blouses and black skirts begin to direct each table to the tables of food. There is bar bq chicken, pulled pork, potato salad, coleslaw, macaroni salad, string beans, green beans, hamburgers, hotdogs, tomato and lettuce salads and assorted sweets.

Before Boswell knew it he is eating and having a good time. He reminds Michelle and the others at the table that good food has the way of creating good feelings. They all agree while attempting to figure out how to eat all the food on their plate. Michelle rubs her belly in an attempt to soothe the baby. Auntie Nannette leans over to whisper in her ear.

"Congratulations, I could not tell."

Michelle blushes, "Thank you. It's not a secret. I just don't show."

"So are you guys going to get married?"

"That's a good question. Something that has yet to be talked about. The whole pregnancy thing is a big enough deal."

"Well, he seems like he has a good head on his shoulder."

"Yes he does. He is my good feeling."

Both women look at Boswell and smile.

"I hope you two are discussing the potato salad recipe because I sure would like it. It something different about it."

"It's celery seed Boswell. She puts celery seed in it. That's the difference," says Auntie Peggy. The whole table erupts in laughter.

"Now the family secret is out," says Boswell.

"Oh no," replies Auntie Nanette, "There many more secrets yet to reveal. Like did you know that Peggy colors her hair?"

"That's not coloring Nanette it's shampoo. Stop, you're lying!"

Before Auntie Nanette can reply Mrs. Brenda Brown is back at the podium. "So that we can leave time to shake what God has blessed you with we need to move on with the program. You all can continue to eat just chew a little quieter."

The banquet hall roars with laughter. "Let me introduce Howard Smith who will read our history."

Howard Smith, a dark- skinned, slim build man with a bald head strolls up to the podium. He clears his throat while adjusting the height of the microphone. The light reflects off of his bald head to make it seem like it's glowing. He starts by saying with his baritone voice, "In the beginning there was just on and his name is J. S. Thomas." Then he

In Search of a Good Feeling

stops and looks out to the audience as applaud immediately fills the air.

At that moment, Boswell feels good inside because finally there is a connection to his past. The feeling causes him to get caught up in the emotion of the moment and he stands up clapping to give honor to his ancestor. Like a ripple in a pond others around him begin to stand until there is no one left sitting. Finally, the clapping ceases and everyone returns to their seat.

Howard Smith continues reading, "JS was born about 1804, as a slave around the Charleston low country area. It is told that his parents were stolen from Africa and sold into slavery. Not much is known about his childhood other than he became a skilled blacksmith. So skilled that he was hired out to other farmers to earn money for his owner. Rumor had it that because he was such a great asset to his owner it was stated in his will that on his death JS would be freed. No one knows if that is true or not. He married a woman named Ruth, and had three sons, John Lee, Paul and Bruce C."

The rest of the reading of the family history becomes a blur to Boswell. The voices in his head are applauding the fact that there was a beginning, but it's just a ploy to get Boswell's attention. Soon their questions begin. *Was he big and black, or small and high yellow? Could he read or write his name?* The voices have a way of making a good thought into a bad one, because that's their role. So Boswell uses a technique that has worked in the past, he just turns his focus back to the moment and the voice slow down their campaign of inquiry. He looks around the room and observes all the smiles on people faces, which makes him feel good. The idea that he is part of something that is bigger than he could ever imagine causes him to tear up. Boswell takes Michelle's hand and holds it.

She leans over to him to ask, "Is anything the matter baby?"

"No, just thinking. I'm glad that you are here with me."

Michelle smiles and squeezes Boswell hand. "I'm glad also. I am having a good time and going to have a great time just as soon as the dancing begin."

By the time Michelle and Boswell enter their hotel room it is late and they are tired. Boswell opens the door and Michelle immediately flips off her shoes and flops onto the bed.

"I know why you are tired. You had the spirit of the boogie tonight and you had it bad. I did even know you could dance like that," says Boswell.

"Shhh not now...sweetie could you rub my feet?"

"Yes dear, but you were the talk of the reunion."

"Yes I was, even some of your relatives were asking about me when I was in the bathroom. They did not know that I was in the stall, but I heard them, then I surprised them when I came out."

"What, wow what did they say?"

"Nothing too negative just asking each other who I came with and how much they like my dress. By the way they did not know too much about you, just that you were Auntie Nanette's nephew from Philly.

"So, what happened when you came out of the stall?"

"I just thanked them for the compliments about my dress and engaged in a little woman talk. We heard the music start up and I said they are playing my song, see you on the dance floor."

In Search of a Good Feeling

"That dance floor saw a different you and after you wore me down you danced with George and anyone else who was left standing."

"I told you I wanted to dance and I did. Remember do not judge the book by the cover until you see it dance," laughs Michelle as Boswell moves his hand up to rub her belly.

"You know I'm ok if our son receives your dancing genes. He might turn out to be a world class dancer."

Michelle shakes her head, "Silly man sorry to disappoint you, yes our daughter will be blessed with the spirit of the boogie but science will be in her future."

Pretending not to hear Michelle's statement Boswell continues on his thought, "Time will tell what he will be but he does have my support if he wants to be a dancer. Anyway, lay on your stomach and relax."

Without a word of protest Michelle positions her body as requested awaiting the good times to begin.

Boswell slides his hand up her legs stopping briefly at the calf muscle massaging them and slowly moves to the thigh muscles softly squeezing as he goes.

She smiles, loving all the attention and wanting to cry out in pleasure and tell Boswell what a wonderful man he is but instead she just cries. Michelle turns around and pulls Boswell down next to her. They embrace and Boswell notices her wet red eyes. "Why you crying?" he asks as he touches her face.

"Because you make me feel so good...thank you."

"You are so welcome my queen." They kiss...

CHAPTER 18

Boswell rises earlier than Michelle which is not unusual. Of the two, Boswell is the early riser. It was programmed into him during his college days that the early bird really does get the worm. When he lived in the dorms, the first one in bathroom was guaranteed hot water and most importantly a clean bathroom. Since those college days he has always gotten up before the sun. He dresses quickly and leaves Michelle asleep in the bed.

It's 7 am, in the morning and the heat is slowly making its presence known to all who are awake. Boswell stops down at the continental breakfast area of the hotel to check out their food offerings. He walks by two people sipping coffee in the lobby, but not too much action this morning. The breakfast area is clean and doubles as a lounge area for most of the day. The food offering surprises Boswell. There are heated containers full of hash browns, bacon, eggs and the South's favorite food item, grits along with assorted breads, coffee and juice. *This breakfast is Southern Hospitality at its finest even if it is at an old rundown hotel off the beaten trail,* thinks Boswell as he gets a black coffee and chocolate chip muffin. He finds a seat next to a window and takes a sip

In Search of a Good Feeling

of his coffee. *Hot and a little bitter just like I like it.* He takes the muffin and slices it in half then in half again before eating it. Boswell slowly allows the sliced muffin to melt in his mouth as he alternates between drinking the coffee and eating the muffin. He looks around at the hotel's interior. It is old and in need of a fresh paint job. As he inspects the hotel, Boswell feels that someone is inspecting him at the same time. Suddenly, he looks to his left and there looking right at him is an old elderly grey haired gentleman. He is sipping his coffee while staring at Boswell.

He gets up and walk up to Boswell. "Excuse me young man, forgive me for looking so hard at you, but you resemble someone who I used to know. What's your name?"

"No problem, my name is Boswell, sir."

"Boswell?" The older gentleman makes a face while continuing shaking his head. "That is sure is a strange name. Boswell, hmm, well I do not know anyone named Boswell. You from down here?"

"No sir, visiting my daddy's folks. We had a reunion last night down at Sullivan hall."

"Yaw did ... What's your last name?"

"Wilkerson?"

"Wilkerson? What's your daddy's name?"

"Thomas Wilkerson," Boswell says with a smile on his face.

"That's it, Thomas, yeah. I knew your daddy. We went to school together. Anyone ever tell you that you look just like him?"

"Wow, you knew my father?"

"Yep, I knew your granddaddy, too. His name was Thomas also. We used to call him Big T and your father Little T."

"What's your name?"

"Charles, Charles Thornton. How the heck you got the name of Boswell? Your name should have been Thomas like your daddy and granddaddy."

"Well I think my mama named me."

Both men were quiet for the moment eyeing each other, attempting to discover more information about the person without asking.

Charles Thornton starts off the next round of questioning "You got any little Boswells running around?"

"No sir…but one is in the oven," Boswell states proudly.

"What are you going to name him?"

"Well we have not discussed names yet, but Boswell is in play."

"Hmm I hope not. His name should be Thomas like your daddy and granddaddy."

In an attempt to change the topic from the naming of his unborn child, Boswell goes to a tried and true subject, the weather. "Hmm looks like it going to be a hot one today."

Mr. Thornton smiles, "Where you from Boswell?"

"Philadelphia sir. Why do you ask?"

"Well, if you are in the south, every day in the middle of the summer no matter where you are at its going to be hot. So telling me that it is going to be hot is like telling me that I am a black man. Tell me something I do not know. Let me ask you something. Have you ever picked cotton or beans?"

"No sir"

"Well me and your daddy did. That's what we did in this here hot summer sun …we picked cotton. Yes your daddy. Do you think that your daddy was too good to pick cotton?"

In Search of a Good Feeling

"No sir, he just never told me about his cotton picking days."

"Well some people like to keep the past in the past which may not be a bad thing but the past has a way of catching up with the present in very strange ways. Yes, we learned the three P's early in life."

"What are the three Ps' sir?"

"Plowin, plantin and pickin. We were hired out to the farmers to work their fields and when we came home had to help work the little plot of land that the family leased from the farmer. If I remember correctly the first chance your daddy got he enlisted in the army. Yep, I think he lied about his age. Your granddad was mad when he found out because it took money away from the family, but again in a way he was happy because your daddy did not go through what he went through growing up in the south."

Boswell is speechless. He is listening beyond the words of Mr. Thornton, concentrating on the melody, the intonation, and the texture of what was coming out of his mouth to help create a picture of the events and of the times.

Suddenly Mr. Thornton says, "It was nice talking to you Boswell. I have to go. It seems that my past has caught up with my present. When I see your dad I will tell him that we met."

"See my dad? My dad is dead."

"Yes I know. See you around. Hopefully I will see you before you will see me." With that statement Mr. Thornton gets up and disappears out of the hotel's door while Boswell continues to sit speechless in his chair.

See my daddy? How the heck will he see my daddy? Mr. Thornton is quite a strange person. He must be suffering from early dementia. He is getting his past and present mixed up thinks Boswell as he remains seated in the breakfast area. He finishes his muffin and with the unsolicited help of his voices attempts to wrap his head around the conversation with Mr. Thornton. Boswell comes to the conclusion that Mr. Thornton was just a little mixed up on his dates and times but otherwise a good guy. He goes over to the breakfast bar and selects a blueberry muffin and fixes a cup of lemon tea for Michelle.

On the way to the room Boswell asks the hotel desk clerk if a Mr. Thornton is a guest at the hotel. After a quick look on the computer the clerk declares without too much emotion, "No, nobody by that name is registered here. Are you sure the last name is Thornton?"

Boswell says, "Yes and thanks. Hey by the way, your breakfast is very good," as he proceeds to the room with Michelle's morning meal in his hand. When he opens the door to the hotel room a just showered Michelle greets him with a gloomy look on her face.

"Good morning sweetie, I see that you could not wait for your queen to awaken from her sleep. What did you have a date this morning?"

Somewhat taken off guard by her question, Boswell immediately points to the tea and muffin saying, "Good morning. I see that you are as beautiful as ever. I just got up to bring you back something to eat. Wasn't that sweet."
"Sorry to jump on you but I had a bad dream and just wanted you. I know I never told you this but I really like being around you and there are times I really need you close to me. You mean a lot to me. Thanks for the food, that's a sweet gesture but why a blueberry muffin?"

In Search of a Good Feeling

Boswell shakes his head. "Slow down Michelle you went from having a bad dream to questioning my choice of muffin while stating in between you miss me and its only 7:30 am." He takes Michelle into his arms smelling her recently shampooed hair and just holds her. Michelle begins to shake.

"The dream was terrible. I dreamed that the baby needed diapers and I had no fingers. I could not find you. I looked and looked. The baby and I was crying. So a crow flew down from a freaking tree and changed the diaper and the baby stopped crying. A freaking crow. I woke up scared and for the first time I really thought about what if we are not prepared…are we enough?"

Boswell holds her closer as the shaking ceases. Her stomach seems a little larger as he touches it. He kisses her ear and says, "Yes, Michelle we may not be enough but we have friends and family that can show us what to do. Scared. I've been scared for the last five months. You always talk about how strong I am and I am so scared that I will let you down. There are some days that I am so close to the edge…you do not know how close you are to the edge until you get there and find out that you have always been there all the time. There are times that I just want to cry. I want someone to hold me and let her draw out the pain, the grief, the suffering that my ancestors and I suffered which I hold inside of me. I keep my balance by remembering my past, the voice of my father is there, my mom's voice is there during happier times. Every now and then I lose my balance and I need to cry. It makes me human. Something triggers something and I cry and sob and then I get my balance again and move closer to the edge. Keeping your balance is hard sometimes. I do not want you to see me as weak, just human so I stand closer to the edge. I just look towards the future with hope and remember my past for strength. However, despite all of that, I am so happy and blessed that I have you in my life, and you are the mother of our child." Within each other's embrace both of them begin to cry, first just a quiet whimper, then their bodies begin to shake and the manifestation of their emotional state moves slowly to a loud outcry, expressing without words the pains of their existence while confirming their need for each other.

They disengage from each other after five minutes of embracing, not knowing what to do with their new found information about each other. Michelle goes to the bathroom and returns with two face cloths rinsed in cold water.

"Place it on your face, it will make you feel better. And thanks Boswell for trusting me with you. I feel very special.

With the face cloth still covering his face Boswell says, "You are special, never forget that."

The coolness of the face cloth does the trick of taking away the sting from crying red eyes. Boswell feels weak and needs to sit down as he sits in the only chair in the hotel room. He is quiet now and reflective. He looks at Michelle with his redden eyes and starts talking randomly. "What I just shared with you about me was quite difficult for me but now instead of feeling energetic I feel weak like Superman around kryptonite. I have presented to you as one person but I revealed another part of me that you did not know existed so I am now scared that you will think less of me."

Michelle moves closer to Boswell. "Over the last 4 months I have been with you on a daily basis and at first it overwhelmed me. It had been awhile since I had been in

In Search of a Good Feeling

such constant contact with a man. What it did allow me to do was to get to see the real Boswell without you knowing it. Not the weekend Boswell who has everything well planned and performs well under pressure. But the Wednesday Boswell who was more real, less shiny and sometimes wrong and that's the person who makes me feel good. Your fear of not revealing the true you can push me away not draw me towards you. I need to know that you are imperfect, scared, and not all knowing. Those human qualities have the power to draw me closer…so close to you because that is the Boswell I seek, not Superman. Michelle smiles, "C'mon on sweetie, go take your shower. We are supposed to be at your aunt's in about an hour."

Without protest, Boswell retrieves the face cloth and marches in to the bathroom closing the door behind him.

The couple arrives at Auntie Nanette on time and Boswell remembers to go in the garage entrance. "Hello," yells Boswell as he enters the kitchen, "Anyone home?"

"Boswell, I see that you can follow directions," yells Auntie Nanette back. "Come on in to the dining room we are in here."

Taking Michelle's hand they enter into one door and out another that leads to the dining room. There sits Auntie Nanette, and Auntie Peggy with a lot of food within their reach. The sisters rise when the couple enter the room and greet them with hugs and kisses.

"Sure is hot out there ain't it?" asks Auntie Peggy.

"Yes ma'am, it sure is," answers the couple in unison.

"I hope you all are hungry because it's time to eat," laughs Auntie Nannette.

Anthony Webb

"Yes ma'am I am here to taste all the southern cooking I can get and you won't have to ask me twice," smiles Boswell.

"Well help yourself," says Auntie Peggy. "We have bacon, sausage, grits, eggs and biscuits. There is coffee and juice if you like. So, Boswell will you bless the food?"

The request surprises Boswell. He cannot remember the last time he was asked to bless some food. His religious rigor has gone lacking ever since he left home for college. God and he have not been on speaking terms for a while and it's not that God has not tried. But being forced to perform on the spot is one of Boswell's greatest talents. Therefore, without missing a beat Boswell states a blessing of the food like he was a deacon of a church. His blessing even surprises Michelle and causes a smile to appear on her face. As Boswell loads up his plate Auntie Nanette pulls Michelle to the side. "Michelle, you are the talk of the family now."

"Why is that Auntie?"

"Well you were quite outgoing last night and you put some of those young folk to shame on the dance floor."

Michelle blushes, "Well Auntie, I like to dance what I can say. Last night, I felt a connection to the music and the people but I tell you today I am paying for it. My feet are still a little sore."

"You made my heart glad last night. I was so happy that you had a good time. Oops, we better get some food before your better half eats it all up."

They look over at the table and Boswell's plate is filled with food. Once the group is settled with their plates, Boswell takes a biscuit to his mouth and proclaims, "These biscuits are unbelievable. Michelle we have to get the recipe."

In Search of a Good Feeling

Michelle replies, "Hey I do not want to know how they are made I just desire to enjoy another person's handiwork and therefore I can keep their memory."

After finishing his second biscuit Boswell asks, "So, does either one of you know anything more about our ancestor J.S. other than what was read last night during the history? I never knew the family history before yesterday. It gave me an emotional chill and I felt such a connection last night to everyone. I was buzzing the rest of the night after hearing the history."

"I did notice a change in you last night. So, it was reading of the history. Ok, it makes sense now, but all I know is what was read. Maybe Nanette knows more than that since she was on the organizing committee," says Auntie Peggy.

"Well I do know a little more. There was some talk of J.S. being a highly skilled blacksmith and made money for his master by being hired out to different plantations. Rumor had it that the family is so diverse because J.S. planted his seed wherever he went."

"Wow, that's deep," says Boswell. "My ancestor could have been a skilled craftsman and a great lover all in one. I really need to find out more about my ancestors. I could be a prince and not know it."

"Boy, laughs Auntie Peggy, you are silly, but if you are interested in your people, you need to spend more time around your people so that you can heard the stories. Remember we are your family."

"Ok, I understand your point. I have been out of the loop too long," says Boswell. "By the way, I had an interesting conversation with a man named Charles Thornton. Do either one of you know anyone by that name? He said that he knew my daddy and granddaddy."

The sisters smile at each other. Auntie Nanette is the first to speak. "Charles Thornton, yes we know of him, and even knew him, but Charles is dead. He passed 10 years ago."

"No," says Boswell. "Dead! That cannot be. I spoke to him today down in the lobby when I went to get some coffee this morning."

"Are you sure Boswell?" says Auntie Peggy. "I attended his funeral. Nanette had to work but I was there. Charles Thornton is dead. I was there."

Boswell shakes his head in disbelief. "He talked about picking cotton and how Daddy did not like to pick cotton so he went to the army."

"Well whoever you talked to was right on that accord. Your daddy hated picking cotton, beans or anything," laughs Auntie Peggy.

"I can remember as a little boy he used to just cry all day because he disliked being in that hot sun, but Charles Thornton is dead. His resting place in over behind the church in the colored folks section of the graveyard not far from our oldest brother, your Uncle Leroy's grave."

"Colored? Who say colored these days? Auntie you are dating yourself," laughs Boswell.

"Sometime nephew dear you are in a situation so long that you never knew that it has changed. Being in a small town like this does that to a person," remarks Auntie Pat with a smile.

Boswell is beaten and the voices in his head are not helping Maybe he dreamed about Mr. Thornton or maybe he is real If he exists or not is too much for him to focus on

In Search of a Good Feeling

at the moment but the idea of a grave yard visit heighten his interest. "So," asks Boswell, "Does anyone knows the location of J.S's grave?"

"No Boswell. There are rumors and myths about the location, but some say his spirit never rested and on a clear night you hear chank, chank, that's J. S. with his hammer putting a shoe on a horse. Others say that he is buried somewhere over near Charleston and died doing a job for his master. He had so many children in the area they buried him somewhere around there. There is another rumor that he made so much money for his master that he was able to buy himself out of slavery and settled some place up north, but again no one knows."

Michelle is quiet, just watching and learning more about Boswell, his people and how he interacts with people other than herself. She wipes her hand with the napkin and then slides them on top of her belly. This has become her default comfort position. It allows Michelle to be in touch with the life form inside of her while at the same time being able to interact with whatever is happening before her. Her quietness gets Auntie Nannette's attention.

"Michelle, you ok?" asks Auntie Nannette. "You a mite quiet over there. Did you have enough to eat, there is plenty more…want some coffee? You did not eat that much."

"No ma'am, I'm fine. Sometimes I get quiet and just listen. Besides my feet are hurting a little. If I may, could I put my feet up? They feel a little swollen."

"No problem, I will get a stool for you." Auntie Nanette disappears thru the doorway and returns quickly with a foot stool. "Here baby," says Auntie Nanette as she places

Michelle's feet on the stool, "I hope this makes you feel better."

"Thank you, that's so sweet," says Michelle as she closes her eyes for a moment as Boswell continues to talk to his aunties.

"So aunties, do you guys believe in spirits?" Both of them look at each other and begin laughing.

"What so funny?"

"Why God is a spirit and they that worship must worship him in spirit and truth," quotes Auntie Pat.

"I must have missed that Sunday School lesson, but I do believe you."

For the moment both sisters are pondering their response, attempting to balance their Christian faith with their non-Christian belief in spirits. Auntie Nanette is the first to speak.

"Well Boswell, what you ask is a mighty good question which I need more time to think about, but for the sake of time I would say yes, I do believe in spirits."

"You what!" shouts Auntie Peggy who is sitting right next to her. "You believe in ghosts! Oh wait until I tell the church missionaries, they will be down here praying for you and anointing you with oil.

"I doubt that. Those women are scared of themselves, but remember my sister, people who live in glass houses should not throw stones. So anyway Boswell why do you ask about spirits?"

"Well I never have given them much thought until I came down here. It seems ever since I stepped out of the rental car I have been made aware of the presence of spirits. First, by Michelle then by Martha."

In Search of a Good Feeling

Hearing her name spoken causes Michelle to open her eyes and look in the direction of the conversation.

"Who is Martha?" asks Auntie Peggy.

"She works around the house where Michelle was born, doing cooking, and cleaning."

"So she is a day worker, a maid?" pops in Aunt Nanette.

"No, she is not a maid, nor is she a day worker because I never hear the Watermans tell her to do anything. She is just there…more of an assistant. Hmmm what I do know is that she is a wonderful cook and has a connection with spirits. Michelle, please help me explain Martha."

Michelle quickly resumes her sleeping posture and shrinks a little in her chair. The last thing she wants to do is to try to explain Martha, so she fakes like she is sleeping.

"Oops, I think she is taking a nap. Let her sleep because when she awakens, I want to go over to see Charles Thornton's grave site before going back to Charleston tomorrow."

Michelle smiles to herself, it worked.

"So how old is Martha?" asks Auntie Nanette.

"That's a good question. Michelle said that Martha was there while she was growing up so she must be as old as you auntie but it's hard to figure how old black folks are sometimes. She seems to have an ageless youth about her combined with a spiritual wisdom."

"Like I told you before, I may know a Martha in passing but the Martha I knew would be more than 80 now.

"Well, I do not think we are talking about the same person. She is quite a spooky person but there is something that draws me closer and closer to her.

"She sounds spooky to me but changing the subject, is Michelle's last name is Waterman?"

"Yes ma'am."

"Peggy, didn't you say that you knew some Watermans out of Charleston?"

"I did but I think I got them mixed up with some Watermans out of Sumter. My memory fails me sometimes."

"No doubt. Like last week when you forgot what day it was," laughs Auntie Nannette.

"Remember what you told me about people in glass houses? So, Boswell you think that Michelle and Martha have some awareness of those in the spirit world?" asks Auntie Peggy with a sneer.

"Yes ma'am I do. Martha's awareness is stronger than Michelle's though. Martha told me that the spirits like me and to trust them...whatever that means."

"We, Black folks will believe in anything that will allow us to escape the pain that we are facing...be it spirits, roots... but my faith is in Jesus!" shouts Auntie Peggy as she jumps and struts around the table with her hand in the air saying repeatedly, "Alleluia" over and over again.

"Darn it Boswell, now you got her started," laughs Aunt Nannette. "Well whatever you believe in Boswell, its personal and do not let anyone take that away from, you not even your aunties."

"Yes ma'am," says Boswell. He gets up and gives his aunties great big hugs.

Michelle awakes from her fake sleep and does the same. Auntie Peggy returns from the kitchen with a bag filled with biscuits and gives them to Boswell.

"Warm them up in a micro wave for about 30 seconds and they will be as good as new. Speaking for myself and silly sister, we have really enjoyed your company and please

In Search of a Good Feeling

come back really soon. We would like to meet the new addition as soon as possible. Boswell if you are still wanting to go to the grave yard turn right on Fish Road and go for about two miles until you get to Euclid Street. Make a right and travel another 15 minutes. The grave yard is on your right. Oak Tree Cemetery…you will not miss it.

CHAPTER 19

Michelle and Boswell sit on a bench in a gazebo located behind the church. Built in the 1840's, the gazebo has two wooden benches facing each other with a hand laid red brick floor. Orange trumpet vines cover the gazebo on the sides and on top. Several honey bees dart in and out of the orange flowers quickly sampling their sweetness. Boswell can faintly hear the sound of a lawn mower as it criss-crosses over someone's nearby front lawn. Suddenly the sun peaks through the gazebo's over hanging branches softly kissing Michelle's face. Boswell is struck by how Michelle's countenance seems to glow in the sun beam. He reaches over to touch Michelle's hand, she smiles. Behind the gazebo lay a sea of head stones in various shapes, sizes and conditions. The couple walk hand in hand into the church's graveyard in search of clues to their past. Soon they split up using the lay out map given to them by one of the graveyard caretakers to identify the headstones. Boswell sees the names on the tombstones;

Lewis Meckel
Born Jan. 30 1828
Died Oct. 30, 1902

In Search of a Good Feeling

Elizabeth Nester, 1844-1935 with an upright tombstone is next to Peter Nester 1834-1890. Boswell wonders if they were married or just brother and sister. Alice Freed born 1878 died 1884...only lived 6 years. Michelle ponders what she died from at such a young age.

They pass into the part of the graveyard where the African – Americans are buried. A fence separates the two worlds. This section of the graveyard is less pleasing to the eye and more run down than the front portion. There is overgrowth everywhere, some of the tombstones have been knocked down and the seating benches are in need of a paint job. The Spanish moss that is growing from the oak trees gives the graveyard an eerie look.

Before driving over to the cemetery, Auntie Nannette warned the couple to be prepared for the apparent difference in appearance between the two sections. She stated that there is a cemetery society for the white northern section who does the upkeep for the grave sites. When the church congregation turned from white to black there was a decision made to sale the church and the graveyard. The purchase agreement included the sale for the northern section where all the whites are buried to be maintain by the Oak Tree cemetery society but there was no mention in the agreement about who is in charge of the upkeep of the south section where only African-Americans and a couple of poor whites are buried. There is no map identifying the location of any of the graves. Michelle looks around thinking, *The graves on our property are in much better condition than this place. There must be a lot of families being haunted by spirits around here.*

One of the headstone reads:

Anthony Webb

Gone Home
Edith, wife of Miles Thomas.
Born in 1849. Died 1919.

Michelle attempts to visualize the life of Edith Thomas with very little to go on other than a name and a couple of dates. How did it feel to be born into slavery? Was Edith a house slave or field slave? The baby began to move inside of Michelle forcing her to stop what she was doing and sit down on one of the benches. She remembers the sisters saying that the last time they had visited the cemetery there was something about being there that was unsettling. She realizes the feeling that the sisters spoke about is a sense of sadness. She detects it all around her, like voices are calling out from the graves searching for a connection. They are tired of being forgotten and seek some type of recognition. Michelle immediately says a quiet prayer of thanks to God and for the voices of the spirits to be recognize.

Boswell turns around to find Michelle in this solemn state with tears in her eyes. Before he can speak Michelle says, "Boswell, I can feel the sadness of the spirits here. This is not a place of rest so I prayed. Yes, I do not know the last time I prayed for anyone, but Michelle Waterman prayed for them and now I feel better."

Boswell nods in agreement, takes her hand and remains silent in his own thoughts. He too feels the sadness in the air, quite a different feeling than he experienced at the graveyard on the Waterman Plantation. They find the grave sites of some of Boswell's family members in the location where his aunts had told them over by the right corner of the property. Auntie Peggy had explained that no one in the family has

In Search of a Good Feeling

been buried in that cemetery since her brother Leroy twenty years ago. After following his aunties' directions, the couple finds Boswell's late Uncle Leroy's grave. His headstone reads:

> Leroy Wilkerson
> A Man of all Seasons
> Birth: 3/3/35
> Death: 5/6/85

Around his grave were as scattering of other possible family members such as Wilma Lou Wilkerson, Paul Wilkerson and Fred Wilkerson. A couple of feet left of Boswell's uncle's grave Michelle discovers the grave of the late Charles Thornton. It is very poorly kept with weeds growing around it and there is a broken off branch of a nearby tree on top of the grave. Michelle waves frantically for Boswell to come over.

"Wow, you found his grave."

"Barely, I really almost tripped over it."

Boswell looks around the grave site. He is sadden about what he sees. He reads the head stone.

> Charles Thornton
> Rest in Peace.
> Or
> Give Them Hell
> Born 4/4/1920 Death 6/ 6/1985

"It does not look like anyone has been here for a while," Boswell tells Michelle. "I will be right back."

"What!" yells Michelle.

She looks around and Boswell is gone. His absence fills her with apprehension. There is a stillness in the air which frightens Michelle. Then a mosquito buzzes by her face, a bird chirps from a nearby tree and slowly the sounds of the cemetery come alive to her ear. She automatically begins to rub her stomach to calm herself and the baby. The moments seem to stretch into days and then weeks and she feels so alone. Then she hears a soft hum all around, it was low but not mournful…it was soothing. Michelle begins to relax and fear is vanishing from her body.

Boswell reappears after five minutes with some garden tools, a garbage bag, and gloves. By this time Michelle is furious with him and he knows it.

"You left me in a grave yard…you left me!" she yells trembling.

"I'm sorry, I'm so sorry."

"Please do not ever leave me again. You promise?"

"Yes, I promise Michelle, never again." Boswell attempts to hold Michelle but she pushes him away and just stands a distance from him. It takes Michelle a while to regain her composure. In the meantime Boswell is cleaning up around Charles Thornton's grave site. He picks the huge branch that is covering the grave and places it next to the fence.

As he bends down to begin picking up some of the debris Michelle's hand reaches down and touches him. Boswell immediately stands up and takes her hand and wraps it around his body. He whispers in her ear, "I will never ever leave you again." He kisses her awaiting lips as they embrace. "When I saw the condition of Mr. Thornton's grave site, I wanted to do something, so I decided to clean it up."

"So where did you get all of this stuff?"

In Search of a Good Feeling

"Well, I figured that grave caretaker probably had some type of equipment, so I asked and he agreed to let me use these items. He said that it's a shame that no one regularly takes care of the south section."

"Ok… well I will help…at least one spirit will stop haunting somebody."

"Huh?"

"Somebody told one of my ancestors that a fellow slave owner had desecrated his slave burial grounds by allowing his cattle to trample through it. The spirits of the dead slaves sought retribution so they haunted the slave master's plantation until his death."

"You don't say. So the man I talked to could have been a spirit?"

"I am not saying. Let's just hurry up because it's hot and the baby is talking to me fierce."

"Ok, you just sit there until our son calms down, this should not take too long."

"Once again silly man, she is not a he."

It takes Boswell about twenty minutes to clean up Charles Thornton's grave site. Sweat is pouring down his face as Michelle sits watching him. Although it is hot and the bugs are beginning to be problematic she has to admit that it has been a good use of time. The grave site does look much better and the baby has calmed down. Michelle watched as the grave site goes from a disgrace to a place of rest for a deceased soul. Through the transformation of the area she is aware of a difference in the feeling in the cemetery since they arrived. The feeling of sadness is no longer present. It has been replaced slowly with a sense of compassion.

Boswell stops and looks at his finished project and then at Michelle. "Ok, I am finished. Hopefully the soul of Charles Thornton finds his grave site a place of rest and stops haunting innocent people like me."

"I am proud of you. You have done a wonderful job, but what's this business about someone haunting innocent people? Did I miss something?"

"Have you been listening? Shsssssh. Anyway, let's go, it's time for a shower."

As Boswell gathers up the items that he has borrowed, Michelle stands before the grave of Charles Thornton holding her stomach while softly humming a song then motions for Boswell to join her. She takes his hand and says a short prayer for the soul of Charles Thornton to be allowed to rest in peace. Boswell stands speechless. He is unable to move from the grave site. It is like his feet are in cement and for some reason he is not to move from this spot until he can absorb what just occurred. Voices speak to him out of the grave saying, "Thank you." He looks to Michelle "Did you hear that?"

"Hear what? All I hear are birds. There you go hearing things again. Are you coming?"

"Nope, not right this minute. I'm just going to sit over there under that tree on the bench and listen to the birds before leaving. I think it will do my soul well just to rest for a moment. Let's just sing that song that you were humming. As the bugs fly around their heads and sweat rolls down their faces Michelle and Boswell along with a chorus of birds sang softly,

In Search of a Good Feeling

Soon I will be done
With the troubles of the world
Troubles of the world
Troubles of the world
Soon I will be done
Troubles of the world
I'm going home to live with God.

No more weepin' and wailin'
No more weepin' and wailin'
No more weepin' and wailin'
I'm going home to live with my Lord.

CHAPTER 20

Their ride back to the Waterman's plantation is uneventful. After stopping by his aunts before leaving, the couple travel on their way down route 26. Traffic is light but for some unknown reason everyone seems to be in a hurry. Passenger cars, 4 wheel drive vehicles and trucks are zooming past Boswell like he is standing still. It's called driving Southern style putting your foot to the pedal or eat my exhaust. Driving has never been Boswell's thing. He cannot understand why people are in love with driving especially long distances. He sees driving as repetitive nothingness, so once he moved to Philly he stopped. He gave it up with very little regret. Living in Philly, although quite difficult at times can be a great place for a person to decrease their carbon footprint by using public transportation. So both Michelle and Boswell chose the road less traveled by deciding not to drive. His friends sometimes question him about the decision and Boswell replies if someone can give up meat and people applaud them is not giving up driving a greater sacrifice than meat? The question generally makes his friends speechless and they change the subject, while Boswell laughs deep inside of himself.

In Search of a Good Feeling

Although Summerville is only about 35 miles from Charleston they seem to be worlds apart. Summerville is rural Southern while Charleston is historic Southern with self-imposed class. While sitting in the lobby of the motel earlier, Boswell picked up a brochure which identified some of Summerville's finer points such as being the best place in the world if one has a lung and throat disorder due to the dry air and sandy conditions. It is also recognized as the birth place for sweet tea, but that claim is being disputed. Charleston in contrast had a welcome sign at the airport that Boswell noticed as he walked thru it boasting to visitors about being named the best city in the world by some national magazine. When he saw the sign, Boswell wondered if there is somewhere on the docks of Charleston's seaport a banner saying, "Welcome to America", where 40% of all slaves landed thus acknowledging Charleston's role in slavery as the slave capital of America. He smiled and doubted its existence. The difference is also reflected in the landscape between the two cities. Boswells notices that the country side from Summerville slowly changed from farmland to light industries the closer he drives to Charleston. A truck full with fruit and vegetables passes Boswell. He wonders if the vegetables were picked by hand or machine or by Blacks or Mexicans. He imagines his father picking watermelons while planning his escape not unlike a slave who seeks his freedom escaping up north. Both were just waiting for the right time when those in charge were unaware of their movements. They took a great risk to be free to see life on their own terms. Boswell wonders if he would have been that brave to run.

Boswell turns off route 26 onto route 17 and travels that for a while before making a right on State Road 11 following

Grandpa's directions to a tee. It's about noon and Michelle's friend, the sun, is making his presence known and making sure that he is not forgotten. Boswell looks across the seat to find his navigator fast asleep. He has noticed that she is beginning to sleep longer now and has added short naps to her repertoire of new behaviors. Boswell continues to have difficulty wrapping his head around the idea that within her stomach lies their combined effort to populate the world. He wonders what his mother will say when one of his sisters tells her that she is a grandmother, because the news will not be coming from him. He knows that his sisters will be thrilled, but his mother's reaction is unknown. Maybe, he thinks, he will not tell them anything and just one day surprised them with the news.

He laughs to himself, *I wonder if Michelle's whiteness would be a concern of the twin? Black women can become very strange animals about their men interacting outside of their race. They need to understand that my choice has little to do with skin color but more about me attempting to get my needs met no manner what race, ethnicity, or size the woman might be.*

He remembers a discussion the twins had with him about dating and how they left upset with his equal opportunity dating view. Boswell told them that dating should not be based on race but on interests so that everyone has an equal opportunity to be a potential date. So when they find out about the relationship the twins probably will not be surprised...just a little disappointed.

Michelle opens her eyes and realizes that she is no longer dreaming. Yes, the car is moving and Boswell is driving it but it's not a dream. She stretches while smiling in his

In Search of a Good Feeling

direction as bits and pieces of her dream comes back to her. They were driving somewhere going very fast but not on a road. A flock of birds were leading them over a forest as the full moon waved at them. That's all she remembers. She starts to tell Boswell about the dream but she thinks better of it. With all of the unexplained things that have occurred on this trip she figures it would just be one more thing to explain.

Before they left to visit his folks, Michelle told Boswell that there are some papers that Grandpa wanted them to see when they return back from Summerville. Although he desired more details about the papers, Michelle refused to tell him anything else and asked him to trust her. Honestly, Michelle did not know anything since the contents of the papers were not made know to her and she promised Grandpa not to talk about them again until they returned. So she made a deal with Boswell. If he did not ask any more about the papers, she would massage his back. So his questions were replaced with deep mmms and ahhs along with a couple of well-placed kisses.

Michelle looks out of the car to notice a lone bird flying in the air ahead of them seeming to announce their arrival. It appears to be saying, "Home again, Home again, the Queen is Home again." They pass old man Bray's place with still no signs of him being around. The hanging Spanish moss on the old weeping willow tree appeared to be waving hello to the couple as the car sped toward its destination.

Boswell turns up the long driveway and the sun is there waiting for Michelle to appear. As Boswell pulls the car in to the backyard a smile comes to the couple's faces because there sitting on the porch is Martha. They exit the car just as a flock of birds take flight while the spirits of the fields acknowledge their arrival with a shout of hello. Boswell is stun by the reception but Michelle acts like nothing has occurred.

He looks towards Michelle and asked," Did you hear that?"

"Hear what the birds?"

"No the voices?"

"Here we go again Boswell. Just let it go."

"But....." before he can say another word Michelle is running up the steps to greet Martha.

"It looks like the birds were correct," says Martha."

"About what?" asks Michelle.

"Well 15 minutes ago I looked outside and saw a flock of crows beginning to perch out here on that there mahogany tree over there. I came outside to see what the fuss was all about and then I heard a crow calling out in the distance. By that time I figured out what was occurring so I went back in the house and fixed you guys some iced tea and ham sandwiches. And I did not forget your oatmeal raisin cookies."

Michelle quickly looks over to the table and there is a pitcher of iced tea, two glasses, two meaty ham sandwiches and a bowl full of cookies.

"Now that's true love," smiles Michelle. "So Martha the birds really told you that we were coming?" "Remember what I told you about asking questions. So where is Boswell?"

In Search of a Good Feeling

Michelle rubs her stomach and points in the direction of the car. "He is getting the bags. Watch it because he is hearing things again. Are my folks around?"

"Nope, but they will be here in a bit. Your Grandpa had to go to the bank for something."

Before another word could be spoken they hear a loud noise behind them and turn around quickly to find Boswell has tripped up the stairs with the luggage. There is a moment of silence as no one seems to know what to do or say.

Finally, Martha says, "Well Boswell I heard that you were hearing things but I did not know that you were also going blind."

Boswell looks up from his position on the floor of the deck with luggage scattered all around him and burst out laughing which causes the women to join in with him.

Michelle helps pull him to his feet saying, "I am sorry that I laughed sweetie but you looked so funny."

"I only stumbled because I heard my name being mentioned," remarks Boswell.

Martha reaches between Michelle to hand Boswell a glass of iced tea. She looks him in the eye. "I glad you are back Boswell. Remember whatever you hear it is for you and no one else. We all do not hear and see the same thing."

Boswell says "Yes ma'am and thanks for the tea."

"Thank the birds Boswell, not me. Like I said before, the spirits like you."

"I'm glad, I think, but how do you that the spirits like me?"

"Ask Michelle what I told her about asking questions. But it is better that they like you than they do not like you, like some around here. Drink your tea and remember I ain't no maid. I have things to do."

Boswell obeys, drinking his iced tea slowly, allowing it to tickle his throat with its cold sweetness. "That's good tea."

"You silly." Martha laughed as she pats Boswell on his head. "Good tea. Everything I touch is good. Now go and help Michelle with them there bags before she falls down like you."

Boswell looks behind him to see Michelle struggling with the luggage and turns quickly back to Martha only to find her gone. He takes the bags and gives Michelle a peck on the cheek while saying, "My dear, I am at your service. By the way what did Martha tell you about asking questions?"

Michelle laughs, "She got you too I see. Well it's like this, do not ask questions that you do not want answers for because in the end you are responsible for any knowledge you gain for the answer."

"Well that sounds like a reasonable request."

"It's only reasonable if the answer benefits you, but what happens if the answer sends you down a deep hole?"

"Hmm, I never thought of that. Well I have been warned," says Boswell as he takes the bags into the house.

Not long after they arrive, Grandpa and Grandma Lizzie return from their trip to town. They enter the kitchen with big smiles on their faces greeting their visitors with hugs and kisses. Martha had their glasses ready filled with iced tea and left two slices of pound cake out for their dining pleasure.

Michelle notices something that she has not seen before. Grandpa had a leather pouch in his possession. After the merriment of the greeting ends, Grandpa excuses himself, takes his iced tea, a slice a cake and the pouch into the study. Grandma Lizzie in the meantime is conversing with Boswell asking him about his family reunion.

In Search of a Good Feeling

Ten minutes later, Grandpa reappears back into kitchen and motions Michelle and Boswell to come with him. They go into the stud. It is one of the few places in the house that Boswell has never entered. The room has two windows with a book shelf lining one of the walls. One side of the room is covered with awards and blue ribbons that Grandpa has won over the years with his hogs. In the middle of the room Grandpa has placed a folding table with a stack of papers on it. Grandpa pulls our three folding chairs and places them around the table.

"Alright, Michelle and Boswell, I have brought you in here to show you the Waterman's papers. I keep many of the final documents in a safe deposit box at the bank. A lot of what you are going to see are copies of originals or copies that have been retyped from the originals. I have laid them out in different piles. You are free to read what you want but you cannot take anything out of this room, understand?"

"Yes sir."

"I am going to leave you two along. Take your time reading the documents but remember that knowledge about your past has the power to free someone and at the same time placing them in a cell. What is done is done. Learn from it."

Grandpa left Michele and Boswell in the study with the Waterman family papers. At first the couple is motionless just staring at the stacks of papers in front of them. Then Boswell picks up the first paper from the first stack and reads it aloud.

Anthony Webb

Waterman History
Liverpool to Charleston
A time to reflect,
The first hundred years

On a shipping dock on Liverpool's waterfront a young lad looks out across the vast water. With the wind blowing in his sandy hair he makes a promise to his friend that one day he would cross that sea to live in the New World because he deserves better than Liverpool can offer a man of his humble background.

James Waterman was born in the year 1780 in Bootle, a small town outside of Liverpool, England. Born to a poor family, the name of his father and mother is not known, Rumor had it that James took up the last name Waterman to rid himself of his terrible past. Although born poor, James worked hard in Liverpool's ship yard. First, becoming a cabin boy then after a couple of years at sea he switched to working on the docks building boats. James became a successful ship builder. First small vessels and later larger transatlantic ships. He married Jill Brown in 1805 and to this union was born Walter James in 1808 and one daughter Mary Lou born 1810. Mary Lou died shortly after birth. He came to America in 1807 after a successful ship building business in Liverpool and purchased land outside of Charleston in 1809. He died in 1842 six months after the death of his wife. Walter James married Lynette Walsh in 1835. To that union came three sons Walter James II, Matthew, and Timothy. When the Civil War broke out Matthew and Walter James II joined the Southern cause and perished fighting at the second Battle of Fort Wagner.

In Search of a Good Feeling

Neither were married. Timothy, the youngest was left back to help his father take care of the estate. He married his childhood sweetheart Michelle Richer two years later and they had two children Timothy II and Julia. Through shrewd negotiations, payment of fines and a benevolent view of the Northern position Walter James was able to keep ownership of the Whitman plantation although the main house was destroyed and most of the valuables were looted by Union troops.

This begins the resurrection of the Waterman family. Timothy with the help of neighbors and hired help began to rebuild the main house of the Waterman Plantation. Mr. and Mrs. Walter James Waterman did not live long enough to live in the new house. In 1868 Walter James was kicked in his head while shoeing a horse and died instantly. After her husband's death, Mrs. Water James Waterman moved in with her sister in Charleston and never returned to the plantation. She died in 1880 of what some say of a broken heart. Thus describes in some detail the first 100 years of the Waterman Family.

Written by Howard Waterman

"Wow," says Michelle. "Howard Waterman is my father, and he must have been the historian for the family. I'm not surprised, he was always telling me this and that about the family. But hearing you say his name sent a shiver down my spine. I have not heard his name in a while." Michelle becomes silent for a moment as a vision of her father appears before her. "Yep that's my dad," she says with a smile. After basking in the spotlight with memories of her father

Michelle picks a document titled, "Last Will and Testament of James Waterman." It is a copy of the original document but it is typed in an Old English font to make it appear to be old. She reads….

I leave and Bequeath to my only son James Waterman II, three tracts of land, two which contains one hundred fifty acres each the other containing three hundred acres all of them on which I now live with all dwellings on land also 12 Negroes; Vissy, Shatar, Fillis, Latty, Farmer, Amoutah, Judith, Ned, Shem, Toney, Joe and Derry Jack with their increase with 10 horses and saddles, and his cattle to him and his heirs forever, in case he should live till the age of 21 years or is married if not to sold at public sale and equally divided amongst all my siblings in England.

The reading of this portion of the Will and Testament of James Waterman makes the couple speechless. Not only by what is said in the will, but how the words have come alive in their minds. Neither look at each other, but stare aimlessly into space pondering on the words that they have heard spoken to life. Boswell slides back in his chair with his hand on his head while Michelle picks up the document to silently read more of it. She stops half way down and points at the document saying to Boswell, "This is the section that I was telling you about…"

Boswell did not move from his slouched position in the chair, the voices in his minds are beginning to stage a war so Michelle reads the following out loud to him.

In Search of a Good Feeling

The creation of the burial place for the slaves

A burial place located somewhere pass the Apple Bend Creek will always be maintained by my descendants to show respect to the slaves that were under our charge. If this request is not honored by my descendants the ownership of the Waterman Plantation and all that is on it would be lost and transferred to the state.

Boswell looks in Michelle's direction. Her eyes are wet and she is rubbing her stomach. He knows that this information is having an effect on her and it is not positive. To lighten the mood Boswell says in a joking manner, "Your ancestors are strange people. They enslave someone, but they provide a burial space to honor them because they are scared that they will be haunted to death….strange very strange." But unfortunately for Boswell the comment goes over Michelle's head and she starts crying.

He goes to comfort her and makes a comment about stopping. She looks into his eyes saying," No Boswell we have less than one day left. I am a researcher. I uncover secrets. That is what I have been trained to do. Let me do what I do, it will be fine." With those words of clarity they hug, kiss and went back reading.

Martha knocks on the door and quietly slides a pitcher of iced tea, and a pile of oatmeal cookies onto the table. "I thought you two might get hungry…enjoy." Before anyone can answer, Martha disappears out of the door. For the next three hours Michelle and Boswell travel back in time to the 1800's in attempt to reconstruct the world that the documents describes.

Michelle opens up a folder labeled "Burial Place". Inside the folder were two sheets of paper, the first containing a drawing of the burial place in the woods. The drawing helped Michelle remember how the burial place is laid out with each mound represented by a square. There are ten rows neatly spaced with a twelve mounds in each row. The rows are lettered from A to J and each mound in the row is numbered from 1-12. Each square has a number and letter on them. The mounds in the first row are labeled 1A, 1B.

A light wind blows the second paper off the table. As Michelle attempts to retrieve it she looks outside and notices the change in weather. The old weeping willow tree branches were swaying back and forth as the sky darkened. Birds began to take flight, going wherever birds go when a storm is approaching.

Michelle remarks, "Wow, sweetie it's getting very dark outside."

Boswell glances up from his reading as the rain starts to fall. Before Michelle can close the window they hear a big roar of thunder followed by a flash of lightning.

The ceiling fan slowly stops and a couple seconds later they hear Grandpa say, "Damn it, we are out of electricity. The lighting must have hit the power generator."

The news deflates the couple's mood but they knew they needed a break from researching the history, so they decided to abandon their work and join the rest of the family.

On the way to the front porch Boswell remarks, "This storm reminds me of the one that occurred when we were in the burial place a couple days ago.

Michelle nods in agreement but keeps her thought to herself. *There is some connection between the storm and the burial place. It's like when we get close to finding out something the powers that be send a storm to stop us. It's the darnest thing. I would not believe it if someone told me, but since I am experiencing it, I have to. I wonder what they are preventing us from finding out about the burial place."*

They find Grandpa, and Grandma Lizzie sitting in their rockers on the front porch watching the storm like it was a television show. The couple take their place on the porch's three seat glider and they too become observers of the natural phenomena. Nothing is said for a while. The only sounds are creaks of the porch furniture accenting the symphony of rain and thunder.

After a series of rumbles of thunder and flashes of lightning Grandma Lizzie is the first to speak. "I have always loved summer storms. As a child we would come out on our old leaking porch and just watch the rain come down and when the storm lessened we always would ask our mama could we go out and play in the rain. She would say, 'You guys can go out and play, but you must be careful about them there snakes...they and frogs come up when it rains in the country.' That was enough to scare us kids from playing outside in the rain. But one day one of our dogs got bitten by a snake and I never liked snakes after that ump... they are ugly slimy creatures."

"Well," says Boswell, "Where I am from we don't have snakes luring in the grass. So right after a storm like this we would race popsicle sticks in the street gutters before all the water disappeared into the sewer. Yes, those were the days."

The reflection on the past seemed to lighten the mood on the porch causing the conversational interaction to increase. The rain began to slack off, going from a storm to a very light mist then to nothing.

Martha appears on the porch with two lanterns and couple of flashlights. "Until the power returns no going into the icebox.. If you are hungry there is some chicken on a platter on the stove and a pitcher of iced tea on the table. Martha picks up one of the flashlights. "I brought these out just in case the lights do not come back on and one of you are still scare of the dark. I have flash lights here."

"I'm not scared of the dark…well not anymore," volunteers Michelle.

"What is that's all about? "Asks Boswell.

Grandpa pipes in, "Well when Michelle came to live with us she was afraid of the dark and being alone so for the first couple of weeks we made a sleeping area for her in our bedroom and she slept there. I gave her as flashlight, so after the day every night she went to sleep with that flashlight next to her."

"I was scared," Michelle adds. "I had never known the night to be so freaking dark. Where I was from we had streets lights so moving here was just a shock to my system. The darkness really scared me and it took me awhile to give up that flashlight. Ha ha."

Suddenly the porch ceiling fans began to move and looking out they saw old man Bray's house light up.

"Well I guess the power is back on," says Martha. "I will just put these back up until next time." Martha scoops up at the lanterns and flashlights and disappears into the house.

"Wait up Martha, I am coming inside with you. The mosquitoes are about to come out and I didn't spray myself yet," says Grandma Lizzie.

In Search of a Good Feeling

"Niter Martha and Grandma," yells Michelle. She turns to Grandpa. "Where does Martha live?"

"Remember what I told you about asking questions," says Grandpa.

"Yeah, Martha told me the same thing."

"Well the truth of the matters is I do not know. I have never inquired so do likewise."

"Yes sir."

Boswell gets up and motions for Michelle to come with him. "Grandpa, do not blame he. Remember she is a researcher and they all are nosey", laughs Boswell. "We better be getting back to what we were doing Michelle." He takes her hand and they walk back into the study. The couple quickly resume their research.

In one pile of documents labeled "Estate Purchases", Boswell sees a copy of an ad from the South Carolina Gazette stating 1847:

The forthcoming sale of Africans from the Windward and Rice Coast: All ages. Connected to the ad is a bill of sale for slaves.

Sale receipt of property

Bought: Slaves Date 1847
March 14Henry about 24 years of age for $1000.00
Clarissa about 13 years of age for $875.00
Guaranteed to be of sound mind and body
Slaves for life
Seller will forgo title and will defend the title of said African slaves
Sold by Lang& Hartfield

Although there were a couple more bills of sale in the pile Boswell did not bother with them. His interest is focused on the one in his hand. The voices in his head are going crazy asking him questions about Henry. *How did he feel about being a slave? Who gave him the name Henry? He's African, did they beat him?. What type of people can sale another human being? How did the Waterman Plantation justify their purchase of another human being?* The questions kept coming without any answers to quell the stream so Boswell places the bill of sale down and sips on some iced tea. The cold sweetness of the tea temporally buffers the voices.

Michelle is working from the same pile of documents as Boswell. Her hair is all over her head, with her researcher's eyes scanning every document that she touches looking to make sense of her family's history. Michelle sips her tea and munches on an oatmeal cookie while she looks blankly on one of the bill of sale. Suddenly she stops munching and tells Boswell to look at what she just found. Boswell hesitantly takes the document from her knowing that it would not be good news and reads:

Bill of Sale

KNOW ALL MEN BY THESE PRESENTS, That I, JS Kershaw
For and in consideration of the sum of one thousand dollars.
To sum in hand paid, at and before the sealing and delivery of these Presents,
by James Waterman

In Search of a Good Feeling

*(the receipt whereof I do hereby acknowledge)
have bargained and sold, and
by these Presents do bargain, sell, and deliver to
the said James
Waterman the male slave JS about 28 years of
age of sound mind
TO HAVE AND TO HOLD the said slave
unto the said James Waterman his Executors,
administrators, and Assigns: to his and this
only proper use and be hoof forever. In Witness
Whereof, I have hereunto set my Hand and Seal
Dated at Charleston on the 4th day of in the year of
our Lord, one thousand eight hundred and fifty
seven and in the 40th year of the Independence of
the United States of America.
Sealed and delivered*

In the presence of William E. Parker

The only thing you can hear in the room is the song of a whippoorwill in the nearby tree. Michelle is waiting for a reaction from Boswell in the form of a verbal response, however none is coming. This new information has even silenced the voices in his head. His initial reaction is to scream until he cannot scream anymore but instead there is calmness brewing inside of him. In looking at the history of Michelle's family, Boswell realizes that within these documents of misery he has found his own history tangled up inside of hers. Although the idea of being a slave on the Waterman's plantation is not a comforting one for Boswell, it does gives him light in a dark place. Instead of feeling sad, bewildered and angry, a sense of peace has intervene within him causing a smile to appear on his face.

Michelle notices the difference and just stands in awe not understanding the source of the transformation. Another whippoorwill joins in outside the window as Boswell begins to softy sing, Amazing Grace, how sweet the sound, that saved a wretch like me. I once was lost but now am found, was blind, but now, I see. The words of the song reverberate in his soul....he has a beginning.

Oh my God...Oh my God, He is really real. A piece of paper declares the existence of my ancestor JS. He is no longer a myth, he is real. The stories about him now have validity, yes he was a slave, bought by James Waterman for one thousand dollars at the age of 28 in 1857. Wait until I tell my aunties, they will be thrilled. Just the idea of finding some information about him that verifies his existence is amazing. Truly I am speechless.

Boswell just sits there examining the document line by line, inspecting the wording while trying to make sense of his find. He feels like a kid in a toy, the good feeling taking over his body, thoughts and emotions. Boswell wants to yell, cry, and sing at the same time. He looks over to Michelle attempting to find a way to share his feeling, but not in words though. He wants her to experience the same feelings that he is feeling and Boswell knows that words sometimes are not the best vehicle for transferring the power of a good feeling. He is stuck in his good mood so he gets up and starts dancing while waving the document in the air.

Michelle observes Boswell for moment. His face is full of expression. His body is moving to some far off beat, maybe to the beat of congas or to a James Brown record. Not understanding why, it could be the contagious nature of the

In Search of a Good Feeling

feeling but Michelle jumps up and joins her man dancing. Shaking her hips, and waving her hands in the air, dancing because it is time to celebrate. It's a feel good time. They dance allowing their bodies to connect with a feeling that has spread throughout their soul and communicating an expression of joy that mere words cannot describe. They end in each others arms with big smiles on their faces, hugging each other as tight as they can. Boswell looks Michelle in her eyes and says,

"Thank you my queen."

"The joy was all mine," replies Michelle.

They release each other grudgingly. In a desire to keep the feeling alive they move closer to each other at the table occasionally touching each other's hand. Soon they are back engaging in the search for something that they have no idea what they are looking for. There is a knock on the door and Martha appears with a pitcher of iced tea.

"Well, this is the last of the tea, you children alright? I heard some commotion in here a little earlier."

"Why thank you Martha, but we are fine. We were just having a celebration of joy," says Boswell.

"Well, I am glad that you can find joy in this here world, that's a good thing. OK, continue your celebration of joy but next time try not to wake the dead," laughs Martha as she disappears as quickly as she appears.

Boswell pours himself another glass of iced tea and begins to sort through some documents.

Suddenly Michelle yells out, "Boswell I do not know what you must be feeling now but you have to look at this, it's freaking incredible." Michelle hands him a copy of something that she has been reading.

Anthony Webb

Certificate of JS a Freeman of Color.

State of South Carolina. Be it known that on the day of the date hereof, JS a free Man of Color, personally appeared before the undersigned notary public of the State of aforesaid duly commissioned and qualified, residing outside the city of Charleston, South Carolina who exhibited to the said Notary a paper purporting to be a certified Copy of a deed of and having requested a copy of the original remaining with me, in the words and figures following, to wit, "To all who shall see these presents, Know ye that I, Walter James Waterman II of the County of High River in the State of South Carolina in consideration of the sum of Five Hundred dollars to me in hand paid by JS my negro man slave and for the further consideration of the esteem and regard, which I have heretofore had and entertained, and still have and entertain for the said JS in consequence of this long and faithful service as a servant; have emancipated and set free and by these presents do hereby emancipate and set free the said JS and liberate him from all claims whatsoever which I my heretofore have had or may now have on the said JS for his services as a slave or servant as aforesaid. And the said JS is hereby permitted and allowed to maintain and enjoy his freedom and emancipation as aforesaid from this day henceforth forever without any claim or hindrance of any person whatsoever and without an account to me or any other person whatsoever hereafter to be rendered so that neither I the said Walter James Waterman II or any other person for me or in my name, any right or interest to the services of the said JS as slave or servant as aforesaid, or any part thereof shall or will challenge claim or demand

In Search of a Good Feeling

at any time or times hereafter, but from all claims and demands therefore shall be wholly debarred and excluded by virtue of these presents. And in fine I the said Walter James Waterman II do hereby declare the said JS to be a free man of Color entitled to all the privileges and immunities secured to a free man of color by the law of the State of South Carolina and by the laws of the United States. In testimony whereof I have hereunto set my hand and seal, the twenty sixth day of April in the year eighteen hundred and sixty.

Signed: James Waterman II

After reading the words on the paper, the voices inside of Boswell's head go into action questioning every and anything. *Free what do you mean free? The Waterman, the family that the mother of your child belongs to enslaved your ancestor and he had to pay to be free. Free? Will your child be free or will the Waterman family make you paid for him? The family of the woman whom you love f bought and owned JS... owned like Grandpa Jed owns those hogs in the back. Free. How can a piece a paper make you free? He was a slave on the Waterman plantation. He might have stepped in the same places like you have stepped. Free! He is free paid for by his own black ass, but was he really free? You have slept with the enemy and now you have made them a baby that you now have to free. You have slave blood...the blood of JS and she, your lover has the master's blood...what type of baby will you create? Think Boswell, how do you feel? Aren't you angry? Don't you have the anger of your ancestor?* "QUIET," yells Boswell to the voices." Just Be Quiet". *I am confused...very confused...I am not connected to my feeling...nor do I know how I should feel....*

*Slavery bad…freedom good…past is the past…unmovable….
who should I blame…since blame is what we do… James
Waterman….make him a slave…buy him….hahaha….can't
do that…angry at Michelle?...she is the mother of our child…
only love for her…am I angry…yes…I am angry that my people
were sold like animals into slavery …yes who would not be…
angry at the thought of slavery…the articles of slavery…angry
because it was not their fault…they were victims…helpless
victims…made to feel less than human just for being the
wrong color…just in the wrong place at the wrong times…..I
am made to feel helpless also because I can do nothing about
the past…nothing…anger placed me into my own prison...
shackled me down like I was a slave...anger prevented me for
seeing …instead of being proud about my past…I avoided it….
unable to look it in the eye…shamed of it...I have allowed
others to tell my history with their own eyes and views…to
have nothing and to gain everything should be celebrated…not
to be shunned…stole from their country, brought to a strange
land and SURVIVED…THERE SHOULD BE SONGS
SUNG, POEMS WRITTEN AND MONUMENTS BUILT
for what my ancestors had to overcome…So I am no longer
confused… anger can no longer hold me in a cage and control
my thoughts…feeling of shame have no place to reside in me
other have celebrated their captivity and survival...so will I….I
am free now and no longer blind…let the celebration begin…*

Boswell is immediately taken back to that day when his ancestor JS gained his freedom. He feels the joy, apprehension, pride, fear and hope all colliding into one at the moment when James Waterman II hands JS his ticket to freedom. A sheet of paper that proclaims his legal status as a free man was all that's it took. A couple of lines on a sheet of

In Search of a Good Feeling

paper that were more powerful than the words on Boswell's degree. A good feeling called victory runs through his body as Boswell places his head in his hands and just starts crying. Crying the pain of his ancestors out of him, the pain of the unknown, the pain of just floating unattached to anyone or anything. Being shut out of his ancestor's birth country and shunned in the country of his birth, Boswell has now found a rock to cleave onto until he gets his footing.

Michelle watches as Boswell goes from one emotional state to another one. She does not attempt to comfort him, but allows him to be. Michelle knew that comfort is not what Boswell needs, but release is what's required, letting go of all that has been weighing him down without him knowing. She whispers softly, "Cry my sweetheart. Cry so the hurt that you have kept hidden can be washed away with your tears allowing the good to emerge from within you. Cry my sweet heart because crying is good for the soul."

Boswell looks up acknowledging Michelle's presence with a smile. She hands him a tissue to wipe his face but Boswell refuses the offer.

"Thanks my dear," he says, "but I'd rather have a wet face than to wipe these tears away. These tears represent something deep inside of me...they came from a place that I did not know existed. I believe to just wipe them away would not honor them so I will let them be."

Unable to resist another moment Michelle suddenly grabs Boswell and begins kissing his face. As she graces his face with her lips she says, "So let me wet your face with my kisses also, let me kiss your tears that run down your face tasting your saltiness. Allow my kisses to represent my love for you that if allowed may have the ability to replace hurt with softness."

Birds continue to sing outside filling the air with a melody of sound while Michelle and Boswell communicate at a level much deeper than words. A loud hoot from an owl reminds the couple of the lateness of the hour. Boswell realizes that he has not heard a siren since he arrived in the south. The night sounds consist of crickets chirping, a hooting owl and an occasional dog barking. He takes Michele's hand as they walk to the backyard. The night sky is lit up with stars. The couple looks up at God's handy work until the mosquitoes force them to quickly end their star gazing. They separate as they go into the house. Michelle kisses Boswell on the cheek and states that she will see him in the morning.

Boswell watches Michelle go up the steps rubbing her stomach. He wanders in to the kitchen in search of one last cookie. As Boswell takes the top off the cookie jar he hears, "Hasn't your mama told you about eating sweets so late at night?"

Boswell turn quickly to see Martha sitting in a chair at the kitchen table. "Wow Martha you scared the heck out of me. I thought that you left. Didn't you?"

"Boswell sometimes you have to answer your own question. Now get you one, OK, two cookies and get to bed because you have a big day tomorrow. It is time you go back home. Philly is calling your name."

"Yes ma'am. We fly out tomorrow night. Philly here we come."

"Remember Boswell, when you do not expect anything…. you receive everything."

In Search of a Good Feeling

"Huh, yes ma'am."

"I have to go now, just remember what I said. Good night." Martha gets up and walks out of the back door.

"Night Martha," says Boswell as he watches her get swallowed up by the darkness of the back yard.

CHAPTER 21

Boswell opens his eyes attempting to figure out if he is still dreaming or not. He quickly looks around and determines that he is not in Philly thus he is not dreaming. Morning comes early in Boswell's world, but this morning is a travel day, so his anxiety is playing havoc with his internal clock. Yesterday had been such a whirlwind of experiences such that some of the unfinished residue must have leaked into his dream world. Boswell remembers bits and pieces of his dream but not enough to make any sense of what really occurred. He remembers flying like a bird and eating some of Martha's biscuits while talking to TJ at the coffee house, but the how, what and why he is not able to figure out.

Remembering something that Smoke told him one day when he was trying to bring the past into the future,' Boswell, today has enough trouble waiting for him without bring in yesterday's miseries, so let it be.'

He ponders the dream for another moment then he lets it go. He sits up in the bed and listens to sounds of night. Other than an infrequent rousing in the tree outside, the only sounds at 3 am are the ticking of the clock and the hum

In Search of a Good Feeling

of the fan. The crickets are even silent. Boswell decides to close his eyes to see if he can go back to sleep.

An hour later Michelle is stirring in her bed. After a night of fit fill sleep she is mentally and physically tired. She looks at the clock and shakes her head. "Four freaking o'clock...this is insane and my journey to motherhood is just beginning, who knew. She rubs her stomach while softly humming a song to the kicking baby. Robbed of her good night's sleep Michelle moves from the bed to her to rocking chair and finds a comfortable spot. Five minutes later she is asleep with a smile on her face. Around six am the sun nudges her wake by flashing its brilliant rays into her eyes little by little. Michelle attempts to fight off the it's approaches but to no avail. The sun is too strong and much too wise. Although the nap is short it serves it purpose, Michelle feels good and the baby is no longer kicking. She showers and dresses quickly.

Yesterday, the combing through the family history was quite simulating. Finding out that some of the history was compiled and written by my father was gratifying, she thought. But I am missing the second sheet of paper about the burial site. I looked but the wind must have blown it somewhere. It's like there is something on the paper that somebody does not want us to discover. I need to talk to Grandpa about the contents of the paper. Michelle slides down the steps as quick as possible. When she enters into the study Grandpa is sitting at the table with a document in his hand drinking coffee.

"Morning Grandpa, you are up early this morning." Her greeting startles him.

"Morning Chellie. Do you always sneak up on people child? Well I could not sleep so I got up. So why are you up?"

"Sorry about that. Well, l sort of had the same problem, trouble sleeping. I do not know if it was the baby or something mysterious. I just had problems sleeping last night which is quite unusual for me. What are you reading?"

He hands her the document. "Oh the family history. Before he can finish the statement Michelle's notices the redness of Grandpa's eyes.

"So I guess from looking through all those papers, you college educated guys have figured out a couple things."

"Well we still have some stuff to read Grandpa," says Michelle. "There is a lot of documents in there and they all are calling our name."

"If you look hard enough you will figure out that The Waterman family lives with a curse."

"A curse. What are you talking about?"

"The Waterman family lives with a curse. Yes dear, if you look closely at the history not one of my ancestors had more than three children and one always died early. It's like the family is paying for the sins of the father.

"What sin Grandpa?"

"I guess that son of mine never told you. Walter James became rich by building slave ships, yes slave ships. It is like God is snatching his descendants away just like the slavers did to their African cargo. My daddy told me about the curse, and that's why we had only one child, your father, and damn it, didn't he die before me? Yes, our family might have benefitted by our ancestor's wealth but we descendants have paid a heavy sorrowful tax for the privilege of being Waterman. Your father, my only son is dead because of some

In Search of a Good Feeling

damn curse. The reason I could not sleep is because those documents were in the house. They have blood all over them and the souls of dead cry out for mercy."

Michelle is quiet as she studies the face of her Grandpa and at the same time feels his pain. After a couple minutes of silence, Michelle takes the document from Grandpa's hands and examines it. She places the document down and looks at her grandfather. She thinks that Grandpa and her father did resemble. They both had the Waterman eyebrows, thick and wide with a narrow nose.

She says to Grandpa, "I do not believe in curses Grandpa. I am an observer of human behavior by my training and I believe that we sometimes fall short but we are redeemed. My forefather's vision might have been a little short sighted, but we must also look at the good it did. Because of the terrible past, it has allowed for a wonderful thing to occur. I became pregnant by the seed of a man whose ancestor was a slave on this plantation. Yes, on this very land a slave named JS toiled under the weight of slavery until he could buy his freedom. The slave named JS is Boswell's direct ancestor and because of JS a life lives in my stomach today."

Grandpa is quiet, as tears begin to roll down his face. The news has sent him into a protective cocoon which allows him to sort out his feelings without expressing them verbally.

"Grandpa whatever curse that you and your dad believed in no longer exists. It has been lifted. Just do what Boswell has told me a thousand times, just let it go." She goes over and kisses Grandpa on the head and from the corner of her eye Michelle spies something under one of the bookshelves.

Grandpa says, "Thank you Chellie. This curse thing has taken a toll on me and I did not want you to share in its misery."

"I understand Grandpa. No worries, the curse stops today."

She gives Grandpa a reassuring hug before investigating what see had observed under the book shelve. Michelle bends down and picks up the object. *Oh My God it's the missing sheet of paper from the Burial place folder. The wind must have blown it under the bookshelf. Wait until I tell Boswell I found it.* After looking at the paper for a moment Michelle quickly excuses herself leaving the room with the paper in her hand. She turns the corner and runs smack into Martha.

"Slow down little girl. Good morning. You almost ran me over."

"Good morning Martha. Sorry I did not see you. I have to show Boswell something, have you seen him?"

"Child I do not know about you sometimes. The man is supposed to run after you not the other way around. I just left him in the kitchen doing his usual; eating."

"Thanks." Michelle runs pass Martha and enters into the kitchen. There sits Boswell with a big smile on his face consuming a breakfast meal of two biscuits, grits, bacon and a cup of coffee. Michelle just stops and looks at him for moment. At first Boswell did not notice her, but something tells him to look to his right, and there she is looking straight at him.

"Good morning Michelle," says Boswell, "how are you doing this morning? Did you sleep well?'"

"Well morning Sweetie, no I did not sleep well thank you for asking. How did you get breakfast before anyone else?"

In Search of a Good Feeling

"Well when I came down the steps looking for you, Martha said that you and Grandpa were having a personal moment and that I should join her and Grandma Lizzie for breakfast. Grandma Lizzie only wanted some coffee because she had to go meet her sister this morning so it left me by myself. Just me and these here biscuits. Did I do something wrong? I did not sleep that well myself either."

"Boswell, I do not think anyone slept well in this house last night. Anyway, I found the second page from the burial area folder. The wind had blown it under one of the book shelves. On this second paper there is a list of individual squares with a name across it. Look at the names."

"Michelle darling, I know that lack of sleep can play havoc on your mental state but I am eating breakfast so can this wait until I'm finish?"

Without a second thought Michelle hands the sheet of paper to Boswell who reluctanty puts down his biscuit.

He quickly scans the name list. He looks at Michelle and says, "Let's go."

"Go where?"

"To the burial place."

"Now?"

"Yes, now Michelle."

Ten minutes later the couple are in the rental car driving towards the burial place. Neither is talking, Michelle is eating a biscuit bacon sandwich thinking, *This will be the last piece of pork that I am going to eat for a long time, and I sure enough going to enjoy it, hmm maybe I should rethink this vegetarian thing.*

The car soon comes to the dry creek bed and Boswell parks it under a tree. It is 8am and sun is doing its thing.

Boswell steps out the car heading for the woods, but Michelle stops him.

"Sweetie, before you go marching in to the woods, how about applying some of this. You will be glad that you did later."

Michelle produces a container of bug stray from her bag and hands it to Boswell. After spraying themselves the couple enters into the woods. There were sounds of life everywhere from the chirping of locust and the buzzing of bumble bees to the early morning songs from the birds. The woods seemed exceptionally alive today. Michelle points to some wild hog's tracks on the trail causing Boswell's mind to go back to their last encounter with hogs. Ten minutes into the walk, Michelle motions for Boswell to stop and sit in the shade of a nearby downed tree.

"What's up?" asks Boswell?"

"Nothing, but since we are leaving today I just want to sit here quietly for a moment and enjoy each other."

"Ok, but Michelle we need to get to the gravesite."

"Yes I know, but I want to tell you something before we get there. I know your time in the south has been an emotional roller coaster and at times you seem to be overwhelmed but I want you to know that you make me feel so good. You have touched my heart in so many ways. When we are not together I still feel a bit of you. I know that you do not like this word but I love you. I know that I love you because I feel butterflies in my stomach when I am around you, like right now."

"Wow, butterflies. Are you serious?"

"Yep."

"Michelle, those are feelings of anxiety not of love," he laughs.

In Search of a Good Feeling

"You are a silly man, very silly, always deflecting. Deflect if you want."

"Well my dear not to interrupt your commentary on me, but truthfully you are a very good feeling for me. You make me feel real. You have allow me to persevere through the painful part of the process of becoming me and I thank you."

Boswell's words make Michelle blush and feel the butterflies inside of her. Wanting to cement the feeling, she hugs Boswell like she has never hugged another man before, tightly but not clingy. She feels his warmth and his growing sexuality. She kissed him on the cheek and then whispers in his ear, "It is time to go." After another squeeze, the couple returns back to the path more connected than ever before.

Fifteen minutes later they come to the clearing. Boswell motions Michelle to stop and listen. Since leaving the car the couple have noticed that birds have been their constant noisy companions during their journey in the woods. When they stop, the birds stop, and now they gather overhead in the trees near the clearing awaiting the couple's next move.

Boswell says, "The birds are quiet now and the wind is picking up."

Michelle does not answer, she just nods her head at Boswell while rubbing her stomach at the same time. Her mind is racing, as fear attempts to take the place of logic. *Every time we mess around with this burial site something super natural always occurs. The wind starts blowing, animal scatter and then the freaking rain comes. I must be crazy in love to be out here with him,* she thinks to herself.

Michelle holds Boswell's hand, walking slightly behind him. Boswell's eyes are fixed on the burial site. Unknown to Michelle, fear is also attempting to get his attention. The quietness in a forest previously teeming with activity is eerie. The bugs have even stop flying around the couple's face. As they reach the fence, Michelle releases Boswell's hand and stops at entrance. Her fears will not allow her to go any further. Boswell goes alone into the burial site. He counts the columns and rows until he finds D-12. As the wind swirls through the trees. Boswell slowly walks over to the plot where his ancestor is buried. He kneels down in front of the plot D-12 to brush off some leaves that have fallen on the wooden tombstone. Not a religious man by any means, something causes Boswell to raise his hands and say "Thank you."

He feels a hand on his shoulder, Michelle reaches down to help pull him up. In her absence, Michelle has gathered some wildflowers which she places on the wooden tombstone. One by one the birds begin to sing from the trees surrounding the clearing. Boswell scoops up some soil from JS's burial plot and places it in a small plastic bag. The couple lingers for a couple of moments listening to the birds but they soon depart. At the edge of the clearing Boswell looks back smiling. He squeezes Michelle's hand while saying,

"I just cannot put this experience in words. I came down here expecting nothing and received everything. I faced my biases, found my roots and experienced some of the best feelings in my life. I have you to thank. You are my good feeling."

"Thank you Boswell, I love you too."

The couple hold each other and Boswell feels the movement of their unborn child as he touches Michelle

In Search of a Good Feeling

stomach. The birds suddenly disperse, flying quickly away. The couple continue their walk to the car. As they turn a bend on the trail they run into Martha. She is just standing there in the middle of the path like she had been waiting on them to appear. She was wearing a long colorful skirt, a white top with an orange head band. Her appearance reminds Boswell of the pictures of an African queen he had seen at the Philadelphia art museum.

"Martha, funny to see you out here?" says Boswell.

"I have come to tell you something."

"But why out in the woods and not at the house?" asks Michelle

"What have I told both of you about asking questions?"

"Oops forgot. OK, we are ready to listen."

"Stop dancing in one place and start using the whole floor."

"Dancing. Martha, what are you talking about? Yes we danced at the reunion and you should have seen Michelle. She danced up a storm. My people are probably still talking about her but what does this have to do with us now?"

Michelle kicks Boswell softly motioning him to hush with her finger.

"Hmm I see that listening is still a skill that you need to work on Boswell. I hope it's not genetic. If it is that baby is going to get it bad. Be like Michelle and just ponder what I am about to say to you for a minute. While you were here you discovered something about your past that was unnerving which caused you to dance in one place but it did not resolve your issue. It was not until you used the whole floor that your issue was no longer an issue, and thus you changed the story."

"Well let me think about it for a moment….hmm that's makes sense, and you are correct as usual. When I was struggling with the slavery issue, I was looking at it through a narrow perspective and it was not until I incorporated different points of views did my issue no longer exist. But how did you know I resolved my issue? I did not tell anyone."

"Boswell, I did not come all the way out here to be questioned about something that has an obvious answer."

"How do you know that I went through such a transformation in my thinking?"

"The spirits told me and they were glad."

> "Martha you are a wonder. After the baby is born we will bring him here for your blessing."
>
> "Excuse me Martha, the baby will be a little girl and I will be honored if you allow us to name her after you."
>
> "Chellie the honor will be all mine. Now give me my hugs, Philadelphia awaits."

Martha took them in her arms and kissed them on their head. They stand, the three of them holding on to each other like their lives depended on it.

Then Martha says, "It is time."

The couple with their wet eyes wave good bye to Martha as she heads into the forest. Soon they hear her singing,

> Deep river, my home is over Jordan,
> Deep river, Lord, I want to cross over into campground.
> Oh, don't you want to go to that gospel feast,

In Search of a Good Feeling

That promised land where all is peace?
Oh don't you want to go to that promised land,
That land where all is peace?
Deep river, my home is over Jordan,
Deep river, Lord, I want to cross over into campground.

"Wow, Martha has a wonderful voice," says Michelle.

"Yes she does," agrees Boswell. When they arrived at the car. Boswell scoops up another hand full of soil and places it in another plastic sandwich bag.

"What now?"

"Well I need to have some evidence to show Smoke when I get to Philly that I had been down south."

"You are silly."

They arrive at the plantation house with Grandpa and Grandma Lizzie waiting for them on the back porch. Michelle could see by their faces that her grandparents were sad that they were leaving. Grandma Lizzie hugs Michelle and told her Betty Jean called to tell her goodbye and said that she was sorry that she did not get a chance to meet Boswell but will next year when you guys bring back the baby.

Michelle smiles between her tears.

Grandma Lizzie turns to Boswell and proceeds to give him a great big hug. She said, It was a joy getting to know you."

Unable to verbally respond Boswell just hugs her back.

Grandpa takes the suit cases to the car while the threesome engages in their good byes.

As the couple approaches, he states, "None of the emotional stuff for me." He shakes Boswell's hand. "Take care of her." He then kisses Michelle on the cheek. "You are so beautiful. I will see you soon." He quickly departs from them to resume his place next to his wife on the back porch.

Before entering the car Boswell thinks he hears a multitude of voices saying, "Farewell blessed one." He looks at Michelle but she is already in the car wiping her wet eyes. So in response Boswell says, "Farewell and thanks." He dips his body into the driver's side seat, starts the car and honks the horn over and over as he slowly steers down the driveway. The couple hear the sound of crows cawing from the tree branches as they pull off into the state road. The old willow tree's swaying branches appear to be waving good bye along with Mr. Bray who has come out to the road to see Michelle off. A crow seems to follow them until they get to the main highway. During their trip home to Philadelphia there is very little conversation only touches and smiles.

One year and a month after the birth of Martha James, Michelle receives a call from Grandma Lizzie informing her about the death of her grandfather. Grandma Lizzie says, "Do not worry yourself about being present for his funeral. We are going to bury him within three days of his death like he stated in his will. He thought most of his friends were local so why wait. Your granddaddy was a strange but funny man. So he will be buried tomorrow bless his soul. But he did want you to be present for the reading of his will since you are one of the few Waterman left. I know all of this is quite sudden but baby girl your Granddaddy lived a very good life. Your visits were such a blessing to him. He got a joy from you being here. Whatever you said to him

In Search of a Good Feeling

really lighten his load. Well, I need to get off of here and start getting ready for tomorrow. 'A woman's work is never done.' Oh yea, the reading of the will is scheduled for 14 days after his burial as stipulated by his wishes, so I will see you in two weeks. Bye now."

Michelle just stands with her mouth open unable to say a word. Then she lets out a scream that wakes Martha James and anyone else who is sleeping.

Boswell runs into the living room and reaches for Michelle. She falls in his arms while saying between her tears, "Grandpa Jed is dead."

The place where the reading of the will is to take place in a conference room in a law office. The room has a large mahogany table with several comfortable looking chairs. The walls are covered with awards for this and certificates for that. There is a coffee and tea service on a table on the side filled with a tray of assorted pastries. As they enter the office the smell of freshly brewed coffee engages the senses. Grandma Lizzie is sitting by herself sipping on some coffee. She is looking quite elegant wearing a grey sweater with a long black skirt. Boswell notices that she looks a little heavier but the weight looks good on her.

The executor of the will is Jackie L. Brown, attorney at law. A tall African-American man with a deep booming voice. He appears to be somewhat annoyed with the couple's late arrival. Also sitting in the office is a woman who reminds Boswell of someone but he is unable to figure out whom. Michelle and Boswell rush over to Grandma Lizzie greeting her with hugs and kisses. The welcome celebration is short lived.

Attorney Brown makes a sound like he is clearing his throat and all talking ceases. Michelle and Boswell quickly find their seats. They hand Martha James over to her great grandmother and greet the unknown woman with smiles.

"I see that all parties that are benefactors on the will of Jed Waterman are finally present. First of all let me introduce myself. I am Jackie Brown, Esquire attorney at law. I was named by Mr. Waterman to be the executor of the will. My role is to make sure that Mr. Waterman's legal wishes are done properly and in order.

Martha James appears to be falling asleep in Grandma Lizzie's arm. She seems to be the only one that's able to relax. Attorney Brown continues, "Does everyone know each other?"

Michelle and Boswell shake their heads no.

"Well let me introduce everyone. To my left is Lizzie Waterman, the wife of the late Jed Waterman. Sitting in front of me is Boswell Thompson and Michelle Waterman. Michelle is the late Jed Waterman's granddaughter and to my right is Yvette Waters, daughter of Martha Waters who was sister of the late Jed Waterman.

With those words, Michelle and Boswell are speechless. *Grandpa had a sister who was black. Oh my God, and Martha was that sister. No way, oh my God,* Boswell screams quietly to himself.

Michelle quickly raises her hand.

"Yes Ms. Waterman.

"Attorney Brown, "I just need some clarity. Are you saying that Martha the same Martha who took care of me when I came to live with my grandparents is kin to me. That she is my great aunt?"

"Yes Ms. Waterman that is what I am saying."

In Search of a Good Feeling

Michelle looks quickly over to Grandma Lizzie.

"Yes, Michelle it is true. Martha was Jed's sister and Yvette over there is her daughter."

Yvette smiles at the couple. "Yep strange but true, Martha is my mama."

Michelle and Boswell do not know if they should cry or scream with joy.

Attorney Brown clears his throat so deep it wakes up Martha James. "Ok people now that everyone knows each other, can we move on to the reading of the will?"

Boswell says, "No not yet." He turns to Yvette and says, "I remember you, I saw you leaving the house one day. So where is Martha? Why isn't she here?"

"My mama went to live with the spirits last summer. Remember when you came down with the baby and she blessed her. She was so happy that day. It was a special time for her. A week later the spirits came for her. It was time... she was tired. She did not want to bother anyone so she told me not to tell anyone too soon. Just wait and you will know when to tell people. So no one knew for quite a while until I spread the news that she went to live with the spirits. My mama believed that we never leave those we love, we just change the matter in which we interact with them."

"So where is she buried?"

"Her desire was to be buried next to her mother, so Mr. Waterman had her buried privately because that was her wish."

'Who was her mother?

"Shed, my mama was a private woman, not one to make a lot of fuss over too much. When I asked why she lived her life in the matter that she did she said, 'I do not make it a habit to answer people's questions about what I do but I will make an exception for you today. I made a promise to my daddy that I would take care of my brother and I believe my word is my bond. Yeah, he is a white boy and I am a colored gal but he is my brother and we should not be defined if we are colored or white, but what's inside of us and how it shows up in what we do.'

"Jed and Martha had a bond deeper than blood, their own special relationship. I did not truly understand it, but I marveled at it. It was their secret. If it had been revealed, maybe they thought it may change what they developed over the years, so it remained a secret. Martha would come over do a little housework, cook, and make sure that Jed and I was doing well, and then go off and do whatever she desired. She never complained, and your grandfather did whatever she told him to do. Jed told me that she had a house built out in the forest," says Grandma Lizzie as she wipe her eyes.

Tears roll down Michelle and Boswell faces but Attorney Brown seemingly untouched by the expression of human emotion clears his throat once again.

"Ok everyone is updated about family business so let's proceed. I will attempt to make this as simple as possible. Let me pass a complete copy of the will to everyone."

Each of the three beneficiaries eyes focus on the document in front of them as Attorney Jackie Brown reads it in a deep grave voice. "To my darling wife, Lizzie Waterman who has stuck with me through thick and thin, I leave all of my stock holdings, my personal bank accounts, our summer home and my two vehicles. To Martha Waterman, my beloved sister whom I do not know what I would have done without I bequest two hundred acres of farm land

In Search of a Good Feeling

which your house surrounds, a tractor, and 100 thousand dollars from the Waterman trust. To my niece, the daughter of our only child I leave to you the Waterman Plantation and everything on it minus the acreage given to Martha and control of the Waterman trust minus the amount given to Martha. Attorney Brown's deep baritone voice is quiet now as everyone in the room attempts to figure how what was just said out of his mouth impacts them. Then from out of nowhere Martha James starts clapping. Grandma Lizzie follows her lead and Yvette, Michelle and Boswell joins in the joyful clapping. Among the clapping and the tears a sense happiness and good feelings emerge within the most unlikely kin folk. Attorney Brown announces that his business is over and that he will be in touch with everyone at a later date.

The white widower along with her black sister-law's daughter, the interracial couple with the biracial child walk down to a nearby eatery for something to eat as a crow in a nearby tree nosily announces its presence.

Anthony Webb

IN SEARCH OF A GOOD FEELING

We are all searching and seeking for those things
that make life complete,
But truly never understanding
how to obtain those very things we look for,
then someone unannounced and unknown
comes into our life.
Suddenly life itself takes on a new meaning,
Time disappears into another dimension.
Simplicity has replace complexity as
the sun shines brightly on all
Nevertheless slowly time reappears and life with
it convoluted ways rudely awakens us.
That someone that had made life so complete is gone
We are left with unfulfilled dreams,
a dull ache in the heart and tearful memories.
But all the pain and joy of this experience
has brought us closer to the meaning of happiness
and that's…….a good feeling